ELEGY FOR APRIL

ELEGY FOR APRIL

BENJAMIN BLACK

ISIS
LARGE PRINT
Oxford

First published in Great Britain 2010
by
Mantle
An imprint of Pan Macmillan

Published in Large Print 2011 by ISIS Publishing Ltd.,
7 Centremead, Osney Mead, Oxford OX2 0ES
by arrangement with
Pan Macmillan
A division of Macmillan Publishers Limited

British Library Cataloguing in Publication Data
Black, Benjamin, 1945–
  Elegy for April.
  1. Quirke, Garret (Fictitious character) - - Fiction.
  2. Pathologists - - Ireland - - Dublin - - Fiction.
  3. Missing persons - - Investigation - - Ireland - -
  Dublin - - Fiction.
  4. Family secrets - - Fiction.
  5. Dublin (Ireland) - - Social conditions - -
  20th century - - Fiction.
  6. Detective and mystery stories.
  7. Large type books.
  I. Title
  823.9'14–dc22

ISBN 978–0–7531–8774–6 (hb)
ISBN 978–0–7531–8775–3 (pb)

Printed and bound in Great Britain by
T. J. International Ltd., Padstow, Cornwall

I

CHAPTER
ONE

It was the worst of winter weather, and April Latimer was missing.

For days a February fog had been down and showed no sign of lifting. In the muffled silence the city seemed bewildered, like a man whose sight has suddenly failed. People vague as invalids groped their way through the murk, keeping close to the house-fronts and the railings and stopping tentatively at street corners to feel with a wary foot for the pavement's edge. Motor cars with their headlights on loomed like giant insects, trailing milky dribbles of exhaust smoke from their rear ends. The evening paper listed each day's toll of mishaps. There had been a serious collision at the canal end of the Rathgar Road involving three cars and an Army motorcyclist. A small boy was run over by a coal lorry at the Five Lamps, but did not die — his mother swore to the reporter sent to interview her that it was the miraculous medal of the Virgin Mary she made the child wear round his neck that had saved him. In Clanbrassil Street an old moneylender was waylaid and robbed in broad daylight by what he claimed was a gang of housewives; the Guards were following a definite line of inquiry. A shawlie in Moore Street was knocked down by a van that did not stop, and now the woman was in a coma in St James's. And all day long the fog horns boomed out in the bay.

Phoebe Griffin considered herself April's best friend, but she had heard nothing from her in a week and she was convinced something had happened. She did not know what to do. Of course, April might just have gone off, without telling anyone — that was how April was, unconventional, some would say wild — but Phoebe was sure that was not the case.

The windows of April's first-floor flat on Herbert Place had a blank, withholding aspect, not just because of the fog: windows look like that when the rooms behind them are empty; Phoebe could not say how, but they do. She crossed to the other side of the road and stood at the railings with the canal at her back and looked up at the terrace of tall houses, their louring, dark brick exteriors shining wetly in the shrouded air. She was not sure what she was hoping to see — a curtain twitching, a face at a window? — but there was nothing, and no one. The damp was seeping through her clothes and she drew in her shoulders against the cold. She heard footsteps on the tow-path behind her but when she turned to look she could not see anyone through the impenetrable, hanging greyness. The bare trees with their black limbs upflung appeared almost human. The unseen walker coughed once; it sounded like a fox barking.

She went back and climbed the stone steps to the door again, and again pressed the bell above the little card with April's name on it, though she knew there would be no answer. Grains of mica glittered in the granite of the steps; strange, these little secret gleamings, under the fog. A ripping whine started up in the sawmill on the other side of the canal and she realised that what she had been smelling without knowing it was the scent of freshly cut timber.

She walked up to Baggot Street and turned right, away from the canal. The heels of her flat shoes made a deadened tapping on the pavement. It was lunchtime on a weekday but it felt more like a Sunday twilight. The city seemed almost deserted, and the few people she met flickered past sinisterly, like phantoms. She was reasoning with herself. The fact that she had not seen or heard from April since the middle of the previous week did not mean April had been gone for that long — it did not mean she was gone at all. And yet not a word in all that length of time, not even a phone call? With someone else a week's silence might not be remarked, but April was the kind of person people worried about, not because she was unable to look after herself but because she was altogether too sure she could.

The lamps were lit on either side of the door of the Shelbourne Hotel, they glowed eerily, like giant dandelion clocks. The caped and frock-coated porter, idling at the door, lifted his grey top hat and saluted her. She would have asked Jimmy Minor to meet her in the hotel but Jimmy disdained such a swank place and would not set foot in it unless he was following up on a story or interviewing some visiting notable. She passed on, crossing Kildare Street, and went down the area steps to the Country Shop. Even through her glove she

5

could feel how cold and greasily wet the stair-rail was. Inside, though, the little café was warm and bright, with a comforting fug of tea and baked bread and cakes. She took a table by the window. There were a few other customers, all of them women, in hats, with shopping bags and parcels. Phoebe asked for a pot of tea and an egg sandwich. She might have waited to order until Jimmy came but she knew he would be late, as he always was — deliberately, she suspected, for he liked to have it thought that he was so much busier than everyone else. The waitress was a large pink girl with a double chin and a sweet smile. There was a wen wedged in the groove beside her left nostril that Phoebe tried not to stare at. The tea that she brought was almost black, and bitter with tannin. The sandwich, cut in neat triangles, was slightly curled at the corners.

Where was April now, at this moment, and what was she doing? For she must be somewhere, even if not here. Any other possibility was not to be entertained.

A half-hour passed before Jimmy arrived. She saw him through the window skipping down the steps and she was struck as always by how slight he was, a miniature person, more like a wizened schoolboy than a man. He wore a transparent plastic raincoat the colour of watery ink. He had thin red hair and a narrow, freckled face, and was always dishevelled, as if he had been sleeping in his clothes and had just jumped out of bed. He was putting a match to a cigarette as he came through the door. He saw her and crossed to her table and sat down quickly, crushing his raincoat into a ball and stowing it under his chair. Jimmy did everything in a hurry, as if each moment were a deadline he was afraid he was about to miss. "Well, Pheeb," he said, "what's up?" There were sparkles of moisture in his otherwise lifeless hair. The collar of his brown corduroy jacket bore a light snowfall of dandruff, and when he leaned forward she caught a whiff of his tobacco-staled breath. Yet he had the sweetest smile, it was always a surprise, lighting up that pinched, sharp little face. It was one of his amusements to pretend that he was in love with Phoebe, and he would complain theatrically to anyone prepared to listen of her cruelty and hard-heartedness in refusing to entertain his advances. He was a crime reporter on the *Evening Mail*, though surely there were not enough crimes committed in this sleepy city to keep him as busy as he claimed to be.

She told him about April and how long it was since she had heard from her. "Only a week?" Jimmy said. "She's probably gone off with some guy. She is slightly notorious, you know." Jimmy affected an accent from the movies; it had started as a joke at his own expense — "Jimmy Minor, ace reporter, at your service, lady!" — but it had become a habit and now he seemed not to notice how it grated on those around him who had to put up with it.

"If she was going somewhere," Phoebe said, "she would have let me know, I'm sure she would."

The waitress came and Jimmy ordered a glass of ginger beer and a beef sandwich — "Plenty of horseradish, baby, slather it on, I like it hot." He pronounced it *hat*. The girl tittered. When she had gone he whistled softly and said, "That's some wart."

7

"Wen," Phoebe said.

"What?"

"It's a wen, not a wart."

Jimmy had finished his cigarette and now he lit a new one. No one smoked as much as Jimmy did; he had once told Phoebe that he often found himself wishing he could have a smoke while he was already smoking, and that indeed on more than one occasion he had caught himself lighting a cigarette even though the one he had going was there in the ash-tray in front of him. He leaned back on the chair and crossed one of his stick-like little legs on the other and blew a bugle-shaped stream of smoke at the ceiling. "So what do you think?" he said.

Phoebe was stirring a spoon round and round in the cold dregs in her cup. "I think something has happened to her," she said quietly.

He gave her a quick, sideways glance. "Are you really worried? I mean, really?"

She shrugged, not wanting to seem melodramatic, not giving him cause to laugh at her. He was still watching her sidelong, frowning. At a party one night in her flat he had told her he thought her friendship with April Latimer was funny, and added: "Funny peculiar, that's to say, not funny ha ha." He had been a little drunk and afterwards they had tacitly agreed to pretend to have forgotten this exchange, but the fact of what he had implied lingered between them uncomfortably. And laugh it off though she might, it had made Phoebe brood, and the memory of it still troubled her, a little.

"You're probably right, of course," she said now. "Probably it's just April being April, skipping off and forgetting to tell anyone."

But no, she did not believe it; she could not. Whatever else April might be she was not thoughtless like that, not where her friends were concerned.

The waitress came with Jimmy's order. He bit a half-moon from his sandwich and, chewing, took a deep draw of his cigarette. "What about the Prince of Bongo-Bongo-land?" he asked thickly. He swallowed hard, blinking from the effort. "— Have you made enquiries of His Majesty?" He was smiling now but there was a glitter to his smile and the sharp tip of an eye-tooth showed for a second at the side. He was jealous of Patrick Ojukwu; all the men in their circle were jealous of Patrick, nicknamed the Prince. She often wondered, in a troubled and troubling way, about Patrick and April — had they, or had they not? It had all the makings of a juicy scandal, the wild white girl and the polished black man.

"More to the point," Phoebe said, "what about Mrs Latimer?"

Jimmy made a show of starting back as if in terror, throwing up a hand. "Hold up!" he cried. "The blackamoor is one thing but Morgan Le Fay is another altogether." April's mother had a fearsome reputation among April's friends.

"I should telephone her, though. She must know where April is."

Jimmy arched an eyebrow sceptically. "You think so?"

9

He was right to doubt it, she knew. April had long ago stopped confiding in her mother; in fact, the two were barely on speaking terms.

"What about her brother, then?" she said.

Jimmy laughed at that. "The Grand Gynie of Fitzwilliam Square, plumber to the quality, no pipe too small to probe?"

"Don't be disgusting, Jimmy." She took a drink of her tea but it was cold. "Although I know April doesn't like him."

"Doesn't like? Try loathes."

"Then what should I do?" she asked.

He sipped his ginger beer and grimaced and said plaintively: "Why you can't meet in a pub like any normal person I don't know." He seemed already to have lost interest in the topic of April's whereabouts. They spoke desultorily of other things for a while, then he took up his cigarettes and matches and fished his raincoat from under his chair and said he had to go. Phoebe signalled to the waitress to bring the bill — she knew she would have to pay, Jimmy was always broke — and presently they were climbing to the street up the damp, slimed steps. At the top, Jimmy put a hand on her arm. "Don't worry," he said. "— About April, I mean. She'll turn up."

A faint, warmish smell of dung came to them from across the street, where by the railings of the Green there was a line of horse-drawn jaunting-cars that offered tours of the city. In the fog they had a spectral air, the horses standing unnaturally still with heads lowered dejectedly and the caped and top-hatted drivers perched in attitudes of motionless expectancy on their high seats, as if awaiting imminent word to set off for the Borgo Pass or Dr Jekyll's rooms.

"You going back to work?" Jimmy asked. He was glancing about with eyes narrowed; clearly in his mind he was already somewhere else.

"No," Phoebe said. "It's my half-day off." She took a breath and felt the wet air swarm down coldly into her chest. "I'm going to see someone. My — my father, actually. I suppose you wouldn't care to come along?"

He did not meet her eye, and busied himself lighting another cigarette, turning aside and crouching over his cupped hands. "Sorry," he said, straightening. "Crimes to expose, stories to concoct, reputations to besmirch — no rest for the busy newshound." He was a good half-head shorter than she was; his plastic coat gave off a chemical odour. "See you around, kid." He set off in the direction of Grafton Street, but stopped and turned and came back again. "By the way," he said, "what's the difference between a wen and a wart?"

When he had gone she stood for a while, irresolute, slowly pulling on her calfskin gloves. She had that heart-sinking feeling she had at this time every Thursday when the weekly visit to her father was in prospect. Today, however, there was an added sense of unease. She could not think why she had asked Jimmy to meet her — what had she imagined he would say or do that would assuage her fears? There had been something odd in his manner, she had felt it the moment she mentioned April's long silence; an evasiveness, a shiftiness, almost. She was well aware of

11

the simmering antipathy between her two so dissimilar friends. In some way Jimmy seemed jealous of April, as he was of Patrick Ojukwu. Or was it more resentment than jealousy? But if so, what was it in April that he found to resent? The Latimers of Dun Laoghaire were gentry, of course, but Jimmy would think she was, too, and he did not seem to hold it against her. She gazed across the street at the coaches and their intently biding jarveys. She was surer than ever that something bad, something very bad, perhaps the very worst of all, had befallen her friend.

Then a new thought struck her, one that made her more uneasy still. What if Jimmy were to see in April's disappearance the possibility of a story, a "great yarn", as he would say? What if he had only pretended to be indifferent, and had rushed off now to tell his editor that April Latimer, a junior doctor at the Hospital of the Holy Family, the "slightly notorious" daughter of the late and much lamented Conor Latimer and niece of the present Minister of Health, had not been heard from in over a week? Oh, Lord, she thought in dismay, what have I done?

CHAPTER
TWO

Quirke had never known life so lacking in savour. In his first days at St John's he had been in too much confusion and distress to notice how everything here seemed leached of colour and texture; gradually, however, the deadness pervading the place began to fascinate him. Nothing at St John's could be grasped or held. It was as if the fog that had been so frequent since the autumn had settled permanently here, outdoors and in, a thing present everywhere and yet without substance, and always at a fixed distance from the eye however quickly one moved. Not that anyone moved quickly in this place, not among the inmates, anyway. *Inmates* was a frowned-upon word, but what else could they be called, these uncertain, hushed figures, of which he was one, padding dully along the corridors and about the grounds like shell-shock victims? He wondered if the atmosphere were somehow deliberately contrived, an emotional counterpart to the bromides that prison authorities were said to smuggle into convicts' food to calm their passions. When he put the question to Brother Anselm that good man only laughed. "No, no," he said, "it's all your own work." He meant the collective work of all the inmates; he sounded almost proud of their achievement.

Brother Anselm was director of the House of St John of the Cross, refuge for addicts of all kinds, for shattered souls and petrifying livers. Quirke liked him, liked his unjudgemental diffidence, his wry, melancholy humour. The two men occasionally took walks together in the grounds, pacing the gravel pathways among the box hedges talking of books, of history, of ancient politics — safe subjects on which they exchanged opinions as chilly and contentless as the wintry air through which they moved. Quirke had checked into St John's on Christmas Eve, persuaded by his brother-in-law to seek the cure after a six-month drinking binge, few details of which Quirke could recall with any clearness. "Do it for Phoebe if no one else," Malachy Griffin had said.

Stopping drinking had been easy; what was difficult was the daily unblurred confrontation with a self he heartily wished to avoid. Dr Whitty, the house psychiatrist, explained it to him. "With some, such as yourself, it's not so much the drink that's addictive but the escape it offers. Stands to reason, doesn't it? Escape from yourself, that is." Dr Whitty was a big bluff fellow with baby-blue eyes and fists the size of turnips. He and Quirke had already known each other a little, professionally, in the outside world, but in here the convention was they should behave as cordial strangers. Quirke felt awkward, though: he had assumed that somehow St John's would afford anonymity, that it would be the least anyone consigning himself to the care of the place could expect, and he was grateful for Whitty's studiedly remote cheerfulness and the scrupulous discretion of his pale gaze. He submitted meekly to the daily sessions on the couch — in fact, not a couch but a straight chair half turned towards the window, with the psychiatrist a largely unspeaking and heavily breathing presence behind it — and tried to say the things he thought would be expected of him. He knew what his troubles were, knew more or less the identity of the demons tormenting him, but at St John's everyone was called upon to clear the decks, wipe the slate clean, make a fresh start — cliché was another staple of the institutional life — and he was no exception. "It's a long road, the road back," Brother Anselm said. "The less baggage you take with you, the better." As if, Quirke thought but did not say, I could unpack myself and walk away empty.

The inmates were urged to pair off, like shy dancers at a grotesque ball. The theory was that sustained daily contact with a designated fellow-sufferer, entailing shared confidences and candid self-exposure, would restore a sense of what was called in here "mutuality" and inevitably speed the process of rehabilitation. Thus Quirke found himself spending a great deal more time than he would have cared to with Harkness — last-name terms was the form at St John's — a hard-faced, grizzled man with the indignantly reprehending aspect of an eagle. Harkness had a keen sense of the bleak comedy of what he insisted on calling their captivity, and when he heard what Quirke's profession was he produced a brief, loud laugh that was like the sound of something thick and resistant being ripped in half. "A pathologist!" he snarled in rancorous delight. "Welcome to the morgue."

Harkness — it seemed not so much a name as a condition — was as reluctant as Quirke in the matter of personal confidences and at first would say little about himself or his past. Quirke, however, had spent his orphaned childhood in institutions run by the religious, and guessed at once that he was — what did they say? — a man of the cloth. "That's right," Harkness said, "Christian Brother. You must have heard the swish of the surplice." Or of the leather strap, more like, Quirke thought. Side by side in dogged silence, heads down and fists clasped at their backs, they tramped the same paths that Quirke and Brother Anselm walked, under the freezing trees, as if performing a penance, which in a way they were. As the weeks went on, Harkness began to release resistant little hard nuggets of information, as if he were spitting out the seeds of a sour fruit. A thirst for drink, it seemed, had been a defence against other urges. "Let me put it this way," he said, "if I hadn't gone into the Order it's unlikely I'd ever have married." He chuckled darkly. Quirke was shocked: he had never before heard anyone, least of all a Christian Brother, come right out like this and admit to being queer. Harkness had lost his vocation, too — "if I ever had one" — and was coming to the conclusion that on balance there is no God.

After such stark revelations Quirke felt called upon to reciprocate in kind, but found it acutely difficult, not out of embarrassment or shame — though he must be embarrassed, he must be ashamed, considering the many misdeeds he had on his conscience — but because of the sudden weight of tedium that pressed down on him. The trouble with sins and sorrows, he had discovered, is that in time they become boring, even to the sorrowing sinner. Had he the heart to recount it all again, the shambles that was his life — the calamitous losses of nerve, the moral laziness, the failures, the betrayals? He tried. He told how when his wife died in childbirth he gave away his infant daughter to his sister-in-law and kept it secret from the child, Phoebe, now a young woman, for nearly twenty years. He listened to himself as if it were someone else's tale he was telling.

"But she comes to visit you," Harkness said, in frowning perplexity, interrupting him. "Your daughter — she comes to visit."

"Yes, she does." Quirke had ceased to find this fact surprising, but now found it so anew.

Harkness said nothing more, only nodded once, with an expression of bitter wonderment, and turned his face away. Harkness had no visitors.

That Thursday when Phoebe came, Quirke, thinking of the lonely Christian Brother, made an extra effort to be alert to her and appreciative of the solace she thought she was bringing him. They sat in the visitors' room, a bleak, glassed-in corner of the vast entrance hall — in Victorian times the building had been the forbiddingly grand headquarters of some branch of the British administration in the city — where there were plastic-topped tables and metal chairs and, at one end, a counter on which stood a mighty tea-urn that rumbled and hissed all day long. Quirke thought his daughter was paler than usual, and there were smudged shadows like bruises under her eyes. She seemed distracted, too. She had in general a sombre, aetiolated quality that grew steadily more marked as she progressed into her twenties; yet she was becoming a beautiful woman, he realised with some surprise and an inexplicable but sharp twinge of unease. Her pallor was accentuated by the black outfit she wore, black skirt and jumper, slightly shabby black coat. These were her work clothes — she had a job in a hat shop — but he thought they gave her too much the look of a nun.

They sat opposite each other, their hands extended before them across the table, their fingertips almost but not quite touching.

"Are you all right?" he asked.

"Yes," she said. "I'm fine."

"You look — I don't know — strained?"

He saw her deciding to decline his sympathy. She glanced up at the high window beside them where the fog was crowding against the panes like compressed gas. Their grey mugs of tea stood stolid on the table top before them, untouched. Phoebe's hat was on the table too, a minuscule confection of lace and black velvet stuck with an incongruously dramatic scarlet feather. Quirke nodded in the direction of the hat. "How is Mrs What's-her-name?"

"Who?"

"The one who owns the hat shop."

"Mrs Cuffe-Wilkes."

"Surely that's a made-up name."

"There was a Mr Wilkes. He died, and she began to call herself Cuffe-Wilkes."

"Is there a Mr Cuffe?"

"No. That was her maiden name."

"Ah."

He brought out his cigarette case, clicked it open, and offered it to her flat on his palm. She shook her head. "I've stopped."

He selected a cigarette for himself and lit it. "You used to smoke — what were they called, those oval-shaped ones?"

"Passing Clouds."

"That's it. Why did you give up?"

She smiled wryly. "Why did you?"

"Why did I give up drink, you mean? Oh, well."

They both looked away, Phoebe to the window again and Quirke sideways, at the floor. There were half a dozen couples in the place, all sitting at tables as far separated from the others as possible. The floor was covered with large, black-and-white rubber tiles, and with the people in it placed just so the room seemed set up for a silent, life-sized game of chess. The air reeked of cigarette smoke and stewed tea, and there was a faint trace too of something medicinal and vaguely punitive. "This awful place," Phoebe said, then glanced at her father guiltily. "Sorry."

"For what? You're right, it is awful." He paused. "I'm going to check myself out."

He was as startled as she was. He had not been aware of having taken the decision until he announced it. But now, the announcement delivered, he realised that he had made up his mind that moment when, in the grounds that day, under the stark trees, speaking of Quirke's daughter, Harkness had turned aside with that bitter, stricken look in his aquiline eye. Yes, it was then, Quirke understood now, that he had set out mentally on the journey back to something like feeling, to something like — what to call it? — like life. Brother Anselm was right: he had a long trek ahead of him.

Phoebe was saying something. "What?" he said, with a flash of irritation, trying not to scowl. "— Sorry, I wasn't listening."

She regarded him with that deprecating look, head tilted, chin down, one eyebrow arched, that she used to give him when she was little and still thought he was her sort-of uncle; his attention had been a fluctuating quantity then, too. "April Latimer," she said. Still he frowned, unenlightened. "I was saying," she said, "she seems to be — gone away, or something."

"Latimer," he said, cautiously.

"Oh, Quirke!" Phoebe cried — it was what she called him, never Dad, Daddy, Father — "my friend, April Latimer. She works at your hospital. She's a junior doctor."

"Can't place her."

"Conor Latimer was her father, and her uncle is the Minister of Health."

"Ah. One of those Latimers. She's missing, you say?"

She stared at him, startled: she had not used the word "missing", so why had he? What had he heard in her voice that had alerted him to what it was she feared? "No," she said firmly, shaking her head, "not missing, but — she seems to be — she seems to have left, without telling anyone. I haven't heard a word from her in over a week."

"A week?" he said, deliberately dismissive. "That's not long."

"Usually she phones every day, or every second day, at the least." She made herself shrug, and sit back; she had the frightening conviction that the more plainly she allowed her concern to show the more likely it would be that something calamitous had happened to her friend. It made no sense, and yet she could not rid herself of the notion. She felt Quirke's eye; it was like a doctor's hand on her, searching for the infirm place, the diseased place, the place that pained.

"What about the hospital?" he said.

"I telephoned. She sent in a note to say she wouldn't be in."

"Until when?"

"What?" She gazed at him, baffled for a moment.

"How long did she say she'd be out?"

"Oh. I didn't ask."

"Did she give a reason not to turn up?" She shook her head; she did not know. She bit her lower lip until it turned white. "Maybe she has the flu," he said. "Maybe she decided to go off on a holiday — they make those junior doctors work like blacks, you know."

"She would have told me," she muttered. Saying this, with that stubborn set to her mouth, she was again for a second the child that he remembered.

"I'll phone the people there," he said, "in her department. I'll find out what's going on. Don't worry."

She smiled, but so tentatively, with such effort, still biting her lip, that he saw clearly how distressed she was. What was he to do, what was he to say to her?

He walked with her down to the front gate. The brief day was drawing in and the gloom of twilight was drifting into the fog and thickening it, like soot. He had no overcoat and he was cold, but he insisted on going all the way to the gate. Their partings were always awkward; she had kissed him, just once, years before, when she did not know he was her father, and at such moments as this the memory of that kiss still flashed out between them with a magnesium glare. He touched her elbow lightly with a fingertip and stepped back. "Don't worry," he said again, and again she smiled, and nodded, and turned away. He watched her go through the gate, that absurd scarlet feather on her hat dipping and swaying, then he called out to her. "I forgot to say — I'm going to buy a car."

She turned back, staring. "What? You can't even drive."

"I know. You can teach me."

"I can't drive either!"

"Well, learn, and then I'll learn from you."

"You're mad," she said, shaking her head and laughing.

CHAPTER
THREE

When she heard the telephone ringing Phoebe somehow knew the call was for her. Although the house was divided into four flats there was only one public phone, down in the front hall, and access to it was a constant source of competitiveness and strife among the tenants. She had been living here for six months. The house was gaunt and shabby, much less nice than the place where she had been before, in Harcourt Street, but after all that had happened there she could not have stayed on. She had her things with her here, of course, her photographs and ornaments, her raggedy, one-eyed teddy bear, and even some of her own furniture that the landlord had let her bring with her, but still she pined for the old flat. There, she had felt herself to be in the busy heart of the city; here, in Haddington Road, it was almost suburbia. There were days when, turning the corner from Baggot Street Bridge, she would look down the long, deserted sweep towards Ringsend and feel the loneliness of her life opening under her like a chasm. She was, she knew, too much alone, which was another reason not to lose a friend like April Latimer.

When she came out on to the landing the fat young man from the ground-floor flat was standing at the foot of the stairs glaring up at her. He was always the first to get to the phone but none of the calls ever seemed to be for him. "I shouted up," he said crossly, "did you not hear?" She had heard nothing; she was sure he was lying. She hurried down the stairs as the young man went back into his flat and slammed the door behind him.

The telephone, coin-operated, was a black metal box bolted to the wall above the hall table. When she lifted the heavy receiver to her ear she was convinced a whiff of the fat young man's carious breath came up out of the mouthpiece.

"Yes?" she said, softly, eagerly. "Yes?"

She had been hoping, of course, hoping against hope that it would be April, but it was not, and her heart that had been beating so expectantly fell back into its accustomed rhythm.

"Hello, Pheeb, it's Jimmy."

"Oh. Hello." He had not written a story about April — she had checked the *Mail* — and now she felt guilty, and foolish, too, for having suspected that he would.

"I forgot to ask you yesterday — did you see if April's key was there, when you called round?"

"What?" she said. "What key?"

"The one she leaves under the broken flagstone at the front door, if she's out and expecting someone to call." Phoebe said nothing. How did Jimmy know about this arrangement with the key when she did not? Why had April never told her about it? "I'll go over now and see if it's there," Jimmy was saying. "Want to come and meet me?"

She walked quickly up towards the bridge with her scarf wrapped round her face and covering her mouth. The fog had lightened but a thin, cold mist persisted. Herbert Place was only one street over, on the other side of the canal. When she got to the house there was no sign of Jimmy. She climbed the steps and pressed the bell in case he had arrived before her and had let himself in, but evidently he had not. She peered at the granite flagstones, trying to spot the one that was loose. Some minutes passed; she felt self-conscious and exposed, thinking someone might come up to her demanding to know why she was still there when obviously the person whose bell she had been ringing was not at home. She was relieved when she saw Jimmy hurrying along the tow-path. He came up through the gap in the black railings and sprinted across the road, ignoring a motor car that had to swerve to avoid him, bleating indignantly.

"Still no sign?" he said, joining her on the top step. He was wearing his plastic raincoat with the unpleasant, acid smell. With the heel of his shoe he pressed down on the edge of a flagstone beside the foot-scraper and a broken corner of it lifted and she saw the dull gleam of two keys on a key-ring underneath.

The mist had penetrated the hall and a faint swathe of it hung motionless like ectoplasm on the stairs. They climbed in silence to the second floor. Phoebe had trod these stairs countless times but suddenly she felt like an intruder. She had not noticed before how worn the carpet was along the outer edge of each step or how the stair-rods were tarnished, and missing at intervals. At the door to April's flat they hesitated, exchanging a look. Jimmy rapped softly with his knuckles. They waited a moment, but no sound came from within. "Well?" he whispered. "Shall we risk it?"

The harsh sound of the key gouging into the lock made her flinch.

She did not know what she had expected to find inside, but of course there was nothing amiss, or nothing that she could see, anyway. April was not the tidiest person in the world, and the clutter in the place was familiar, and reassuring: how could anything really bad have happened to someone who had washed those nylons and left them draped there over the fire-guard in front of the grate? And look at that cup and saucer on the coffee-table — the rim of the cup marked with a crescent of scarlet lipstick — and that half-consumed packet of Marietta biscuits, so ordinary, so homely. All the same, there was something unignorable in the atmosphere, something tensed and watchful and sullen, as if their presence were being registered, and resented.

"Now what?" she said.

Jimmy was squinting suspiciously about the room, as usual playing the hard-bitten reporter; in a moment he would have his notebook and his pencil out. Phoebe could not remember exactly where she had met Jimmy, or when. It was strange: she seemed to have known him an impossibly long time, yet she knew almost nothing about him; she was not even sure where he lived. He was garrulous, and talked tirelessly on every subject except himself. She wondered at the fact that April had let him know about the door key under the stone. Had others been let in on this arrangement? It struck her that if she was the only one that April had not told then perhaps it was not so strange that her friend had stopped calling her — perhaps April did not think of her as a friend at all, only an acquaintance to be taken up or dropped according to whim. If that was the case then she did not need to be so concerned. She was beginning to feel enjoyably aggrieved, but then it occurred to her that Jimmy, whom April had told about the key and therefore must consider a true intimate, had not heard from her either; nor had anyone else in their circle, so far as she knew.

As if he had read her thoughts — sometimes he showed an uncanny knack of clairvoyance — he asked her now: "How well do you think you know her? April, I mean."

They were standing in the middle of the room. It was cold, she still had her scarf wound round her throat, and although her hands were thrust deep in the pockets of her coat she could feel the chill tips of her fingers tingling. "As well as anyone, I think," she said. "Or thought I did. We used to talk nearly every day, you know. That's why I was worried not to hear from her in the first place." He was still glancing about, nodding, and gnawing his upper lip at one corner. "What about you?" she asked.

"She was always a good contact."

"A contact?"

"At the hospital. If there was a story going, some high-up knocking someone down when he was drunk or a suicide that was covered up, I could always depend on April to slip me the details."

Phoebe stared. "April told you about things like that?" It was hardly credible. The April that she knew, that she had thought she knew, surely would not pass that kind of information to a reporter, even one who was her friend.

"It wasn't anything confidential she was giving out," Jimmy said defensively. "A call to her would save me time, that's all. You don't know what it's like, working to deadlines." It was not attractive, that whining, hard-done-by tone that he fell into sometimes. He walked to the window and stood looking out. Even from the back he had a vexed, resentful aspect. She knew of old how quick he was to take umbrage; she had seen it happen so often.

"You realise," she said, "we've been talking about her all this time in the past tense?"

He turned, and they looked at each other.

"There's the bedroom," Jimmy said, "we haven't looked there."

They went in. The untidiness here was worse than in the living room. The wardrobe doors were open wide, the clothes inside crowded together and pulled about anyhow. Intimate items of clothing lay crumpled on the floor where they had been stepped out of and forgotten about. An old black Remington typewriter stood on a desk in the corner, and all around it were piled textbooks and papers and bulging ring-binders, almost covering up the telephone, an old-fashioned model with a metal winder on the side for connecting up to the operator. There was a cup there, too, containing the dried and cracked dregs of coffee that even yet gave off a faint, bitter aroma. April was a coffee addict and drank it all day long, half the night, too, if she was on a late shift. Phoebe stood and looked about. She felt she must not touch anything, convinced that if she did, the thing she touched would crumble under her fingers: suddenly everything was breakable here. The smell of the week-old coffee, and of other things — face powder, dust, slept-in bedclothes — that mingled, stale smell that bedrooms always have, made her feel nauseous.

Strangely, the bed was made, and to a hospital standard of neatness, the blanket and the sheets tucked in all round and the pillow as flat and smooth as a bank of snow.

Jimmy spoke behind her. "Look at this." A narrow plywood door with louvred panels led into the tiny, windowless bathroom. He was in there, bending over the hand-basin. He looked over his shoulder at her, and even as she came forward she felt herself wanting to hang back. The hand-basin was yellowed with age and had stains the colour of verdigris under each of the two taps. Jimmy was pointing to a faint, narrow, brownish streak that ran from the overflow slot at the back almost to the plug-hole. "That," he said, "is blood."

They stood and stared, hardly breathing. But was it so remarkable, after all, a tiny bit of blood, in a bathroom? Yet to Phoebe it was as if an innocuously smiling person had turned to her and opened a palm to show her something dreadful. She was feeling definitely sick now. Images from the past teemed in her mind, flickering as in an old newsreel. A car on a snowy headland and a young man with a knife. An old man, mute and furious, lying on a narrow bed between two tall windows. A silver-haired figure impaled, still twitching, on black railings. She would have to sit down, but where, on what? Anything she leaned her weight on might open under her and release horrors. She felt as if her innards were turning to liquid, and suddenly she had a piercing headache, and seemed to be staring into an impenetrable red fog. — Then, unaccountably, she was half sitting, half lying in the bathroom doorway with the louvred door at her back, and one of her shoes had come off, and Jimmy was squatting beside her, holding her hand.

"Are you all right?" he asked anxiously.

Was she? She still had that piercing headache, as if a red-hot wire had been pushed in through the centre of her forehead. "I'm sorry," she said, or tried to say. "I must have — I must —"

"You fainted," Jimmy said. He was looking at her closely, with what seemed to her a faintly sceptical light, as if he half suspected her swoon had been a pretence, a bit of attention-seeking histrionics.

"I'm sorry," she said again. "I think I'm going to be sick."

She struggled up and stumbled forward on her knees and huddled over the lavatory bowl with her hands braced on the seat. Her stomach heaved but nothing happened save a dry retching. When had she eaten last? For a moment she could not remember. She drew back and sat down suddenly on the floor, her legs folding themselves awkwardly under her.

Jimmy went out to make tea in the alcove next to the living room that passed for a kitchen, from where she heard him filling the kettle and taking crockery out of the cupboard. She wanted to lie down on the bed but could not bring herself to do it — it was April's bed, after all, and besides, the severity with which it had been made up was forbidding — and instead sat on the chair in front of the piled-high desk, shaking a little still, with a hand to her face. The pain behind her forehead had spread downwards and was pressing now on the backs of her eyes. "The milk was off," Jimmy said, setting a cup and its saucer before her on the desk. "There's plenty of sugar, though, I put in three spoonfuls."

She sipped the scalding, bittersweet tea and tried to smile. "I feel a fool," she said. "I don't know that I've ever fainted before." She looked at Jimmy over the steaming rim of the cup. He was standing before her with his hands in the pockets of his trousers, his head on one side, watching her. He was still wearing that smelly raincoat. "What shall we do?" she said.

He shrugged. "I don't know."

"Go to the Guards?"

"And say what?"

"Well, that — that April hasn't been heard of, that we went into her flat and it was empty, that there was a bloodstain in the sink." She stopped. She could hear herself how weak it sounded, weak and fanciful.

Jimmy turned away and paced the floor, weaving a path among April's scattered underthings. "She could be anywhere," he said, almost impatiently. "She could be on a holiday — you know how impulsive she is."

"But what if she's not on a holiday?"

"Look, she could have got sick and gone home to her mother." Phoebe snorted. "Well, she could," he insisted. "When a girl is sick her first instinct is to fly back to the nest." Where, she wondered, was the nest that Jimmy would fly home to, if he was sick, or in trouble? She imagined it, a cramped, whitewashed cottage down an unpaved road, with a mountain behind, and a dog at the gate growling, and a figure in an apron wavering uncertainly in the dimness of the doorway. "Why don't you phone her?" he said.

"Who?"

"Her mother. Mrs Latimer, old ironsides."

It was, of course, the obvious thing to do, the thing she should have done first, but the thought of speaking to that woman daunted her. "I wouldn't know what to say," she said. "Anyway, you're right, April could be anywhere, doing anything. Just because she hasn't called us doesn't mean she's — doesn't mean she's missing." She shook her head, and winced as the pain pulsed anew behind her eyes. "I think we should meet, the four of us, you, me, Patrick, Isabel."

"A conference, you mean?" he said. "An emergency council?" He was laughing at her.

"Yes, if you like," she said stoutly, undeterred. "I'll call them and suggest we meet up tonight. The Dolphin? Seven thirty, as usual?"

"All right," he said. "Maybe they'll know something — maybe one of them will even have heard from her."

She rose and went out to the kitchen, carrying the teacup. "Who knows?" she said over her shoulder. "They might have gone off somewhere together, the three of them."

"Without telling us?"

Why not? she thought. Anything is possible — everything is. After all, April had not told her about the key under the stone. What else might she have kept secret from her?

CHAPTER
FOUR

Quirke's flat had the sheepish and resentful air of an unruly classroom suddenly silenced by the unexpected return of the teacher. He put down his suitcase and walked through the rooms, peering into corners, examining things, not knowing what he expected to find, and found everything as it had been on the morning of Christmas Eve when the taxi had come to take him, sweating and shaking, to St John's. This was obscurely disappointing; had he been hoping for some outrageous violation, the windows smashed, his belongings plundered, his bed overturned and the sheets shat on? It did not seem right that all here should have remained intact and unaffected while he was away suffering such trials. He returned to the living room. His overcoat was still buttoned. There had been no fire lit in the flat for nearly two months and the air felt colder in here than it had outside. He plugged in the one-bar electric fire, hearing himself grunt as he leaned down to the socket; immediately there was a scorched smell as the reddening coil burned off the weeks of dust that had accumulated on it. Then he went into the kitchen and turned all four burners of the gas stove on to full, and lit the oven, too, and set it to high.

Malachy Griffin had not ventured past the front doorway, where he stood now framed with the landing behind him, in his grey mackintosh and woollen muffler, watching Quirke grimly claiming back his territory. Malachy was tall and gaunt with thinning hair; his rimless spectacles gave to his eyes a teary shine.

"Can I get anything for you?" he asked.

Quirke turned. "What?" He was at the big kitchen window, with his hands in the pockets of his overcoat. He had a lost, vague look. Fogged light fell down on him from the window, a thin, silvery misting.

"You'll need provisions. Milk. Bread."

"I'll go up in a while to the Q and L."

A faintly desperate silence fell. Quirke wished his brother-in-law would either leave or come inside and shut the door. Yet at the same time he did not want him to go, not yet: even Malachy's company was preferable to being left alone with himself in these suddenly estranged and sullen surroundings. He began to open a cupboard door, then stopped. He laughed. "Christ, I was about to pour us both a drink!"

"Why don't we go up to the Shelbourne?" Malachy said. "You probably didn't have any breakfast, did you?" He was thinking how Quirke's largeness — that great head, those massive shoulders — made him seem all the more vulnerable, now.

"I don't eat much, these days. The metabolism changes when the booze is taken away. Like a baby that's been weaned, I suppose."

The gas jets hissed and spluttered, spreading a faint, flabby warmth on the air.

"All the same," Malachy said, "you have to —"

"Don't say I have to keep my strength up."

There was another silence, this time offended a little on Malachy's side. Quirke waved a hand in irritated apology, shaking his head. He turned off the gas. "All right, let's go," he said.

The atmosphere outdoors had the texture of wetted, cold cotton. Malachy's car was parked at the kerb; although Malachy had picked him up in it from St John's, it was only now that Quirke recognised it, with a dull shock, as the big old black Humber once owned by Judge Garret Griffin, his adoptive father. The Judge, now dead, was Malachy's natural father; he had done them both great wrong. Why was Malachy driving the wicked old man's motor car — what was it, a gesture of forgiveness and filial piety?

Quirke suggested that they walk. They set off along Mount Street, their footsteps rising up a beat late behind them. There was coal dust from the city's fireplaces suspended in the fog; they could feel the grit of it on their lips and between their teeth. At the corner of Merrion Square they turned left in the direction of Baggot Street.

"By the way," Quirke said, "do you know that young one at the hospital, Conor Latimer's daughter?"

"Latimer? Which department is she in?"

"I don't know. General, I imagine. She's a junior."

Malachy pondered; Quirke could almost hear the sound of his brain working, as if he were flicking through a set of file cards; Malachy prided himself on his memory for detail, or used to, before Sarah died and he lost interest in such things. "Latimer," he said again. "Yes. Alice Latimer — no, April. I've seen her about. Why?"

The traffic lights at the corner of Fitzwilliam Street, turning red, pierced through the mist with an unnatural and almost baleful brightness.

"Phoebe knows her. They're friends." Malachy was silent. Mention of Phoebe always made for constraint between the two men: after all, Phoebe had grown up thinking Malachy, not Quirke, was her father. "It seems," Quirke said, clearing his throat, "she hasn't been heard from for some time."

Malachy did not look at him. "Heard from?"

They turned right on to Baggot Street. A tinker woman in a tartan shawl accosted them, doing her piteous whine; Quirke gave her a coin and she gabbled a blessing after them.

"Phoebe is worried," Quirke said. "It seems they're in the habit of speaking every day on the phone, she and the Latimer girl, but it's been a week or more since she had a call from her."

"Has she been at work, April Latimer?"

"No — sent in a sick-note."

"Well, then."

"Phoebe is not convinced."

"Yes," Malachy said after a pause, "— but Phoebe does worry." It was true; for one so young Phoebe had known a disproportion of misfortune in her life — betrayal, rape, violent deaths — and how would she not fear the worst? "What about the family?" Malachy asked. "Bill Latimer would be her uncle, yes? Our esteemed Minister." They both smiled grimly.

"I don't know," Quirke said. "I don't think Phoebe has spoken to them."

"And the brother? Hasn't he rooms in Fitzwilliam Square?"

"Oscar Latimer — is he her brother?"

"I think so." Malachy was brooding again. "She has a bit of a reputation, so I hear," he said, "the same Miss, or I should say Dr, Latimer."

"Yes? A reputation for what?"

"Oh, you know, the usual. Drinks a bit, goes about with a fast crowd. There's a fellow at the College of Surgeons, I forget his name. Foreigner." He paused, frowning. "And that one from the Gate, the actress, what do you call her? — Galway?"

"Isabel Galloway?" Quirke chuckled. "That's fast, all right."

They were crossing at the top of Merrion Street when a green double-decker bus appeared suddenly out of the fog, bearing down on them with a roar, and they had to skip in haste to the safety of the pavement. A reek of porter from the doorway of Doheny & Nesbitts made Quirke's stomach heave.

"So she might have gone to England, in that case," Malachy said, and gave a little cough.

Quirke knew what "gone to England" was a euphemism for. "Oh, come on, Mal," he said drily. "Wouldn't she have got one of the likely lads at the hospital to help her with any little problem in that line?"

Malachy did not reply, and Quirke, amused, glanced at him and saw his mouth tightened in a deploring pout. Malachy was consultant obstetrician at the Hospital of the Holy Family and did not take kindly even to the suggestion that April Latimer or anyone else could have got an illegal abortion there.

At the Shelbourne, outside the revolving glass door, Quirke balked. "I'm sorry, Mal," he muttered, "I can't face it." The thought of all that chatter and brightness in there, the winking glasses and the shining faces of the morning drinkers, was not to be borne. He was sweating; he could feel the wet hotness on his chest and on his forehead under the rim of his hat, which was suddenly too tight. They turned and trudged back the way they had come.

Not a word was exchanged between them until they got to the Q and L. Quirke did not know why the shop was called the Q and L, and had never been curious enough to ask. The proprietor — or more properly the proprietor's son, since the shop was owned by an ancient widow, bedridden these many years — was a fat, middle-aged fellow with a big moon face and brilliantined hair slicked flat. He always seemed dressed up for the races, in his accustomed outfit of checked shirt and bow tie and canary-yellow waistcoat, tweed jacket and cream-coloured corduroy slacks. He was prone to unpredictable, brief displays of skittishness — he might suddenly yodel, or grin like a chimp, and more than once Quirke had been present to witness him essay a few dance steps behind the counter, clicking his fingers and stamping the heels of his chestnut-brown brogues. Today he was in undemonstrative mood, due to the dampening effects of the fog, perhaps. Quirke bought a Procea loaf, six eggs, butter, milk, two small bundles of kindling, a packet of Senior Service and a box of Swan Vestas. The look of these things on the counter flooded him suddenly with a wash of self-pity.

"Thanky-voo," the shopman said plumply, handing over change.

In the flat Quirke unplugged the electric fire — it had made little impression on the big, high-ceilinged room — and crumpled the pages of an ancient copy of the *Irish Independent* and put them in the grate with the kindling on top and lumps of coal from the scuttle and set a match to the paper and stood back and watched the flames catch and the coils of heavy white smoke snake upwards. Then he went into the kitchen and scrambled two eggs and toasted slices of bread under the gas grill. Malachy accepted a cup of tea but would eat nothing. "My God," Quirke said, suspending the teapot in mid-pour, "look at us, like a pair of old biddies on pension day." They had been married to two sisters. Quirke's wife Delia had died in childbirth, having Phoebe; Malachy's Sarah had succumbed to a brain tumour two years ago. Being a widower suited Malachy, or so it seemed to Quirke; it was as if he had been born to be bereaved.

Angelus bells were tolling from all quarters of the city.

40

Quirke sat down at the table, still in his overcoat, and began to eat. He could feel Malachy watching him with the melancholy shadow of a smile. A sort of intimacy, however uneasy, had developed between the two of them since Sarah's death. They were indeed like two sexless cronies, Quirke reflected, two ageing androgynes shuffling arm in arm down the wearying middle stretch of life's long road. Malachy's thoughts must have been running on the same lines, for now he startled Quirke by saying: "I'm thinking of retiring — did I tell you?"

Quirke, teacup suspended, stared at him. "Retiring?"

"My heart is not in it any more," Mal said, lifting and letting fall his left shoulder, as if to demonstrate a deficiency of ballast on that side.

Quirke set down his cup. "For God's sake, Malachy, you're not fifty yet."

"I feel as if I was. I feel about eighty."

"You're still grieving."

"After all this time?"

"It *takes* all this time. Sarah was —" He faltered, frowning; he did not know how to begin listing the things that Sarah had been. After all, they had loved her, Quirke as well as Malachy, each in his way.

Mal smiled miserably and looked up at the grey light in the window beside the small table where they sat. He sighed. "It's not Sarah, Quirke, it's me. Something has gone out of my life, something that's more than Sarah — I mean, that's different from Sarah. Something of *me*."

Quirke pushed his plate away; his appetite was gone, not that it had been keen to start with. He sat back on the chair and lit a cigarette. Malachy had been reminding him of someone and now he realised who it was: Harkness, but without the apostate Christian Brother's invigorating bitterness and biting scorn.

"You have to hold on, Mal. This is all there is, this life. If something is gone out of it for you it's your job to replace it."

Malachy was gazing at him, his eyes hardly visible behind those gleaming lenses; Quirke felt like a specimen being studied under a glass. Now Mal asked softly: "Don't you ever just want it to be — to be done with?"

"Of course," Quirke answered impatiently. "In the past couple of months I thought at least once a day it might be best to go, or to be gone, at least — the going itself is the thing I don't care for."

Malachy considered this, smiling to himself. "Somebody asked, I can't remember who, *How can we live, knowing that we must die?*"

"Or you could say, how can we *not* live, knowing that death is waiting for us? It makes just as much sense — more, maybe."

Now Malachy laughed, or at least it was a sort of laugh. "I never knew you to be so enthusiastically on the side of life," he said. "Dr Death, they call you at the hospital."

"I know that," Quirke said. "I know what they call me." He tipped the ash of his cigarette into his saucer and saw Malachy's nostrils twitch in distaste. "Listen, Mal, I'm going to buy a car. Why don't you come and help me pick one out?"

Now it was Malachy's turn to stare. He could not take it in. "But you can't drive," he said.

"I know I can't," Quirke answered wearily. "Everyone keeps telling me that. But I can learn. In fact, I've already decided the model I have my eye on." He waited. "Aren't you going to ask me what it is?"

Malachy was still staring at him owlishly. "But why?" he asked.

"Why not? I have a sack of money I've been accumulating all these years, it's time I bought something with it, for myself. I'm going for an Alvis."

"What's that?"

"Best car the British ever built. Beautiful thing. I knew a fellow that had one — Birtwhistle, at college, remember, who died? Come on, we'll go up to Crawford's. There's a chap there, Protestant, dependable. I did a PM last year on his aged mother, who unaccountably fell downstairs and broke her neck the day after she'd made her will." He winked. "Shall we go?"

Malachy drove the Humber as if it were not a machine but a large, fuming, unpredictable beast he had been put in unwilling charge of, holding the steering-wheel at arm's length and groping about with his feet after the pedals down in the dark. He muttered to himself, under his breath, bemoaning the fog and the poor visibility and the recklessness of the drivers of the other vehicles they encountered along the way. At the corner of St Stephen's Green, as they were turning on to Earlsfort Terrace, they narrowly missed colliding with a CIE delivery cart drawn by a high-stepping Clydesdale, and were followed for twenty yards and more by the drayman's bellowed curses.

"You know," Malachy said, "I used to take pride in my job of helping mothers to bring their babies into the world. Now I look at the world and I wonder if I did more harm than good."

"You're a fine doctor, Mal."

"Am I?" He smiled at the windscreen. "Then why can't I heal myself?"

They went on a little way in silence, then Quirke said, "Isn't despair one of the big mortal sins? Or do you not believe in that kind of thing any more?"

Malachy said nothing, only smiled again, more bleakly than ever.

They parked on Hatch Street — it took Malachy fully five minutes to manoeuvre into a space twice the length of the Humber — and Quirke, shaken after the short but harrowing drive, was wondering if he should reconsider the idea of owning a car. On the pavement he put on his hat and turned up the collar of his coat. The sun somewhere was trying to shine, its weak glow making a sallow, urinous stain on the fog. As they walked towards the showrooms on the corner Malachy said worriedly: "This fellow's mother, the one that fell downstairs — when you did the post-mortem on her, you didn't — I mean, you wouldn't —?"

Quirke heaved a sigh. "You never really did have much of a sense of humour, did you, Mal?"

The showroom smelt of steel and leather, fresh paintwork, clean engine oil. A number of small, gleaming cars stood about the floor, looking self-conscious at the incongruity of being indoors but all the same conveying a bright and eager impression, like puppies in a pet shop. The salesman's name was Lockwood and he was indeed, Mal saw, every inch the image of a Protestant, which probably meant that he was not one at all. He was tall and painfully thin — it seemed his long bones must rattle when he moved — wearing a grey, chalk-striped, double-breasted suit and brown suede shoes with arabesques of holes punched in the toecaps. He had pale, poached eyes and a moustache that might have been painted on with an extra-fine watercolour brush; he was young but balding already, his high forehead giving him a startled, hare-like look. "Good morning, Dr Quirke," he said, "though it's not very good, I suppose, with that blessed fog that it seems will never lift."

Quirke introduced Malachy, then said without preamble: "I'm here to buy an Alvis."

Lockwood blinked, then a slow, warm light came into his eyes. "An Alvis," he breathed, in a hushed tone, reverently. "Why, of course." A very special model had come in just that week, he said, oh, very special. He led the way across the showroom floor, tensely chafing his long-boned hands; Quirke guessed he was calculating the commission he would earn on the sale and unable to believe his luck. "It's a TC108 Super Graber Coupé, one of only three manufactured so far, by Willowbrook of Loughborough — that's right, three only. Hermann Graber, Swiss master designer. Six-cylinder, three-litre, hundred b.h.p. Independent front suspension, Burman

F worm and nut steering box, top speed one-oh-three, nought to sixty in thirteen point five. Look at her, gentlemen — just look at her."

It was indeed a magnificent machine, black, gleaming, low-slung, displaying a restrained elegance in every line. Quirke, despite himself, was awed — was he really to become the possessor of this sleek, polished beast? As well take a panther home with him.

Malachy, to Quirke's surprise, had begun to ask questions that revealed an impressive knowledge of these machines and their attributes. Who would have thought old Mal would know about such things? But here he was, gravely pacing around the car, stroking his chin and frowning, and talking about crankshafts and Girling shocks — Girling shocks? — and valve gears and pushrod overheads, with Lockwood following happily at his heels.

"Maybe you should buy it, not me," Quirke said, trying not to sound peeved, and failing.

"I used to be interested," Malachy said diffidently, "when I was young — don't you remember? All those motoring magazines you used to try to steal from me."

Quirke did not remember, or did not care to. He looked at the car again and felt alarmed and giddy — what was he letting himself in for? — as if he had been enticed out on a tightrope and had frozen in fright midway across. Yet there was no going back. He wrote out the cheque, holding his breath as he filled in all those noughts, but managed all the same to hand it over with something of a flourish. Lockwood tried to maintain his salesman's professional smoothness but little smiles kept breaking out on his long face, and when Quirke made a weak joke about *driving a hard bargain* the young man lost all control and giggled like a schoolgirl. It was not every day of the week, or every year of the decade, for that matter, that a customer walked in off the street and bought an Alvis TC108 Super Coupé.

Quirke, who had not admitted to Lockwood that he did not know how to drive, was relieved to hear that the car would not be ready for the road until it had been given a "thorough look-see under her skirts", as Lockwood put it, by the company's engineers. Quirke had a vision of these men, advancing like a troop of surgeons, white-coated and wearing rubber gloves, each one carrying a clipboard and gripping a brand-new shiny spanner. He could collect the car the following day, Lockwood said. The fog was pressed like lint against the showroom's broad, plate-glass windows.

"Tomorrow, right," Quirke said. "Right." But tomorrow he would not be any more capable of driving than he was today.

Peregrine Otway was a son of the manse. He said it of himself, frequently, with a comical and self-mocking shrug. He seemed to consider it the most pertinent fact there was to know about him. If he made a blunder, forgot to change the sump oil or left a broken windscreen wiper unfixed, he would say, "What else can you expect, from a son of the manse?" and then would do his fat, gurgling laugh. His parents had sent him to one of the minor English public schools and he had retained the accent: "Very useful, when you're running a backstreet garage — everyone thinks you're a duke in disguise, slumming it." His premises, in a mews off Mount Street Crescent beside the Pepper Canister Church, round the corner from Quirke's flat, consisted of a low, cave-like space, reeking of oil and old exhaust smoke, barely big enough for a car and room to work on it — he had excavated a hole in the floor the length and depth of a grave, that afforded what he called "underbody access", a formulation from which he derived much innocent glee. At the front there was a single petrol pump, which he locked with a giant padlock at night. He was large and soft and fresh-faced, with a shock of dirty-blond hair and babyishly candid eyes of a remarkable shade of palest green. Quirke had never seen him in anything other than a boiler suit caked with immemorial oil and rubbed to a high, putty-coloured shine, shapeless and roomy yet painfully tight-fitting under the arms.

Wondering how on earth the new car was to be collected, Quirke had thought at last of Perry Otway, and on his return from the showrooms, when Malachy had departed, he went round to see him.

"An Alvis?" Perry said, and gave a long, expiring whistle.

Quirke sighed. He had begun to feel like a plain man married to a famously beautiful wife; the purchase of the car had been thrilling at first and conducive to quiet pride, but the owning of it was already, before he had even driven it, becoming a burden and a worry. "Yes," he said, with an attempt at airiness, "a TC108 Super —

ehm — Super —" He had forgotten what the damned thing was called.

"Not a Graber?" Perry said breathlessly, with a look almost of anguish. "A Graber Super Coupé?"

"You know the model, then."

Perry did his other laugh, the one that sounded like an attack of hiccups. "I know *of* it. Never seen one, of course. You know there are only —"

"— three of them in the world, yes, I know that, and I've just bought one of them. Anyway, the thing is, I need someone to collect it for me, from the showrooms —" Quirke could see Perry getting ready to ask the obvious question and went on hurriedly "— since I haven't renewed my licence. And then I need somewhere to keep it." He looked doubtfully past Perry's shoulder into the interior of the workshop, which was lit by a single naked bulb suspended on a tangled flex from the ceiling.

"I have a couple of garages along here," Perry said, pointing up the lane with his thumb. "I'll do you a good price on the rent, of course. We can't leave an Alvis sitting out on the street to be ogled and pawed at by any Tom, Dick or Harry, can we, now?"

"Then I'll phone them and say you'll be up to fetch it? When?"

Perry took an oil-soaked rag from the kangaroo pouch at the front of his boiler suit and wiped his hands. "Right now, old man," he said, laughing. "Right now!"

"No, no — the fellow up there said they'd have to check it over and so on, and let me have it tomorrow."

"That's rot. I'll toddle up and get it — they know me at Crawford's."

Quirke did not go with him, certain that if he did he would be shown up this time for the fraud that he was. Instead he went to his flat and made another pot of tea. Over the past weeks he had come to detest the taste of tea with a passion that it would not have seemed so harmless and commonplace a beverage could call forth. What he wanted, of course, was a good stiff drink, Jameson whiskey for preference, although in the latter weeks of his most recent binge he had developed a craving for Bushmills Black Label, which was a Northern brand not easy to find down here in the South. Yes, a smoky dive somewhere, with a turf fire and dim men talking together in the shadows, and a tumbler of Black Bush in his fist, that would be the thing.

Time passed, and with a start he came to and realised that he had been standing in a sort of trance beside the kitchen table for fully five minutes, dreaming of drink. He was angry with himself. Was it not disgust with what drink had done to him that had convinced him to check himself into St John's, disgust and shame at the bruiser and brawler he had become, reeling through the streets in search of a pub that he had not already been barred from? At eight in the morning on Christmas Eve he had ended up at the Cattle Markets in an awful dive packed with drovers and buyers, everyone drunk and shouting, including him. He had looked up and found himself confronting his reflection in the pockmarked mirror behind the bar, hardly recognising the bleared and bloodshot, grey-faced hulk slumped there with his hat clamped on the back of his head, with his fags and his rolled-up newspaper and his ball of malt, the drinker's drinker —

The doorbell buzzed, making him jump. He went to the window and looked down into the street. It was Perry Otway, of course, with the Alvis.

CHAPTER
FIVE

The Dolphin Hotel on Essex Street in Temple Bar had been the little band's meeting place from the start. No one remembered which of them it was that had first chanced on it, but given the nature of the establishment it was probably Isabel Galloway. The Dolphin was a well-known watering-place among the theatrical crowd, but the people who frequented it were mostly of a previous generation, blue-suited old boys with carbuncular noses, and well-preserved women of a certain age in fauvist lipstick and too much rouge. The wood-panelled bar was rarely crowded, even on Saturday nights, and the restaurant was not bad, if they felt like eating there and were in funds. Phoebe in her heart thought the little band a little pretentious — when had they started calling themselves by that Proustian label? — yet she was glad of her place amongst them. They were not the Round Table and the Dolphin was not the Algonquin, but they, and it, would do, for this small city, in these narrow times. There were five of them, exclusively five: Patrick Ojukwu, or the Prince; Isabel Galloway the actress; Jimmy Minor, April Latimer and Phoebe. Tonight, however, they were four only, a subdued quartet.

"I don't see why we're being so concerned," Isabel Galloway said. "We all know what April is like."

"It's not like her to disappear," Jimmy said sharply. There was always a mild friction between Jimmy and Isabel, who tossed her head now and gave a histrionic sigh.

"Who says she's disappeared?" she asked.

"We told you, we went to her flat, Phoebe and I. It was obvious she hadn't been there since Wednesday week, which was the last time Phoebe spoke to her."

"Of course, she could just have gone away," Phoebe urged, as she had urged so many times already, on the principle that she might be encouraged to believe it herself if she saw that the others did.

Jimmy gave her a scathing look. "Gone away where?"

"You're the one who told me I was being hysterical," Phoebe said, aware that she was flushing and annoyed at herself for it.

"But, sweetheart, you *were* being hysterical," he said, in his Hollywood twang. He gave her one of his smiles, not the real, irresistible one, but the smirking mask he had learned to put on, to charm and cajole. She sometimes asked herself if she really liked Jimmy; he could be sweet and affecting, but there was something dour and surly in his nature, too.

No one spoke for a time, then Isabel said: "What about the sick note she gave to the hospital?"

"We've all sent in sick notes without being at death's door," Jimmy said, turning to her and letting the smile drop. His legs were so short that even though the chair in which he sat was of normal height his feet did not quite reach the floor. He turned to Patrick Ojukwu. "What do you think?" he asked, unable to suppress an edge of truculence in his voice.

It was April who had met Ojukwu first and introduced him to the little band. He had been accepted more or less readily; Jimmy had shown the least enthusiasm, of course, while Isabel Galloway, as April drily observed, had attempted to climb into his lap straight off. They were all, even Jimmy, secretly gratified to have amongst them a person so handsome, so exotic and so black. They liked the sense his presence in their midst gave to them of being sophisticated and cosmopolitan, though none of the four except Phoebe had travelled farther abroad than London. They welcomed too, with grim satisfaction, the looks they got when they were in his company, by turns outraged, hate-filled, fearful, envious.

"I do not know what to think," Patrick said. He leaned forward and set his glass of orange juice on the table — he did not drink alcohol, in compliance with some unspecified religious or tribal prohibition — then sat back again and folded his arms. He was large, slow-moving, deep-voiced, with a great barrel chest and a round, handsome head. A student doctor at the College of Surgeons, he was the youngest of them yet was possessed of a grave and mysterious air of authority. Phoebe was always fascinated by the sharp dividing line along the sides of his hands where the chocolaty backs gave way to the tender, dry pink of the palms. When she pictured those hands moving over April Latimer's pale, freckled skin something stirred

54

deep inside her, whether in protest or prurience she could not tell. Perhaps it was her own skin she was imagining under that dusky caress. Her mind skittered away from the thought in sudden alarm. "I can't understand," Ojukwu said now, "why no one has spoken to her family."

"Because," Isabel Galloway said witheringly, "her family doesn't speak to her."

Ojukwu looked to Phoebe. "Is it true?"

She glanced away, towards the fireplace, where a tripod of turf logs was smouldering over a scattering of white ash. Two old codgers were in a huddle there, seated in armchairs, drinking whiskey and talking about horses. She had a sense of the winter night outside hung with mist, the streetlights weakly aglow and the nearby river sliding silently along between its banks, shining, secret and black. "She doesn't get on with her mother," she said, "I know that. And she laughs about her uncle the Minister, says he's a pompous ass."

Ojukwu was watching her closely; it was a way he had, to gaze steadily at people out of those big protuberant eyes of his that seemed to have so much more white to them than was necessary. "And her brother?" he asked softly.

"She doesn't ever mention him," Phoebe said.

Isabel gave her actor's laugh, going *ha ha ha!* in three distinct, descending tones. "That prig!" she said. She was the oldest one of the little band — none of them knew her age and did not dare to guess — yet she was lithe and slim, unnaturally pale, with a sharply angled face; her hair was of a rich, dark, almost bronzen colour, and Phoebe suspected that she dyed it. Isabel twirled the gin glass in her fingers and recrossed her famously long and lovely legs. "The Holy Father, they call him."

"Why?" Ojukwu asked.

Isabel inclined languidly towards him, smiling with imitation sweetness, and patted the back of his hand. "Because he's a mad Catholic and famously celibate. The only poking Dr Oscar ever does is —"

"Bella!" Phoebe said, giving her a look.

"They're *all* prigs, the lot of them!" Jimmy Minor broke in, with a violence that startled them all. His forehead had gone white, as it always did when he was wrought. "The Latimers have a stranglehold on medicine in this city, and look at the state of the public health. The mother with her good works, and the brother whose only concern is to keep french letters out of the country and the maternity hospitals full. And as for Uncle Bill, the Minister of so-called Health, sucking up to the priests and that whited sepulchre in his palace out in Drumcondra — ! Crowd of hypocrites."

An uneasy silence followed this outburst. The pair of horse-fanciers by the fireplace had stopped talking and were looking over with a mixture of curiosity and disapproval.

"I still think," Patrick Ojukwu said, "that someone should speak to Mrs Latimer, or to April's brother. If there is disagreement between them and April, and she does not keep in touch, they may not know she has not been heard from."

56

The other three exchanged uneasy glances. The Prince was right, the family should be alerted. Then Phoebe had an idea. "I'll ask my father," she said. "He probably knows the Minister, or Oscar Latimer, or both. He could speak to them."

Isabel and Jimmy still looked doubtful, and exchanged a glance. "I think one of the four of us should do that," Jimmy said, avoiding Phoebe's eye. "April is our friend."

Phoebe looked at him narrowly. They all knew where Quirke had been for the past six weeks. They knew too of her and Quirke's history together, or not together, rather. Why should they trust him to approach the Latimers? "Then I'll phone her brother," she said stoutly, looking round as if inviting them to challenge her. "I'll phone him tomorrow, and go to see him."

She stopped. She did not feel half as brave or decisive as she was pretending to be. The thought of confronting the famously prickly Oscar Latimer made her quail. And from the way Jimmy and Isabel shrugged and looked away it seemed they were no more enthusiastic for her to talk to him than they had been when she offered her father as a spokesman. Of the three, Patrick Ojukwu had the most enigmatic expression, smiling at her in a strange way, broadening his already flat, broad nose and drawing back his lips to show her those enormous white teeth of his all the way to the edges of gums that were as pink and shiny as sugarstick. He might almost have been mocking her. Yet behind that broad smile he, too, she sensed, was uneasy.

Despite her misgivings, that night when she got home she called Oscar Latimer, from the telephone in the hallway. His office number was the only one she could find in the directory and she was sure he would not be there, at eleven o'clock at night — she knew very well that she was calling him now in the certainty that she would not get him, and she was startled when the receiver was picked up after the first ring and a voice said softly: "Yes?" Her impulse was to hang up immediately, but instead she went on standing there with the phone pressed to her ear, hearing her own breath rustling in the mouthpiece, a sound like that of the sea at a great distance, the waves rising and falling. She thought it must be the wrong number she had dialled but then the voice again said: "Yes?" as softly as before, and added: "Oscar Latimer here. Who is this, please?" She could not think what to say. The hall around her suddenly seemed unnaturally quiet, and she was afraid that as soon as she began to speak the fat young man would come storming out of his flat to rail at her for making noise and disturbing him. She said her name, and had to repeat it, more loudly, though still speaking barely above a whisper. There was another silence on the line — perhaps he did not recognise her name, for why should he? — then he said: "Ah. Yes. Miss Griffin. What can I do for you?" She asked if she could see him, in the morning. After the briefest pause he said she might come at half past eight, that he could give her five minutes, before his first patient was due. He hung up without saying goodbye, and without asking what it was she wanted to see him about. She

58

supposed he thought she must be in trouble; probably girls in trouble phoned him all the time, at all hours of day and night, since he was the best-known doctor, in his line, in town.

She was halfway up the stairs when she stopped and came back down again, and fished more pennies out of her purse, and put them in the slot and dialled Quirke's number. She could not think if there had been an occasion before in her life when, as now, she craved so much the sound of her father's voice.

Next morning at twenty minutes past eight she arrived on foot at the corner of Pembroke Street and Fitzwilliam Square and spotted the unmistakable figure of Quirke, enormous in his long black coat and black hat, waiting for her in the half-light of dawn. Got up like this he always made her think of the blackened stump of a tree that had been blasted by lightning. He greeted her with a nod and touched a fingertip to her elbow through the sleeve of her coat, the only intimacy between them he ever seemed willing to permit himself. "You realise," he said, "it's not everyone I'd venture out for at this hour of the morning, in this weather." He turned and together they set off diagonally across the road, the fog clutching wetly at their faces. "And to call on Oscar Latimer, into the bargain."

"Thanks," she said drily. "I appreciate it, I'm sure." She was remembering the look that Jimmy and Isabel had exchanged at the Dolphin last night, but she did not care: she needed Quirke with her today, to give her support and keep her from losing her nerve.

They climbed the steps of the big four-storeyed terraced house and Quirke pressed the bell. While they waited Phoebe asked him if he had telephoned the hospital, and he looked blank. "To enquire about April," she said, "the sick note she sent in — did you forget?" He said nothing but looked stonily contrite.

There was a smell of coffee in the hallway; Oscar Latimer not only had his consulting rooms but also lived here, Phoebe recalled now, in a bachelor apartment on the two top floors, in what April used to describe scornfully as unmarried bliss. Why had she not remembered that? — it accounted, of course, for his answering the phone so late last night.

The nurse who let them in had a long, colourless face and large teeth; her bloodless nose narrowed to an impossibly sharp, purplish tip that was painful to look at. When Quirke introduced himself she said: "Oh, *Doctor*," and seemed for a second on the point of genuflecting. She showed them into a cold waiting room where there was a large rectangular oak dining-table with twelve matching chairs — Phoebe counted them. They did not sit. On the table were laid out the usual magazines, *Punch*, *Woman's Own*, *The African Missionary*. Quirke lit a cigarette and looked about for an ash-tray, coughing into his fist.

"How are you?" Phoebe asked him.

He shook his head. "I don't know yet, it's too early in the day."

"I mean, since you — since you came home."

"I bought a car."

"You did?"

"I told you I was going to."

"Yes, but I didn't believe you."

"Well, I did." He looked at her. "Don't you want to know what it is?"

"What is it?"

The nurse with the nose put her head in at the door — it was as if a hummingbird had darted in its beak — and told them Mr Latimer would see them now. They followed her up the stairs to the first floor, where her master had his rooms.

"An Alvis," Quirke said to Phoebe, as they climbed. "I suppose you've never heard of an Alvis."

"Have you learned to drive?"

He did not answer.

Oscar Latimer was a short, slight, brisk young man, smaller somehow than it seemed he should be, so that when she was standing in front of him, shaking his hand, Phoebe had the peculiar impression that she was seeing him at some distance from her, diminished by perspective. He had an air of extreme cleanliness, as if he had just finished subjecting himself to a thorough going-over with a scrubbing brush, and exuded a sharp, piny scent. His hand in hers was neat and warm and soft. He had freckles, like April, which made him seem far younger than he must be, and his boyish fair hair was brushed sharply away on both sides from a straight, pale parting. He had the beginnings of a moustache; it was no more than a few bristling, ginger tufts. He glanced at Quirke with faint surprise. "Dr Quirke," he said. "I didn't expect you this morning. You're well, I hope?" He had stepped back and with an adroit little dive had got in behind his desk and was already settling himself before he had stopped speaking. "So, Miss — Griffin," he said, and she caught the slight hesitation; she had never considered abandoning the name Griffin and calling herself Quirke instead — why should she have, when Quirke had not given her his name in the first place? "What can I do for you?"

She and Quirke had seated themselves on the two small chairs to right and left in front of the desk. "It's not about me that we've come," she said.

The little man looked sharply from her to her father and back again. "Oh? Yes?"

"It's about April."

Quirke was smoking the last of his cigarette, and Latimer with one finger pushed a glass ash-tray forward to the corner of the desk. He was frowning. "About April," he said slowly. "I see. Or rather, I don't see. I hope you're not going to tell me she's in trouble again."

"The thing is," Phoebe said, ignoring the implications of that word *again*, "I haven't heard from her, and none of her other friends have either, since a week from last Wednesday. That's nearly — what is it? — nearly twelve days."

There was a silence. She wished that Quirke would say something to help her. He was studying a large photograph hanging among framed degrees on the wall behind the desk, showing Oscar Latimer, in a dark suit and wearing some kind of sash, shaking hands with Archbishop McQuaid; what was it Jimmy Minor had called McQuaid? — *that whited sepulchre in his palace out in Drumcondra*. The Archbishop wore a sickly

62

smile; his nose was almost as sharp and bleached as that of Latimer's nurse.

Oscar Latimer drew back the cuff of his jacket and looked pointedly at his watch. Sighing, he said: "I haven't seen my sister since — well, I don't remember when it was. She long ago cut herself off from the rest of us and —"

"I know there was — there was tension between her and your mother," Phoebe said, in an effort to sound conciliatory.

Latimer gave her a look of cold distaste. "She as good as disowned her family," he said.

"Yes, but —"

"Miss Griffin, I don't think you understand what I'm telling you. As far as we're concerned, I mean the family, April is a free agent, beyond our influence, outside our concern. She's gone twelve days, you say? For us, she left much longer ago than that."

The room was silent again. Quirke was still gazing distractedly at the photograph.

"I didn't say she was gone," Phoebe said quietly, "only that I haven't heard from her."

Latimer let fall another sharp little sigh and again consulted his watch.

Quirke at last broke his silence. "We wondered," he said, "if April might perhaps have been in touch with her mother. Girls tend to cleave to their mothers, in times of difficulty."

Latimer regarded him with amused disdain. "Difficulty?" he said, as if holding the word up by one corner to examine it. "What do you mean by that?"

"As Phoebe says, your sister hasn't been heard from, that's all. Naturally her friends are worried."

Latimer fairly hopped where he sat. "Her friends?" he cried — it was almost a bleat. "Don't talk to me about her friends! I know all about her friends."

Quirke let his gaze wander again over the walls and then refixed it on the little man behind the desk. "My daughter is one of those friends," he said. "And your sister is not beyond *their* concern."

Latimer set his small neat hands flat before him on the desk and took a long breath. "My sister, since she became an adult, and indeed for long before that, has caused nothing but distress to our family, and to her mother in particular. Whether she's in *difficulty*, as you put it, or just off somewhere on one of her periodic romps I frankly don't care. Now, if you'll excuse me I have a patient waiting." He stood up, making two tripods of his fingers and pressing them to the desk and leaning forward heavily on them. "I'm sorry, Miss Griffin, that you're worried, but I'm afraid I can't help you. As I've said, my sister and her doings stopped being of any consequence to me a long time ago."

Quirke rose, turning his hat slowly in his hands. "If you do hear from her," he said, "will you phone us, either Phoebe or me?"

Latimer looked at him again with that disdainful almost-smile. "I won't be the one to hear from her," he said purringly, "you can be certain of that, Dr Quirke."

On the step outside Phoebe violently pulled on one glove and then the other. "Well," she said through her teeth to Quirke, "you were a great help. I don't think you even looked at him."

"If I had," Quirke said mildly, "I think I'd have picked up the little squirt and thrown him out of the window. What did you expect me to do?"

They walked along the square under the silent, dripping trees. There was some morning traffic in the street now, and muffled office workers hurried past them. The dawn seemed to have staled before it had fully broken, and the grey light of day seemed more a dimness.

"Is he a good doctor?" Phoebe asked.

"I believe so. Good doctoring doesn't depend on personality, as you've probably noticed."

"I suppose he's fashionable."

"Oh, he's that, all right. I wouldn't care to have him pawing me, but I'm not a woman."

They stopped on the corner. "Malachy is going to give me a driving lesson today," Quirke said. "In the Phoenix Park."

Phoebe was not listening. "What am I going to do?" she said.

"About April? Look, I'm sure Latimer is right, I'm sure she's off on an adventure somewhere."

She stopped, and after walking on a pace he stopped too. "No, Quirke," she said, "something has happened to her, I know it has."

He sighed. "*How* do you know?"

She cast about, shaking her head. "When we went in there first, into that room of his, I felt such a fool. The way he looked at me, I could see he thought I was just another hysterical female, like the ones I suppose he sees every day. But as he talked I became more and more — I don't know — frightened."

"Of him?" Quirke sounded incredulous. "Frightened of Oscar Latimer?"

"No, not of him. Just — I don't know. I just had this feeling, I've had it all week, but in that room it became — it became *real*." She looked down at her gloved hands. "Something has happened, Quirke."

He put his hands into the pockets of his overcoat and looked at the toecaps of his shoes. "And you think Latimer knows what it is that's happened?"

She shook her head. "No, it's nothing to do with him, I'm sure it's not. It wasn't anything he said or did. Just this certainty got stronger and stronger inside me. I think —" She stopped. A coal cart went past, drawn by an old brown nag, the black-faced coalman with his whip perched atop the piled full sacks. "I think she's dead, Quirke."

CHAPTER
SIX

The lounge of the Hibernian Hotel was almost full at mid-morning, but Quirke found a table in a corner, beside a palm in a tall Ali Baba urn standing on the floor. He was ten minutes early, and was glad he had brought a newspaper to hide behind. After only six weeks in the cotton-wool atmosphere of St John's he had become accustomed to the regulated life there, and now he wondered if he would ever readjust to the real world. Two pinstriped businessmen at a table next to his were drinking whiskey, and the sharp, smoky smell of the liquor came to him in repeated wafts, suggestive and blandishing. He had not thought of himself as an alcoholic, just a heavy drinker, but after the latest six-month binge he was not so sure. Dr Whitty at St John's would offer no judgement — "I don't deal in labels" — and probably it did not matter what his condition was called, if it was a condition. Only he was afraid. He was already past the middle of his life; up to now there had seemed nothing that he could not influence or alter, with more or less effort; to be an alcoholic, however, was an incurable state, whether he were to drink or not. That is a sobering thought, he told himself, and grinned behind his paper and bared his teeth.

When he saw Inspector Hackett come into the lounge he knew he had chosen the wrong meeting-place. The detective had stopped just inside the glass doors and was scanning the room with an air of faint desperation, nervously clutching his old slouch hat to his chest. He was wearing a remarkable overcoat, more a longish jacket, really, black and shiny, with toggles and epaulettes and lapels six inches wide with sharp tips. Quirke half rose and waved the newspaper, and Hackett saw him with evident relief and made his way across the room, weaving between the tables. They did not shake hands.

"Dr Quirke — good day to you."

"How are you, Inspector?"

"Never better."

"I wish I could say the same."

They sat. Hackett put his hat on the floor under his chair; he had not taken off his coat, which at close quarters was even more extraordinary: it was made of a synthetic, leather-like material, and squeaked and creaked with every move he made. Quirke signalled to a waitress and ordered tea for them both. The detective had begun to relax, and sat with his knees splayed and his hands clamped on his thighs, regarding Quirke in that familiar, genially piercing way of his. These two had known each other for a long time.

"Were you away, Doctor?"

Quirke smiled and shrugged. "Sort of."

"Have you not been well?"

"I was in St John of the Cross since Christmas."

"Ah. That's a hard place, I hear."

"Not really. Or, at least, it's not the place that's hard."

"And you're out now."

"I'm out."

The waitress brought their tea. Hackett looked on dubiously as she set out the silver pots, the bone-china cups, the plates of bread-and-butter and an ornamental stand of little cakes. "By the Lord Harry," he said, "here's a feast." He stood up and struggled out of his coat; when the waitress made to take it from him he instinctively resisted, clutching it to him, but then bethought himself and surrendered it, his forehead reddening. "Herself at home makes me wear it," he said, sitting down again, not looking at Quirke. "The son sent it to me for a Christmas present. He's in New York now, making his fortune among the Yanks." He picked up the silver tea-strainer and held it gingerly between a finger and thumb, inspecting it. "In the name of God," he murmured, "what is this yoke?"

In all the time that Quirke had known Inspector Hackett he had not ever been able to decide if what he presented to the world were truly himself or an elaborately contrived mask. If it was, then it was fashioned with cunning and subtlety — look at those boots, those farm labourer's hands, that shiny blue suit of immemorial provenance; look at those eyes, merry and watchful, that thin-lipped mouth like a steel trap; look at those eyebrows. Now he lifted his teacup with a little finger cocked, took a dainty slurp, and set it down again in its saucer. There was a shallow pink dent across his forehead where his hatband had pressed into the skin. "It's grand to see you, Dr Quirke," he said. "How long has it been now?"

"Oh, a long time. Last summer."

"And how is that daughter of yours? — I've forgotten her name."

"Phoebe."

"That's right. Phoebe. How is she getting on?"

Quirke stirred his tea slowly. "It's her I wanted to talk to you about."

"Is that so?" The policeman's tone had sharpened but his look was as bland and amiable as ever. "I hope she's not after getting herself into another spot of bother?" The last time Hackett had seen Phoebe was late one night after the violent death of a man who had been briefly her lover.

"No," Quirke said, "not her, but a friend of hers."

The detective produced a packet of Player's and offered it across the table; the look of the cigarettes, arrayed in a grille, made Quirke think, uneasily, of the Alvis.

"Would that," Hackett asked delicately, "be a female friend, now, or —?"

Quirke took one of the offered cigarettes and brought out his lighter. The men at the next table, who had been sitting forward almost brow to brow and murmuring, suddenly threw themselves back in their chairs, purple-cheeked and raucously laughing. One of them wore a bow tie and a wine-coloured waistcoat;

70

both had a shady look about them. Strange to think, Quirke thought, that the likes of these two were free to knock back all the whiskey they wanted, in the middle of the morning, while he was not to be allowed a single sip.

"Yes," he said to the policeman, "a girl called April Latimer — well, a woman, really. She's a junior doctor at the Holy Family." The frond of palm leaning beside him was distracting, giving him the sense of an eavesdropper attending eagerly at his elbow. "She seems to be — missing."

Hackett had relaxed now and seemed even to be enjoying himself. He had eaten four fingers of bread-and-butter and was eyeing the stand of cakes. "Missing," he said distractedly. "How is that?"

"No one has heard from her in nearly a fortnight. She hasn't been in contact with her friends or, it seems, anyone else, and her flat is empty."

"Empty? You mean her stuff is cleared out of it?"

"No, I don't think so."

"Did someone get in to have a look?"

"Phoebe and another friend of April's got in — April leaves a key under a stone."

"And what did they find?"

"Nothing. Phoebe is convinced that her friend is — that something has happened to her."

The detective had started on a cream cake, and ate as he spoke. "And what about — um — this girl's — ah — family?" A dab of whipped cream had attached itself to his chin. "Or has she any?"

"Oh, she has. She's Conor Latimer's daughter — the heart man, who died? — and her uncle is William Latimer."

"The Minister? Well." He wiped his fingers on a napkin. The fleck of cream was still on his chin; Quirke was wondering if he should point it out. "Have you talked to him — to the Minister — or to her mother? Is the mother alive?"

"She is." Quirke poured more tea and gloomily added milk; he could still smell that whiskey from the next table. "I went with Phoebe to see her brother this morning — Oscar Latimer, the consultant."

"Another doctor! Merciful God, they have the market cornered. And what had he to say?"

The whiskey drinkers were leaving. The one in the bow tie gave Quirke what seemed to him a smirk of pity and contempt; were his troubles written so starkly on his face?

"He said nothing. It seems his sister is the black sheep of the family and there's little contact any more. Frankly, he's a sanctimonious little bastard, but I suppose that has nothing to do with anything."

Hackett had at last located the cream on his chin and wiped it off. His tie, Quirke noted, was a peculiar dark-brown colour, like the colour of gravy. The hat-line across his forehead had still not faded. "And what," he asked, "would you be expecting me to do? Would your daughter, maybe, want to report her friend to us as missing? What would the family think of that?"

"I strongly suspect the family would not like that at all."

72

They pondered, both of them, in silence for a time.

"Maybe," the inspector said, "we should go round and have a look at the flat ourselves. Do we know where the key is kept?"

"Phoebe knows."

Hackett was idly examining a loose thread in the cuff of his suit jacket. "I have the impression, Dr Quirke," he said, "that you're less than eager to let yourself get involved in this business."

"Your impression is right. I know the Latimers, I know their kind, and I don't like them."

"Powerful folk," the inspector said. He glanced at Quirke from under his thick brows and gently smiled, and his voice grew soft. "Dangerous, Dr Quirke."

Quirke paid the bill and Hackett's storm-trooper's coat was returned to him. They walked through the lobby and out on to the steps above Dawson Street. Either the fog was down again or an impossibly fine rain was falling, it was hard to tell which. Motor cars going past made a frying sound on the greasy tarmac.

"I'd say now, Dr Quirke," Hackett said, fitting his hat on to his head with both hands as if he were screwing on a lid, "— I'd say it's power you don't like, power itself."

"Power? I suppose it's true. I don't know what it's for, that's the trouble."

"Aye. The power of power, you might say. It's a queer thing."

Yes, a queer thing, Quirke reflected, squinting at the street. Power is like oxygen, being similarly vital, everywhere pervasive, wholly intangible; he lived in its atmosphere but rarely realised that he was breathing it. He glanced at the dumpy little man beside him in his ridiculous coat. Surely he knew all there was to know about power, the having of it and the lack of it; together they had tried, some years back, to bring down another influential family in this city, and had failed. For Quirke, the memory of that failure rankled still.

They went down into the street. Quirke said he would call up Phoebe and arrange for her to meet them at April Latimer's flat when she left work that evening, and Hackett said he would make sure to be there. Then they turned and went their separate ways.

Malachy arrived at his flat at two, and they walked round to the garage in the lane off Mount Street Crescent and met Perry Otway, who handed over the key to the lock-up garage where the Alvis was waiting. The galvanised-iron door opened upwards on a mechanism involving a big spring and sliding weights, and when Quirke turned the handle and pulled on it the door resisted him at first but then all at once rose up with an almost floating ease, and for a moment his heart lifted too. Then he saw the car, however, lurking in the shadows, agleam and motionless, fixing him with a silvery stare from its twin headlamps. Childish, of course, to be intimidated by a machine, but childishness was an unaccustomed luxury for Quirke, whose real childhood was a forgotten bad dream.

He had thought that for Malachy, too, the Alvis would revive something from his youth, some access of daring he must once have had, but he drove it as he did

74

the old Humber, at arm's length, muttering and complaining under his breath. They went by way of Stephen's Green to Christ Church and down Winetavern Street to the river and turned up towards the Park. The mist was laden with the doughy smells of yeast and hops from Guinness's brewery. It was the middle of the afternoon and what there was of daylight had already begun to dim. Even Malachy's driving could not subdue the power and vehemence of the car, and it swished along as if under its own control, gliding around corners and bounding forward on the straight stretches with a contained, animal eagerness. They crossed the bridge before Heuston Station and went in at the Park gates and stopped. For a time neither of them stirred or spoke. Malachy had not turned off the ignition yet the engine was so quiet they could hardly hear it. The trees lining the long, straight avenue in front of them receded in parallel lines into the mist. "Well," Quirke said, with forced briskness, "I suppose we'd better get on with it." He was suddenly filled with terror, and felt a fool already, before he had even got behind the wheel.

Learning to drive, however, turned out to be disappointingly easy. At first he had trouble operating the pedals and more than once mistook the accelerator for the brake — the engine's howled rebuke quickly taught him the distinction — and getting the hang of the knight's move on the gearstick when shifting into third was tricky, but he soon mastered it. Of course, Malachy cautioned, in a faintly aggrieved tone, he would not find it all such smooth going when he had to deal with traffic. Quirke said nothing. His hour of excited anticipation and anxiety was over; now he was a driver, and the car was just a car.

They came to the Castleknock Gate and Malachy instructed him in how to make a three-point turn. As they drove back the way they had come they passed by another learner driver, whose car was executing a series of jumps and lurches, like a bucking horse, and Quirke could not suppress a smug smile, and then felt more childish still.

"When are you coming back to work?" Malachy asked.

"I don't know. Why — have there been mutterings?"

"Someone asked a question at a board meeting the other day."

"Who?"

"Your chap Sinclair."

"Of course." Sinclair was Quirke's assistant and had been running the department on his own for the past half-year while Quirke was first drinking and then drying out. "He wants my job."

"You'd better come back and make sure he doesn't get it, then," Mal said, with a faint, dry laugh.

They came to the gates again and Malachy said it would be best if he were to take over and drive them back to Mount Street, but Quirke said no, he would go on, that he needed experience of real road conditions. Had he a licence, Malachy enquired, was the car insured? Quirke did not answer. A bus had swerved out of the CIE garage on Conyngham Road and was bearing down on them at an angle from the right.

Quirke trod on the accelerator and the car seemed to gather itself on its haunches for a second and then leaped forward, snarling.

The mist was dispersing over the river and there was even a watery gleam of sunlight on the side of the bridge at Usher's Island. Quirke was considering the dilemma of what he was to do with the car now that he had bought it and mastered the knack of driving. He was hardly going to use it in the city, he who loved to walk, and for whom one of life's secret pleasures was luxuriating in the back of taxis on dark and rain-smeared winter days. Perhaps he would go for spins, as people always seemed to be doing. *Come on, old girl*, he would hear a driver say to his missus, *let's take a spin out to Killiney, or up to the Hellfire Club or the Sally Gap*. He could do that; he rather thought not, though. What about abroad, then, put the old motor on a ferry and pop over to France? He pictured himself swishing along the Côte d'Azur, with a girl by his side, her scarf rippling in the warm breeze from the open window, he blazered and cravated and she sparkling and pert, smiling at his profile, as in one of those railway posters.

"What are you laughing at?" Malachy asked, suspiciously.

At College Green a white-gauntleted Guard on point duty was waving them on with large, stylised beckonings. The car sped into the turn at Trinity College, the tyres shrieking for some reason. Quirke noticed Malachy's hands clasped in his lap, the knuckles white.

Quirke said: "Did you ask at the hospital about April Latimer?"

"What?" Malachy sat as if mesmerised, his eyes wide and fixed on the road. "Oh, yes. She's still out sick."

"Did you see the note?"

"Note?"

"The sick note that she sent in."

"Yes, it said she has the flu."

"That's all?"

"Yes."

"Did it indicate how long she'd be out for?"

"No, it just said she had the flu and wouldn't be in. That was a red light, by the way."

Quirke was busy negotiating that tricky change into third gear. "Typed or hand-written?"

"I can't remember. Typed, I think. Yes, typed."

"But signed by hand?"

Malachy pondered, frowning. "No," he said, "now that you mention it, it wasn't. Just the name, typed out."

At the corner of Clare Street a boy with a schoolbag on his back stepped off the pavement into the street. When he heard the blare of the horn he stopped in surprise and turned and watched with what seemed mild curiosity as the sleek black car bore down on him with its nose low to the ground and its tyres smoking and the two men gaping at him from behind the windscreen, one of them grimacing with the effort of braking and the other with a hand to his head. "God almighty, Quirke!" Malachy cried, as Quirke wrenched the steering-wheel violently to the right and back again.

Quirke looked in the mirror. The boy was still standing in the middle of the road, shouting something after them. "Yes," he said thoughtfully, "it wouldn't do to run one of them down. They're probably all counted, in these parts."

He considered taking the car round to Phoebe's flat to show it off to her and Hackett but thought better of it, and walked instead. It was dark now, and the air was again thickening with mist. A pair of early whores were loitering under the side wall of the Pepper Canister. One of them spoke to him softly as he went past and when he did not reply she called him an obscene name and both the young women laughed. The light from the lamp on Huband Bridge was a soft, grey globe streaming outwards in all directions. It glimmered on the stone arch and made a ghost of the young willow tree leaning on the canal bank there. He was remembering Sarah, as he always did when he passed by this spot. They used to meet here sometimes, Quirke and she, and walk along the tow-paths, talking. Strange to think of her in her grave. Dimly for a moment he seemed to catch the babbling voices of all of his dead. How many corpses had passed under his hands, how many bodies had he cut up, in his time? I should have done something else, been something else, he thought — but what? "A racing driver, maybe," he said aloud, and heard his own sad laughter echo along the empty street.

Phoebe was waiting for him on Haddington Road, standing on the step outside the house where she lived.

"I came down because my bell isn't working," she said. "It hasn't been for weeks. I can't get the landlord to fix it, and when anyone knocks, the bank clerk in the ground-floor flat looks daggers at me." She linked her arm in his and they set off up the road. She asked if he had remembered to enquire about April at the hospital. He lied and said he had seen the sick note and described it as Malachy had told him. "Then anyone could have written it," she said.

"Yes — but why?"

Hackett was pacing by the canal railings. His hat was on the back of his head and his hands were clasped behind him and there was a cigarette wedged in the corner of his wide, thin-lipped, froggy mouth. He greeted April warmly. "Miss Griffin," he said, taking her hand in both of his and patting it, "you're a sight for sore eyes, on such a damp and dismal evening. Tell me, are you well in yourself?"

"I am, Inspector," Phoebe said, smiling. "Of course I am."

They crossed the road, the three of them, and climbed the steps to the house, and Phoebe lifted the broken corner of the flagstone and took the keys out of the hole. The hall was in darkness and she had to feel along the wall for the light switch. The light when it came on was feeble, and seemed to grope among the shadows, as if the single bulb dangling from the ceiling had grown weary long ago of trying to penetrate the gloom. The brownish-yellow shade might have been fashioned from dried human skin.

"It seems to be a very quiet house," Inspector Hackett said as they climbed the stairs.

"Only two of the flats are occupied," Phoebe explained, "April's and the top-floor one. The ground floor and the basement seem to be permanently empty."

"Ah, I see."

Inside April's flat it seemed to Phoebe that everything had darkened somehow and become more shabby, as if years not days had passed since she had last been here. She stopped just inside the doorway, with the two men crowding behind her, and glanced into the kitchen. There was a sharp, rancid odour that she did not remember; probably it was the sour milk that Jimmy had forgotten to throw out, though it seemed to her sinister, like the smell that Quirke sometimes gave off when he had come recently from the morgue. Yet to her surprise she found that she was less uneasy now than she had been the last time. Something was gone from the air, the atmosphere was hollow and inert. Phoebe firmly believed that houses registered things that we do not, presences, absences, losses. Could it be the place had decided that April would not be coming back?

They went into the living room. Quirke began to light a cigarette but thought it would be somehow inappropriate and put away the silver case and lighter. Inspector Hackett stood with his hands in the pockets of his bulky, shiny coat and looked about him with a keen, professional eye. "Do I take it," he said, eyeing the books and papers everywhere, the stained coffee cups, the nylons on the fire-guard, "that this is the way Miss Latimer is accustomed to living?"

"Yes," Phoebe said, "she's not very tidy."

Quirke had walked to the window and was looking out into the darkness, the light coming up from a streetlamp laying a sallow stain along one side of his face. Through the trees across the road he could see faint gleams of moving canal water. "She lives on her own, does she?" he asked, without turning.

"Yes, of course," Phoebe said. "What do you mean?"

"Has she got a flatmate?"

She smiled. "I can't think who would put up with April and her ways."

The policeman was still casting about this way and that, pursed and sharp-eyed. Phoebe suddenly found herself regretting that she had brought these men here, into April's place, to pry and speculate. She sat down on a straight-backed chair by the table. In this room she was more than ever convinced that April was gone from the world. A shiver passed through her. What a thing must it be to die. Quirke, glancing back, saw the look of desolation suddenly on her face and came from the window and put a hand on her shoulder and asked if she was all right. She did not answer, only lifted the shoulder where his hand was and let it fall again.

Hackett had gone into the bedroom, and now Quirke, turning aside from his silent daughter, followed after him. The policeman was standing in the middle of the cluttered room, still with his hands in his pockets, gazing speculatively at the bed in all its neat, severe four-squareness.

"You can't beat medical training," Quirke said.

Hackett turned. "How's that?"

Quirke nodded at the bed. "Apple-pie order."

"Ah. Right. Only I thought that was nurses. Do doctors get trained how to make a bed?"

"Female ones do, I'm sure."

"Would you think so? I daresay you're right."

The floor was of bare boards thickly varnished. With the toe of his shoe the detective kicked aside the cheap woollen rug beside the bed; more bare wood, the varnish a shade paler where the rug had shielded it from the light. He paused a moment, thinking, it seemed. Then, with a brusqueness that startled Quirke, he leaned forward and in one swift movement pulled back the bedding — sheets, blanket, pillow and all — baring the mattress to its full length. There was something almost indecent in the way he did it, Quirke thought. Again the policeman paused, gazing on his handiwork and fingering his lower lip — the mattress bore the usual human stains — then he lifted back the skirts of his squeaky coat and with an effort, grunting, he knelt down and leaned low and scanned between the floorboards along the paler space by the side of the bed where the rug had been. He straightened, still kneeling, and took from the pocket of his trousers a small, pearl-handled penknife on a long, fine chain and leaned forward again and began to scrape carefully in the gaps between the boards. Quirke leaned too and looked over the policeman's shoulder at the crumbs of clotted, dark dust that he was salvaging. "What is it?" he asked, although he already knew.

"Oh, it's blood," Hackett said, sounding weary, and sat back on his heels and sighed. "Aye, it's blood, all right."

CHAPTER
SEVEN

Mrs Conor Latimer lived in widowed splendour in a large, four-storeyed, cream-painted house at the exact centre of one of Dun Laoghaire's grander terraces, set well back from and above the road and looking across the waters of the bay to Howth Head's distant hump lying whale-like on the horizon. She might have been taken for a wealthy Protestant lady of the old school had she not been Catholic and proud of it, fiercely so. She was no more than middle-aged — she had married young and her husband had died unexpectedly, and tragically, while she was still in her prime — and there were more than a few gentlemen of her acquaintance, not all of them indigent by any means, who might have ventured an interesting proposal, had they not all been so wary of her piety and alarmed by the coolness of her manner. She did good works; she was renowned for her charitable dedication, and notorious for the relentless-ness with which she went about screwing money out of many of the better-off of her co-religionists in the city. She was a patroness of many social institutions, including the Royal St George Yacht Club, whose clubhouse she could see when she stepped out of her front door. She had the ear of a goodly number of those at the pinnacle of power in society, not only that of her brother-in-law, the Minister of Health, whom privately she considered not half the man her husband had been, but of Mr de Valera himself and those in his immediate circle. The Archbishop, too, as was well known, was her intimate friend and, indeed, frequent confessor, and many an afternoon his vast black Citroën was to be seen discreetly parked on the seafront near the gate of St Jude's, for Dr McQuaid was famously fond of Mrs Latimer's homemade buttered scones and choicest Lapsang Souchong.

It was all, Quirke considered, surely too good to be true.

He had encountered Mrs Latimer on a number of occasions — her husband's funeral, a fund-raiser for the Holy Family Hospital, a Medical Association dinner that Malachy Griffin had cajoled him into attending — and remembered her as a small, intense woman possessed, despite her delicate stature, of a steely and commanding manner. She was said to model her public image on that of the Queen of England, and at the IMA dinner she had worn, unless he had afterwards imagined it, a diamond tiara, the only such that he had ever seen, in real life, on a real head. What he recalled most strongly of her was her handshake, which was unexpectedly soft, almost tender and, for a fleeting second, eerily insinuating.

Inspector Hackett had asked Quirke to accompany him when he went to call on this formidable lady. "You speak the lingo, Quirke," he said. "I'm from

Roscommon — I have to have a pass before they'll let me set foot in the Borough of Dun Laoghaire."

So the following morning they went out together to Albion Terrace. Quirke drove them in the Alvis. He had a spot of trouble at Merrion Gates — he did something with the gear stick and the clutch together that made the engine stall — but otherwise the journey was uneventful. Hackett was greatly admiring of the machine. "There's nothing like that smell of a new car, is there?" he said. "Are these seats real leather?"

Quirke, whose mind was elsewhere, did not reply. He was thinking of that line of desiccated blood that Hackett had dug out of the gaps in the floorboards of April Latimer's flat; it seemed to him now like nothing so much as a trail of gunpowder.

"Whoa!" Hackett cried, throwing up a hand. "I think, you know, that lorry had the right of way."

They parked outside the gate of St Jude's and walked up the long path between wet lawns and bare flowerbeds. Quirke had the feeling that the house with its many windows was looking down its nose at them. "Remember now," Hackett said, "I'm counting on you to do the talking." Quirke suspected that the policeman, for all his show of nervous reluctance, was enjoying himself, like a schoolboy being taken for a treat to the house of a testy but promisingly rich relative.

The door was opened to them by a red-haired girl who was already blushing. The old-fashioned maid's uniform that she wore, black pinafore and a lace collar and a mob-cap with lace trim, sat awkwardly on her, like a cut-out dress on a cut-out cardboard doll. She saw them into a drawing room off the hall and took their coats and hurried away, saying something that neither of them caught. The room was large and crowded with massive items of gleaming, dark-brown furniture. In the bay of the window there was a plant in a large brass pot that Quirke suspected was an aspidistra.

"So this," said Hackett, "is how the other half lives."

"This room looks to me," Quirke said, glancing about dismissively, "like a priest's parlour."

They went and stood side by side at the big sash window. The fog was light today and they could almost make out Howth, a flat dark shadow on the horizon. A fog horn boomed close by, making them jump.

Ten minutes had passed before the maid appeared again. She led them up the broad staircase. "Isn't it terrible cold?" she said. Hackett winked at her and she blushed again, more deeply this time, stifling a giggle.

She showed them into a long, chill room with three great windows looking out on the sea. There were chintz-covered armchairs and a number of small, dainty tables dotted about bearing cut-glass vases of dried chrysanthemums; a long white sofa was positioned opposite the windows, seeming to lean back in dazed admiration of the view; there was also a grand piano, which somehow had the look of not having been played for a very long time, if ever. The air was scented with the slightly charred aroma of china tea. Mrs Latimer was seated at an antique writing-desk with a leather-bound appointments diary open before her. She wore a dress of scarab-green silk tightly cinched at the waist. Her fair, not quite red hair was carefully waved and set. A coal fire burned in the marble fireplace. Over the mantelpiece there was an oil portrait of a pale girl in a white blouse standing in a splash of sunlight in a summer garden, easily recognisable as a younger version of the woman sitting at the desk, who paused now and waited a moment before looking up at the two men standing by the doorway. She smiled with her lips. She held a silver propelling pencil poised in her fingers; Quirke had once possessed a pencil like that; it had been used to stab a man who richly deserved stabbing.

"Thank you, Marie," Mrs Latimer said, and the maid bobbed her head and shot out backwards, as if she had been jerked on the end of a rope.

"Mrs Latimer," Quirke said. "This is Inspector Hackett."

The woman stood up from the desk and advanced, extending a hand. It was from her, Quirke saw, that her son had got his bird-like quickness. She still had something of the fine-boned delicacy of the girl in the portrait. Hackett was turning the brim of his hat in his fingers. Mrs Latimer looked from Quirke to him and back again, seeming unimpressed by what she saw. "A policeman and a doctor," she said, "come to talk to me about my daughter. I feel I should be worried." She gestured towards a small table before the fireplace where silver tea things were set out. "Can I give you some tea, gentlemen?"

They sat down on three straight chairs and Mrs Latimer, wielding the teapot, spoke of the weather, deploring the fog and the February damp. Inspector Hackett watched her, lost in admiration, it seemed, of the woman's poise, her measured cadences. "It's particularly hard on the poor," she said, "at this time of year, with coal so scarce still, all these years after the war, and everything so dear, as well. In the Society of St Vincent de Paul we're barely able to keep up with demand, and every winter it seems to get worse."

Quirke was nodding politely. The tea in his cup smelt to him of boiled wood. Neither he nor Hackett had told Phoebe about the blood between the floorboards by April Latimer's bed; they would not tell this woman of it, either.

She stopped speaking, and there was a silence. Hackett cleared his throat. Out in the bay the fog horn boomed again.

"My daughter, Phoebe," Quirke said, "— do you know her?"

"No," Mrs Latimer said. "She's one of my daughter's friends, I think?"

"Yes, she is. She tells me she hasn't heard from April for the past two weeks. She's worried. It seems she and your daughter see each other frequently, and if they don't meet they talk on the telephone."

Mrs Latimer sat very still, gazing at a point of reflected light on the lid of the teapot, with a cold smile dying on her lips. "Do I understand you to say, Mr Quirke, that you called in the Gardaí because your daughter hasn't heard from one of her friends for a week or two?"

Quirke frowned. "If you want to put it that way, yes," he said.

Mrs Latimer nodded, the last of her smile becoming a faint, wry grimace of amusement. She stood up from the table and crossed to the piano and fetched an ebony cigarette box and came back and sat down again. She opened the box and offered it, and the men each took a cigarette, and Quirke brought out his lighter. Mrs Latimer accepted a light, bending to the flame and touching the back of Quirke's hand with a fingertip.

"As you can see," she said, "I'm not as surprised or puzzled by your visit as I might have been. My son told me, of course, Mr Quirke, that you and your daughter went to see him. Tell me" — she turned a penetrating stare full on Quirke; her eyes were green and seemed to glitter — "is your daughter all right? I mean, does she suffer from nerves, that kind of thing? My son seems to think she does. I've heard she has had some — some troubles in her life."

Before Quirke could reply Hackett cleared his throat again and leaned forward. "The thing is, Mrs Latimer," he said, "no one else has heard anything from your daughter either. She hasn't been in work for the past fortnight. And her flat is empty."

Mrs Latimer transferred her green gaze to him and smiled her icy smile. "Empty?" she said. "How do you mean? Has April moved out?"

"No," the policeman said, "her things are all still there. There doesn't even seem to be a suitcase gone. But there's no sign of your daughter."

"I see." She sat back on her chair and folded one arm and cupped an elbow in a palm, holding her cigarette beside her cheek. "And where do you think she's gone to?" she asked, in a tone of no more than polite enquiry.

"We were hoping," Quirke said, "that you might know."

Mrs Latimer laughed, making a hard, small sound, like the tinkling of a silver bell. "I'm afraid I know very little about my daughter's doings. She doesn't — she doesn't confide in me." She glanced at them both and shrugged. "She's something of a stranger to us, I mean the rest of the family, and has been for some time. She leads her own life. It's how she wants it, it seems, and that's how it is."

Hackett sat back, frowning. Quirke put down his cup — he had not touched the tea.

"So you have no idea where she might have gone, or" — he paused a second — "or who she might be with?"

He could see her turning over the implications of his question, the second part of it in particular.

"I've told you," she said, "she leads her own life." Becoming brisk suddenly, she stubbed her half-smoked cigarette into the glass ash-tray on the table before her. "I can't afford to let myself be concerned about her. April hardened her heart against us, rejected all we stand for, gave up her religion. She lives amongst God knows what kind of people, gets up to things I dare not speculate on. Of course, I'm not indifferent. She is my daughter, I have to love her."

"Would you rather you didn't?" Quirke said, before he could stop himself.

"Didn't what — love her?" Again that green glitter. "You're impertinent, Mr Quirke."

"Doctor."

"Forgive me. Doctor. I'm used to a different kind of medical man. Besides, from what I hear you're not exactly in a position yourself to challenge anyone on the duties of a parent."

Quirke only looked at her, almost but not quite smiling, and Hackett half lifted his hand as if to forestall some violent movement. They heard from downstairs the sound of the front doorbell ringing. Mrs Latimer turned aside, and set down her cup on the tray. "That will be my brother-in-law," she said. "I asked him to call in."

Bill Latimer came into the room chuffing like a steam train, his hand already out, smiling his broad, cold smile. He was large and heavy, not fat, with a wide, bony face and thick brown wavy hair; he was much favoured, it was said, by women voters. He moved with surprising lightness, even grace, and Quirke recalled that he had been some sort of athlete in his college days. "God!" he said. "Isn't the weather dire?" He shook hands with both men, addressing Quirke by name. His sister-in-law he greeted with a glancing peck to the cheek and walked past her to the table by the fireplace. "I'd kill for a cup of tea," he said. "Will you ring for Maisie or Mary or whatever she's called, and tell her to bring up an extra mug."

Mrs Latimer was wearing her chilly smile again. "This is china," she said. "I'll get Marie to make some indian for you."

He laughed, turning to her. "Christ, Celia," he said, "it's far from china tea we were reared." He rubbed his hands and held them out to the fire, then turned and lifted the flap of his jacket and offered his backside to the heat. He looked at Hackett and then at Quirke. "So," he said, "that niece of mine is causing heartache again, is she? What is it this time — another boyfriend from the criminal classes?"

Mrs Latimer had tugged a bell-pull on the wall beside the fireplace and now Marie the maid entered and was told a pot of tea was required — "Real tea, mind!" Latimer said, with mock severity — and she went off again, grinning from the effect of the Minister's jovial charm. When she had closed the door behind her they sat down all four at the little table, and Latimer accepted a cigarette from the ebony box. Hackett briefly repeated what he and Quirke had already said to Mrs Latimer. The Minister sat back on his chair and laughed loudly; it was a laugh without humour or warmth, a noise only. "For the Lord's sake!" he said, "she's probably off down the country somewhere with some fellow" — he broke off and turned to his sister-in-law — "I'm sorry, Celia, but you know as well as I do what she's like." He turned back to Quirke again. "A terrible tearaway, I'm afraid, the same April. Our very own black sheep."

Quirke and the policeman said nothing. The silence yawned, and then Mrs Latimer, as at a signal, tapped her hands briskly on her knees and stood up, smoothing the pleats of her dress. "Well," she said, "I have things to be doing — I'll leave you three gents to it." She crossed to the desk and took up the diary and her propelling pencil and, casting back at them a brittle, brilliant smile, left the room, shutting the door softly behind her.

Latimer sighed. "It's hard on her, you know," he said. "She doesn't show it but it is. That daughter of hers was wild from the start." He sat back and gave the two men a hard look each. "So: what have you to tell me?"

Hackett shifted on his chair. "We went to the young woman's flat," he said. "To have a look."

"How did you get in?"

"She leaves a key under a stone, for her friends," Quirke said. "My daughter came with us, to show us where the key was."

"And?"

Hackett hesitated. "I think, Mr Latimer, there's cause for concern."

Latimer glanced at his watch. "Concern over what?"

"It didn't look to us like she's gone away," Hackett said. "There are two suitcases in the wardrobe in her room. And all her makeup and stuff is there — I can't imagine a girl going off without her lipstick."

"Maybe she's staying with a friend? Or as I said already, maybe she's shacked up somewhere with some fellow."

"Either way she'd have taken her things with her."

The politician and the policeman eyed each other levelly.

"Then where the hell is she?" Latimer demanded angrily.

They all had finished their cigarettes and now Quirke brought out his silver case and offered it round. Latimer rose with a sigh and went to the fireplace and stood leaning an elbow on the mantelpiece, looking into the burning heart of the coals. "That little bitch has caused nothing but trouble since the day she was born. Her father dying didn't help — she was only nine or ten, I think it was. Who knows what it does to a child when she loses her father? That's the charitable view. I'm inclined to think she'd have been the same even if Conor had lived." He put a hand into his trousers pocket and nervously jingled coins. "It's in the blood," he said. "Her grandfather, my father, was a gambler and a drunkard." He gave his empty laugh again. "The sins of the fathers, eh?" He looked at Hackett. "What else did you find?"

Again Hackett hesitated. "There was a bloodstain beside her bed."

Latimer stared. "Blood?"

"Cleaned up," the policeman said. "But of course you can't ever really get rid of blood, as I'm sure you know. It always leaves a tell-tale trace" — he glanced at Quirke — "isn't that so, Doctor?"

With a violent movement Latimer pushed himself away from the mantelpiece and began to pace the room, so that Quirke and the policeman had to swivel on their chairs to keep him in view. He stopped, staring at the floor and scowling. "What about the bed?" he asked. "Was there blood there, too?"

"You'd expect that, wouldn't you, if it was on the floor," Hackett said, "but I didn't find any. Only between the floorboards. I have a couple of my fellows in there now, going over the place."

Latimer set off pacing again, smoking his cigarette tightly in rapid, sharp drags. "This is not what I expected to hear," he said, as if speaking to himself. "This is serious." He stopped, turned. "It is serious, isn't it?"

Hackett lifted his shoulders and let them drop again. "We'll have to see what the forensics fellows say. I'll have their report tomorrow."

"Who are they," Latimer asked sharply, "these fellows? They'll report direct to you, yes? — they won't go blabbing around the place?" Inspector Hackett chose not to reply but sat as stolid as a frog, gazing before him. "I mean," Latimer said, "I wouldn't want Celia to hear any tittle-tattle before — before there was anything official known."

Quirke could see him going over in his mind the implications for himself and his reputation should it turn out that his niece had come to a scandalous end. "Mr Latimer," he said, "how much do you know about your niece, about the way she lives, and who she knows?"

Latimer turned on him. His brow was flushed and there was an ugly light in his eyes. "Are you the detective now, asking the questions? Why are you here, anyway?"

Quirke gave him a long look. "My daughter came to me," he said quietly, "because she was worried about her friend, and wanted me to do something."

"So you called in the Guards before you even spoke to the family."

"I spoke to April's brother."

"So you did, yes," Latimer said with another ugly laugh. "I don't imagine you got much out of him." He came back to the fireplace again and stood facing Quirke and the policeman. "Look," he said, "you know what we're dealing with here. We can't control this young woman, we have no hold over her. She's a stranger to us. God knows what she's been getting up to in that flat — a black Mass or something, it wouldn't surprise me."

"So you don't know," Hackett said, "who she might have been friendly with?"

Latimer stared at him. "What do you mean, friendly?"

"Going with — you know."

"A boyfriend?" His look darkened. "A lover? Listen, Inspector — What's your name again? Hackett, sorry, yes. I don't know how many other ways you want me to say this — April cut herself off from us. She blamed the family for everything, trying to run her life, keeping her from being free, being too respectable — the usual stuff, and all an excuse to get out from under any authority and live it up, doing whatever she liked —"

"I'm told she's a good doctor," Quirke said. "I asked about her at the hospital." It was not true, but Latimer was not to know it.

Latimer did not like to be interrupted. "You did, did you?" he said. "So now you're carrying out surveys, are you, issuing questionnaires? What are you? — a

98

pathologist, isn't that right? I've heard of you. I thought you had retired, on health grounds."

"I was in St John of the Cross," Quirke said.

"Nerves, was it?"

"Drink."

Latimer nodded, smiling nastily. "Right. Drink. That's what I heard." He was silent for a moment, looking Quirke up and down with a contemptuously measuring eye. Then he turned to Hackett. "Inspector," he said, "I think we'll call it a day. I can't help you about April, no one in this house can. Let me know what you find out about the bloodstain or whatever it was. I'm sure there's some simple explanation." Again he consulted his watch. "And now I'll say good day to you."

He stood before them, waiting, and they got to their feet slowly and turned towards the door. The fog horn once more sounded its blaring note. Outside on the road again Quirke would not speak, and kicked the Alvis hard in one of its rear wheels, for which show of fury he got nothing save a bruised toe.

CHAPTER
EIGHT

The Shakespeare was one of the few pubs where two unescorted women could meet for a drink without being stared at or even asked to leave by the barman. "Well, it is the works canteen, you know," Isabel Galloway would say. All the actors from the Gate Theatre round the corner drank there, and during intervals half the men in the audience would come hurrying down and throw themselves into the crush in order to get a real drink, instead of the sour wine and ersatz coffee on offer in the theatre bar. The place was small and intimate and easy-going, and in certain lights, with enough people in, and enough drink taken, it could seem the height of sophistication, or at least as high as could be hoped for, in this city.

Phoebe and Isabel met by arrangement at seven o'clock. At that hour there were few customers, and they sat at a table in a corner by the window and were not disturbed. Phoebe had a glass of shandy; Isabel was drinking her usual gin and tonic. "I'm resting for the next fortnight," she had said, in her weariest drawl, "so this is going to have to be your treat, darling." She was wearing a green feather boa and the little pillbox hat that Phoebe had got for her at a discount from the

Maison des Chapeaux where she worked. Her unnervingly long nails were painted scarlet, and her lipstick was scarlet to match. Phoebe as always was captivated by her friend's extraordinary complexion, its porcelain paleness and fragility set off by the merest touches of rouge placed high on her cheekbones, and those vivid lips, sharply curved and glistening, that looked as if a rare and exotic butterfly had settled on her mouth and clung there, twitching and throbbing. "Well," she asked now, "what's the latest? Has April escaped from the white slave trade and come back to tell the tale?"

Phoebe shook her head. "My father and I went round to her flat yesterday," she said. "With a detective."

Isabel opened her eyes very wide. "A detective! How exciting!"

"There's not a sign of her there, Bella. Everything in the flat is just as she left it — she might have walked out to go to the shop and not come back. She can't have gone away, she took nothing with her. It's as if she vanished into thin air."

Isabel shook her head with her eyelids lightly closed. "Darling, no one vanishes into the air, thick or thin."

"Then where is she?"

Her friend looked away, and busied herself searching in her purse. "Have you got a cigarette? — I seem to be out."

"I've given up smoking," Phoebe said.

"Oh, my God, you haven't, have you? You're becoming more virtuous every day, a nun, practically, I can't keep up with you — not, mind you, that I want to." Phoebe said nothing. There was a sourness sometimes to Isabel's tone that was not appealing. "I suppose," she said, "you wouldn't like to buy some fags for me? I really am broke." Phoebe reached for her purse. "You're such a darling, Pheeb. I feel a complete slut compared to you. Gold Flake — a packet of ten will do."

At the bar, while she waited for the barman to give her the cigarettes and fetch her change, Phoebe recalled an evening that the little band had spent here three or four weeks previously. Isabel had been in a play that closed after five performances and her friends had gathered in the Shakespeare to console her. There were the usual stares from the other customers — Patrick seeming not to notice, as always — nevertheless it had turned into a jolly occasion. April was there, gay and sardonic. They had drunk a little more than they should have, and when they came outside at closing time the streets were glittering with frost, and they walked under the sparkling stars round to the Gresham in hope of persuading the barman there, an avowed and ever hopeful admirer of Isabel's, to give them a nightcap. In the lobby they laughed too loudly and spent some time shushing each other, putting fingers to each other's lips and spluttering. To their disappointment Isabel's fan was not working that night and no one would give them a drink, and instead Patrick invited them back to his flat up by Christ Church. The others had gone with him but something, a vague yet insurmountable unwillingness — was it shyness? was it some obscure

102

sort of fear? — made Phoebe lie and say she had a headache, and she took a taxi home. When she got home she was sorry, of course, but by then it was too late: she would have felt a fool turning up at Patrick's door at dead of night, pretending that her headache had suddenly vanished. But she knew that something had happened at Patrick's that night; no one would talk about it next day, or in the days after that, but it was their very silence that told her something definitely had occurred.

She brought the packet of cigarettes back to the table.

"Tell me what the detective said," Isabel urged, tearing at the cellophane with her scarlet nails. "No, wait — first tell me what he was like. Tall, dark and handsome? Was he the Cary Grant type, all smooth and sophisticated, or big and dangerous, like Robert Mitchum?"

Phoebe had to laugh. "He's short, pasty and plug-ugly, I'm afraid. Hackett is his name, which suits him, somehow. I met him before, when —" She stopped, and a shadow fell across her features.

"Oh," Isabel said. "You mean in Harcourt Street, when all that —"

"Yes. Yes, then." Phoebe found herself nodding, very rapidly, she could not stop; she was like one of those figures on a poorbox that nod when a penny is put in, and her breathing had quickened too. She closed her eyes. She must get hold of herself. She would not think of that night in Harcourt Street, the breeze coming through the wide-open window and the man below on the area railings, impaled there.

Isabel put a hand on hers. "Are you all right, darling?"

"I'm fine. I just — Really, I'm fine."

"Have a real drink, for goodness' sake. Have a brandy."

"No, I'd rather not. It's just sometimes, when I remember —" She sat back on the seat; it was upholstered in plush the colour of watered wine; she put her hands down at her sides and somehow the texture of the nap comforted her, reminding her, she did not know why, of childhood. "Isabel," she said, "what happened that night at Patrick's? You remember, after the show had folded and we all came here and got drunk, and you and the others went off with Patrick afterwards to his flat."

Isabel made herself busy detaching an imaginary flake of tobacco from her lip. "What do you mean," she said, looking away and frowning, "what do you mean, what happened?"

"Something did. You all kept very quiet about it, and Jimmy was even more sarcastic than usual."

"Oh, I don't remember. We were drunk, as you have so sweetly reminded me, though you weren't, I'm sure, since you're such a *good* girl." She smiled with mock sweetness. "I suppose there must have been a row or something — you know how Jimmy is with Patrick when he has a drop taken." Phoebe waited. She was calm now, in a horrible sort of way. Isabel, still not looking at her, gave a vexed little sigh that did not sound quite right, that was like a stage sigh. "Yes, all right, yes, there was a row. It blew up over nothing, as usual. Jimmy wanted to walk April home — he was in his chivalrous mode — and April wouldn't go. Eventually I persuaded him to stop sulking, and said why didn't he walk *me* home?"

"And then?"

"And then we left. Jimmy and I. It was a lovely night, frost everywhere and not a soul on the streets. It would have been quite romantic if it had been anybody other than Jimmy."

Isabel was lighting a second cigarette from the butt of the first one. Phoebe wondered if she was imagining it, or were her friend's hands shaking ever so slightly? Was she telling the truth about that night?

"And April stayed there?" Phoebe asked. "With Patrick?"

"Well, I'm sure it depends what you mean by *stayed*, darling." Now at last she turned her face and looked full at Phoebe, as if defiantly, with an odd, hard light in her eyes. "Wouldn't you say?"

It seemed to Phoebe that the lamps in the bar had suddenly dimmed. She tasted something sour at the back of her throat. How they wait to ambush us, our true emotions, she thought.

"I really do think," Isabel was saying, in her husky stage drawl, "that too much is made of these late-night incidents. No one is himself, half crazy on drink and looking for hidden significance in every littlest thing. Of course, I may have missed a lot, since at that time of night I'm usually so drained after two or three hours standing on a stage shrieking at people who do nothing but shriek back at me, the same thing, over and over, every night. All *I* ever want to do is crawl into bed with a hot-water bottle, and the only stiff thing I want near me is a drink."

Phoebe felt as if she had struggled through a dense and thorny thicket and come out into an ashen, waste place. "So they were lovers," she said flatly.

"What?" Isabel stared, and gave what sounded like a forced laugh. "Do you know, I don't think I've ever heard that word used in real life, outside the theatre? Lovers, indeed!"

"Well, weren't they — aren't they?"

Isabel shrugged. "My dear," she said in her jaded, worldly way, "you really have the most vivid imagination, for the convent girl you pretend to be. Patrick, of course, must be fairly bursting with primitive urges — but lovers? I can't quite see it, can you? You know what April is like."

"What do you mean, what she's like?"

"Well, I rather think there's a lot more talk there than action. In my experience the ones who seem the keenest goers turn out to be virgins in the end." She patted her friend's hand. "How quaint you are, darling Phoebe, quaint and adorably strait-laced. Are you jealous? You're blushing — you *are* jealous. Mind you, I can understand it. He is quite a hunk of dusky manhood, isn't he?" Her voice had hardened and there was that cold, bitter light in her eyes again.

"Yes," Phoebe said, "yes, he's very — he's very beautiful."

106

Isabel looked at her. "For God's sake," she said sharply, "don't say you're smitten, too."

Phoebe would not weep: weeping would bring no comfort to her suddenly wrung heart. She was sure, whatever Isabel said, that April and Patrick had been lovers. The notion of it had often crossed her mind, but she had never really believed it; now she did. Once planted, the conviction would not weaken. And Isabel was right, she was jealous. But the worst of it was she did not know which of them she was jealous of, April, or Patrick.

No, she would not weep.

And then, of course, next day she had to go and make a fool of herself. She knew she should not do it but she went ahead and did. She reasoned that since it was her lunch hour she could pretend, if she had to, that she was out for a stroll. Ridiculous, of course: who would believe that anyone would stroll all the way from Grafton Street up to Christ Church in this weather? She had not really expected to see him; after all, what were the chances that he would be at home in the middle of the day? Not that she had any intention of calling on him. What, then, was she thinking of? It was childish; she was like a schoolgirl hanging about the streets hoping for a glimpse of some boy she had a crush on. She told herself to stop being stupid and turn back, yet on she went, through the foul, damp air, and when she turned from Christchurch Place into Castle Street there he was! She saw him walking towards her from the other direction, in his brown duffel coat and a woollen scarf, carrying a string bag of groceries. He did not spot her right away and she thought of turning on her heel and fleeing, but she knew it was too late — he would see her then, surely, running away, and would think her an even bigger fool, and furthermore she would know herself for a coward. So she went on, forcing herself to seem as surprised as he must be.

"Phoebe!" he said, stopping, with that big smile of his. "How good to see you."

"I was — I was meeting someone," she said. "Over at the cathedral. A friend of mine. I just left her." She was babbling, she could hear herself. "I forgot you lived in this street. I'm on my way back to work."

Patrick was still smiling. He must know she was lying. What would he think she was doing here? — Would he realise she must have been hoping he would be there and she would meet him? "Come in for a minute," he said. "It's so cold."

It was a shabby little house that he lived in, with a narrow front door painted in wavy lines and varnished to look like wood. He had the upstairs flat; she had never been in it before. His landlady occupied the ground floor — "She is out," he said, "so there is no need to worry." The hall was laid with cheap lino and the stairs were steep and had a dank smell. He had done what he could to make the tiny bleak living room seem homely, with coloured posters on the walls and a bright-red blanket draped over the back of an old armchair. She was aware of the bed in the corner but would not allow herself to look at it. His desk was a folding card-table set up under the window. On it, beside a green Olivetti portable typewriter and a stack of textbooks, stood a framed photograph of a middle-aged couple in tribal costume, the woman wearing an elaborate headdress. There was a telephone on the floor beside the bed; she noticed it was an old-fashioned one, like April's, with that winder on the side.

"Have you had your lunch?" Patrick asked. "I was going to make something." Phoebe was gazing at a small bronze figure on the window-sill: it was of a big-eyed, fearsome-seeming warrior in a spiked helmet brandishing an elaborate spear or some sort of long, ornamental sword, broad at the tip. "From Benin," Patrick said, following her gaze. "It is an Oba — a king, or ruler. Do you know about the Benin bronzes?"

Phoebe shook her head. "I'm sorry."

"Oh, no need. Very few people up here know about Benin — African art can never be sophisticated in European eyes. This piece is a copy, of course."

He went into an alcove where there was a sink and a wall cupboard and, perched precariously on a shelf, a Baby Belling electric stove, hardly bigger than a hatbox, with a single cooking ring. He filled a kettle and put it on the ring to boil, and began to unpack the string bag on the draining-board. "Would you like coffee, or tea?" he asked. "I have cheese, and bread, and dates. Are you hungry?"

"I love dates," she said, though she had never tasted them before.

He had no pot and made the coffee in a saucepan instead. The coffee was black and bitter and she could

109

feel the grounds like sand between her teeth, yet she thought she had never tasted anything so wonderful and exotic, so redolent of elsewhere. They sat facing each other across a little low table, she in the armchair with the red blanket and he perched on a comical little three-legged stool. The dates were sticky and had a taste like the taste of chocolate. Over the rim of the mug she watched Patrick's hands. They were large and almost square, with very thick fingers that seemed to caress with elaborate tenderness the things they touched. Here, like this, in his own place, amongst his own things, he seemed younger than he did elsewhere, boyish, almost, and a little shy, a little vulnerable. "Would you like some cheese?" he asked. When he spoke the last word his lower lip was drawn down and she glimpsed the pink inside of his mouth, more crimson than pink, a dark, secret, soft place. From the corner of her eye she saw that he had put her coat on the bed; it lay at an angle with one sleeve outflung; it might have been her, prostrate there.

"I lied," she said. "I wasn't meeting a friend. I wasn't meeting anyone."

"Oh?" He showed no surprise, only smiled again. When he smiled he had a way of dipping his large head quickly down to one side and up again, which made him seem awkward and happy at the same time.

"The truth is I came up here in the hope that I'd see you. And what a strange coincidence, meeting you in the street. I could hardly believe it when I saw you."

"Yes, a coincidence. I decided to stay at home today" — he nodded towards the table with its pile of books —

"to study." He ate with small, deft, quick movements, strange to see in one so broad and solid, those big fingers bunched and lifting morsel after morsel to his lips, those lips that seemed dry, and were cracked, and yet looked soft, too, soft as some kind of dark, ripe fruit. "Why did you want to see me?" he asked.

She drank her coffee, holding the mug in both hands, huddled into herself. She continued trying not to see the coat on the bed, but there it was, sprawled there, at once blameless and suggestive. "I don't know," she said. "I suppose I wanted to talk about April. I keep thinking — oh, I don't know. I keep thinking of the things that could have happened to her." She looked at him almost beseechingly. "Do you think she'll come back?"

He said nothing for a while. Outside, a bell chimed the hour, and a moment later another bell rang, farther off, from St Patrick's. Only this city, she thought, would have two cathedrals within a few hundred yards of each other, and both of them Protestant. At last Patrick said: "Did anyone talk to her family?"

"My father and I went to see her brother. He knew nothing, he said, and cared nothing, either. They always hated each other, he and April."

"And Mrs Latimer?"

"Yes, my father went to see her, too. He went with a detective."

Patrick stared at her, his eyes, the orbs themselves, seeming to grow larger, the whites swelling. "A detective?" he said. "Why?"

"My father knows him — I do, too, sort of. His name is Hackett. It's all right, he's very — discreet."

111

Patrick looked aside, nodding slowly, thinking. "And what did she say, Mrs Latimer?"

"Nothing either, I think. Her brother-in-law was there, April's uncle, the Minister. The family is uniting to protect itself, my father says. I suppose they think April has done something that will harm their precious reputation, which is probably all they care about." Why was she speaking like this, so bitterly, with such resentment, suddenly? What business was it of hers what the Latimers said or did not say, what they did or did not do? None of that would bring April back. And then, the next moment, she was shocked to find herself looking into Patrick's great, broad, flat-nosed face and asking: "Do you love her?"

At first she thought he was not going to answer, that he would pretend she had not spoken or that he had not heard or understood her. He blinked slowly; there were times when he seemed to exist at a different pace from everything around him.

"I don't know what you mean," he said simply, his voice very deep and deliberate. "Do you mean, am I *in* love?" She nodded, with lips compressed. He smiled, and opened his hands wide before her, showing her those broad, pink palms. "April is wonderful," he said, "but I think it would not be easy to be in love with her."

"People don't expect being in love to be easy, do they?" she said. "I wouldn't expect it to be easy — I wouldn't *want* it to be."

Patrick lowered his head and flexed his shoulders slowly, as if he felt something being drawn in around him.

112

"It's all right," Phoebe said, and had to stop herself from reaching out and touching his hand, "it's none of my business. Tell me about the Benin bronzes."

He put down his coffee mug and rose and walked to the window. How lightly he moved, in a swaying prance, big and yet strangely delicate, like, she realised, yes, like her father. He took up the bronze figure from the sill and weighed it in his hands. Outside, she saw, it had begun to rain, in an absent-minded sort of way.

"Benin was a great city," he said, "at the heart of a great empire. The Bini people were ruled from earliest times by the Ogisos, the sky-kings. Ekaladerhan, son of the last Ogiso, was banished and lived among the Yoruba people, where he changed his name and became the great Oduduwa, ruler of the city of Ife. When the elders of the Bini people sent to plead with Oduduwa to return and be their Oba, he sent his son instead, and the dynasty continued. The Portuguese were the first Europeans to come, then the Dutch, and then, of course, the British. At the end of the last century a handful of British representatives were killed in the city, and the famous Punitive Expedition was launched, the palace of the last Oba was sacked and its treasures were destroyed or stolen. Most of the bronzes from the palace are now in —" he gave a brief, dismissive laugh "— the British Museum." He stopped, still hefting the warrior thoughtfully, his eyes hooded. She could tell it was a tale he had often told, and had become a kind of performance, a kind of chant. She imagined April sitting here where she was sitting, watching him at the window with the bronze figure in his hand. What did she know about April or about this man from Africa? What did she know about her friend Isabel Galloway, for that matter, or Jimmy Minor — what did she know? Everyone, she thought, is a stranger.

"Is that where you're from," she asked, "— from Benin?"

"No," he said. "No, I am an Igbo. I was born in a small village, on the Niger, but I grew up in Port Harcourt. Not a very pretty place."

She did not care where he was born, what city or cities he had lived in. She felt all at once bereft by his talk of these so far-off places, where she would never be, which she would never know. The rain whispered against the window, as if it, too, had a story to tell her.

"Do you miss it, your home?" she asked, trying not to let him hear the woe in her voice.

"I suppose I do — we all miss our home, don't we, when we leave it?"

"Oh, but you haven't left, have you?" she said quickly. "I mean, you'll go back. Surely they need doctors in Nigeria?"

He gave her a sharp, sly glance, and his smile turned chilly. "Of course — we need everything. Except missionaries, maybe. Of them, we have enough."

She did not know what to say to this; she supposed she had offended him, it seemed so easy to do. He put the figure back on the sill carefully, in the spot where it had been — was it a holy thing for him, reaching down to the deep roots of his past? — and came back and sat down opposite her again on the wooden stool.

114

"You know that's a milking stool?" she said. "I can't think where you got it from."

"It was here when I came. Perhaps Mrs Gilligan was a milkmaid when she was young." He laughed. "Mrs Gilligan is my landlady. If you knew her you would see the joke. Hair curlers, headscarf, cigarette. The cows would not like her, I think." He picked up a crumb of cheese in that way that he did, bunching his thick fingers, and put it thoughtfully into his pink mouth. "Sometimes," he said, and his tone was suddenly changed, "sometimes it's hard, here, for me. I get tired — tired of the way I am looked at, tired of the scowls, the muttered remarks."

"You mean, because you're — because of your colour?"

He plucked up another morsel from his plate. "It does not relent, that is what is the worst of it. I forget sometimes, about my —" he smiled, making a little bow of acknowledgement "— my colour, but not for long. There is always someone to remind me of it."

"Oh!" she said, appalled. "I didn't mean — I mean I —"

"Not you," he said. "Not my friends. I'm lucky to have such friends — you cannot know how lucky."

There was a long silence. They listened to the sibilant sound of the rain on the window-panes.

"I'm sorry I asked you that about April," Phoebe said. "About your being — about her —"

"About my being 'in love' with her?" He did that little bob of his head again, smiling. "I could not afford

115

to love someone like April. There is April herself, what she is like, and then there is, too, my 'colour'."

"I'm sorry," she said again, in a small voice, looking down.

"Yes," he said, almost as softly, "so am I."

When, five minutes later, she came out into the street — Patrick stood in the doorway looking after her as she walked away — she felt more confused than ever. While she was sitting with him and he was talking to her she had thought she understood, in some way beyond the actual words he had spoken, what he was saying, but now she realised that she had understood nothing. It was strange — what was there to understand? What had she expected him to say, what had she wanted him to say? She had wanted him to tell her, to reassure her, that he and April had not gone to bed together that night after the drinks at the Shakespeare, not that night or any other, but he had not told her that. Perhaps it was her fault, perhaps she had asked the wrong question, or asked the right one but framed it in a mistaken way; yes, perhaps that was it. Yet what other words could she have used?

The fine rain fell and gleamed on the cobbles with what seemed a malignant intent, and she had to pick her way along carefully for fear that she would lose her footing and fall. But she was falling. She felt something opening inside her, dropping open like a trapdoor, creaking on its hinges, and all underneath was darkness and uncertainty and fear. She did not know how she knew, but she did know, now, without any remaining shadow of doubt, that April Latimer was dead.

116

★ ★ ★

It was in the afternoon when Inspector Hackett telephoned. "Wouldn't February make you want to emigrate?" he said, and did his gurgling laugh. Quirke, in his flat, had been asleep on the sofa with a book open on his chest. How unfair it was, he thought, with a warm rush of self-pity, that even though he had not taken a drink in weeks he still found himself falling into what might be drunken dozings, from which he would wake with all the symptoms of a hangover. "Did I disturb you?" the policeman asked, with amusement. "Were you in the middle of something, as they say?" He paused, breathing. "The lads from the forensics gave me their report. That was blood, all right. A couple of weeks old, too. There must have been a big splash that someone mopped up."

Quirke rubbed his eyes until they smarted. "How big?"

"Hard to say."

"What about the bed — how is it there were no bloodstains on it?"

"There were, if you looked close enough, which apparently I didn't. Only on the side, a few little specks. Must have been a rubber sheet or something under her."

"Oh, Lord." He was picturing the girl, a faceless figure in a shift, with one shoulder-strap fallen down, sitting on the edge of the bed with her head hanging and legs splayed and the blood falling on the floor, drop by frightening drop.

117

For a time neither spoke. Quirke gazed at the window, at the rain, at the already darkening day.

"What's significant," Hackett said, "is the kind of blood it was."

"Oh, yes? What kind was it?"

"They have some technical name for it, I can't remember — it's written down here somewhere." There was the sound of papers being riffled through. "Can't find the blasted thing," the policeman muttered. "Anyway, it's the kind that would be there after a miscarriage, or —" He paused.

"Or?"

"What would you medical men call it — a termination, is that the word?"

CHAPTER
NINE

Inspector Hackett had always been inquisitive, too much so, as he sometimes thought and as it sometimes proved. He supposed it had to be a good trait in a policeman — he often thought it was the thing that had led him into the Force in the first place — but it had its drawbacks, too. "Snoop" had been his nickname when he was at school, and sometimes he would get a punch in the face or a kick in the backside for poking too eagerly into what was none of his business. It was not that he particularly wanted to get hold of secrets for their own sake, or to find out things that would give him an edge over those whose secrets they were. No, the source of his itch to know was that the world, he was sure, was never what it seemed, was always more than it appeared to be. He had learned that early on. To take reality as it presented itself was to miss an entirely other reality hidden behind.

He clearly remembered the moment he was first given a glimpse into the veiled and deceptive nature of things. He could not have been more than eight or nine at the time. He was walking down an empty corridor one day in school and glanced into a classroom and saw a Christian Brother alone there, sitting at a desk, crying. Long ago as it was, he could still call up the entire scene in his memory and it would be as if he were there again. It was morning, and the sun was shining in through all the big windows along the corridor; he remembered the way the sunlight fell on the floor in parallelograms with skewed, slender crosses inside them. Why there was no one around except for him and the Christian Brother, or why he was there or what he was doing, he did not recall. There must have been a football match or something on and someone had sent him back to the school on an errand. He saw himself walking along and coming up to the open doorway of the classroom and looking in and glimpsing the Brother sitting there all by himself, not at his own desk at the top of the class but at one of the boys' desks in the front row, although it was much too small for him. He was crying, bitterly, in silence, with his mouth slackly open. It was shocking, but fascinating, too. The Brother was one of the easier masters, young, with red hair brushed straight back like a cock's comb, and he wore black, horn-rimmed glasses. He was holding something in his hand — a letter, was it? — and the tears were streaming down his face. Maybe someone had died, though he would hardly have got the news of a death by letter. Or was it a telegram, maybe? Later, at the lunch break, he saw the same Brother in the school yard, supervising the boys, and he seemed as he always did, smiling and joking and making pretend swipes at fellows with the leather strap. How had he recovered his composure so readily, with not a sign of his earlier sorrow? Was he still grieving inside and covering it up,

120

or had the tears been just the result of a passing weakness, and were they forgotten now? Either way, it was strange. It was disturbing, too, of course, but it was the strangeness that stayed with him, the out-of-the-ordinariness of the spectacle of a grown man sitting there at the too-small desk, crying his heart out, in the middle of an otherwise ordinary morning.

From that day on he thought of life as a voyage of discovery — scant and often trivial discovery, it was true — and himself as a lone look-out among a shipful of purblind mariners, casting the plumb-line and hauling it in and casting it again. All around lay the surface of the ocean, seeming all that there was to see and know, in calm or tempest, while, underneath, lay a wholly other world of things, hidden, with other kinds of creatures, flashing darkly in the deeps.

The early twilight was coming on when he climbed the steps again to the house in Herbert Place and fetched the key from under the broken flagstone and let himself in. The hall was silent, and dark save for a faint glow from the streetlamp coming through the transom, but he did not switch on the light, out of a vague unwillingness to disturb the lie of things. The house was in the ownership of the estate of Lord Somebody — he had forgotten the name — who lived in England, an absentee landlord. He had looked up *Thom's Directory* and found only two tenants listed, April Latimer, and a Helen St J. Leetch. Quirke's daughter had told him which flat this other person, this Leetch person, lived in but he could not remember what she had said. He knocked on the door of the ground-floor flat, but from

121

the hollow sound his knuckles made he knew it was unoccupied. He climbed past April's door on the first floor without stopping and continued on, leaning on the banister rail and breathing hard. The landing above was so dark that he had to feel along the walls for the light-switch, and when he found it and flicked it no light came on. There was no light either under the door here, and when he leaned down and put an eye to the keyhole he could see nothing within but blackness. Yet one of his policeman's extra senses told him this flat was not empty. He raised a hand to knock, but hesitated. Something was near him, some presence; all at once he could feel it. He was not fanciful; it was by no means the first dark place he had stood in with a human presence nearby making not a sound, not even breathing, for fear of being found and pounced on. He cleared his throat, the noise sounding very loud in the silence.

When he knocked on the door it was immediately wrenched open with a bang and a waft of dead, cold air came out at him. "What do you want?" a hoarse voice demanded, rapid and urgent. "Who are you and what do you want?"

He could see her dimly against a vague glow that must be coming in from the street through a window behind her. She was a stark, stooped form, leaning on something, a stick it must be. She gave off a stale smell, of old wool, tea leaves, cigarette smoke. She must have heard him coming up the stairs and waited for him, pressing herself against the door inside, listening.

"My name is Hackett," he said, in a voice deliberately loud. "Inspector Hackett. Are you Mrs Leetch?"

"Helen St John Leetch is my name, yes yes — why?"

He sighed; this was going to be a tricky one. "Do you think I could come in, Mrs —"

"Miss."

"— just for a minute?"

He heard her fingers scrabbling along the wall and then a weak bulb above her head came on. Halo of tangled grey hair, face all fissures, a sharp, black, gleaming eye. "Who are you?" Her voice now was surprisingly firm; commanding, he might have said. She had what he thought of as a refined accent. Protestant; relic of old decency. Every other house in these parts would have a Miss not Mrs St John Leetch, waiting behind the door for someone, anyone, to knock.

"I'm a detective, ma'am."

"Come in, then, come in, come in, you're letting in the cold." She shuffled a step backwards in a quarter-circle, making angry jabs at the floor with her stick. She wore a calf-length skirt that seemed made of sacking, and at least three woollen jumpers that he could count, one over the other. Hen's claw, agued, on the handle of the stick. She spoke headlong, staccato, her dentures rattling. "If it's about the rent you're wasting your time."

"No, ma'am, it's not about the rent."

Tentatively he stepped inside. He had a glimpse of a darkened kitchen with lurking furniture shapes and a tall sash window, curtainless. The air was very cold, and felt damp. He hovered uncertainly. "In there, in there!" she said, pointing. "Go on!"

She shuffled after him into what he supposed was the living room and turned on the light. The place was a chaos. Things were dumped everywhere, clothes, pairs of shoes, outmoded hats, cardboard boxes overflowing with jumbles of ancient stuff. There was a strong smell of cat, and when he looked closely he saw a sort of slow billowing in a number of places under the dumped rags, where stealthy creatures crept. When he turned he was startled to find the woman standing immediately at his shoulder, scrutinising him. "You're not a detective," she said, with broad contempt. "Tell the truth — what are you? Some sort of a salesman? Insurance, is it?" She scowled. "You're not a Jehovah's Witness, I hope?"

"No," he said patiently, "no, I'm a policeman."

"Because they come here, you know, knocking at the door and offering me that magazine — what is it? — *The Tower*? I took it once and the fellow had the cheek to ask me to pay sixpence for it. I told him to be off or I'd call the police."

He took out his wallet and showed her his dog-eared identity card. "Hackett," he said, "Inspector Hackett. You see?"

She did not look at the card but went on peering at him with deep suspicion. Then she pressed something into his hand. It was a box of matches. "Here," she said, "I've been trying to get that blasted fire going, you can do it for me."

He crossed to the fireplace and crouched by the gas fire and struck a match and turned the spigot. He looked up at her. "There's no gas," he said.

She nodded. "I know, I know. They turned it off."

He got to his feet. He realised he had not taken off his hat, and did so now. "How long have you lived here, Miss Leetch?"

"I can't remember. Why do you want to know?"

A scrawny black-and-white tomcat came slinking out from under a pile of yellowed newspapers and wrapped itself sinuously around his ankle, making a deep gurgling sound.

"Did you — do you know Miss Latimer," he asked, "in the flat below? Dr Latimer, I mean."

She was looking past him at the dead gas fire, scowling. "I could die," she said. "I could die of the cold and then what would they do?" She started, and stared at him, as if she had forgotten he was there. "What?" Her eyes were black and had a piercing light.

"The young woman," he said, "in the flat downstairs. April Latimer."

"What about her?"

"Do you know her? Do you know who I mean?"

She snorted. "Know her?" she said. "Know her? No I don't know her. She's a doctor, you say? What kind of a doctor? I didn't know there was a surgery in this house."

Rain had begun to fall again: he could hear it hissing faintly in the trees across the road. "Maybe," he said gently, "we could sit down for a minute?"

He put his hat on the table and drew out one of the bentwood chairs. The table was round, with bowed legs the ends of which were carved in the shape of a lion's claws. The top of it had a thick, dull sheen and was sticky to the touch. He offered the chair to the woman, and after a moment of distrustful hesitation she sat down, and leaned forward intently with her hands clasped one over the other on the knob of her stick.

"Have you seen her recently?" Hackett asked, taking a second chair for himself. "Miss Latimer, that is — Dr Latimer?"

"How would I see her? I don't go out."

"You've never spoken to her?"

She put her head back and looked at him with incredulous disdain. "Of course I've spoken to her, how would I not have spoken to her? — she lives down there below me. She does my shopping."

He was not sure that he had heard her correctly. "Your shopping?"

"That's why I have nothing in the house — I'm practically starving."

"Ah, I see," he said. "That's because she's been gone for the last while?"

"That, and the cold in here, I'm surprised I haven't perished already." Her clouded gaze had turned cloudier still. There was a lengthy silence, then she came back to herself. "What?"

In a corner of the room under a pile of what might have been blankets there was a brief, violent scuffle accompanied by hissings and spittings. Hackett sighed again; he might as well give up, he would get nothing here. He took up his hat. "Thank you, ma'am," he said, rising. "I'll be on my way and leave you in peace."

She too stood up, with effortful, corkscrewing motions on the pivot of her stick. "I suppose she's off with that fellow," she said.

Hackett, who had begun to turn in the direction of the door, stopped. He smiled. "Which fellow would that be, now?" he asked softly.

It took a long time, and even then he did not really know what it was he had got hold of, or even if it was anything. Gradually it became clear, if that was the word, that in the chaotic lumber-room that was Miss St John Leetch's understanding, the fellow that April might have gone off with was not one but many. The words came out in a tumble. She was by turns indignant, mocking, aggrieved. There were names, a person called Ronnie, it seemed — "Ridiculous, awful!" — and figures coming and going at all hours of day and night, men, women, too, shadowy and uncertain, a gallery of phantoms flitting on the stairs while she hid on the lightless landing, watching, listening. Yet one figure in particular she kept returning to, indistinct as the rest and yet to her, it seemed, singular.

"Creeping about and hiding from me," she said, "thinking I would not see him, as if I were blind — pah! I was noted for my clear sight, always, always noted for it, my father used to boast of it, *My Helen*, he would say, *my Helen can see the wind*, and my father did not boast of his children lightly, I can tell you. Lurking there, down on the stairs, skulking in the shadows, I'm sure there were times when he took the bulb out of the

127

socket so I could not turn on the light, but even when I didn't see him I could smell him, yes, with that perfume he always wears, dreadful person, some kind of pansy I'm sure, trying to conceal himself in the space under the stairs, oh, quiet as a mouse, quiet as a mouse, but I knew he was there, the brute, I knew he was there —" Abruptly she stopped. "What?" She stared at Hackett in a puzzled fashion as if he too were an interloper who had suddenly materialised in front of her.

"Tell me, now," he said, very softly, cajoling, as if to a child, "tell me who it was."

"Who was who?"

She tilted her head to one side and squinted at him sidelong, her eyes narrowed and her lips pursed. He could see the grime of years lodged in the wrinkles of her cheeks. He tried to picture her young, a long-boned beauty, walking under trees in autumn, leading a bridled bay. *My Helen, my Helen can see the wind.* "Was it a boyfriend, do you think?" he asked. "Or maybe a relative? — a brother, maybe? — or an uncle, calling on her?"

She was still fixed on him with that sly, sideways regard, and now suddenly she laughed, in delight and derision. "A relative?" she said. "— How could he be a relative? He was black!"

128

CHAPTER
TEN

Quirke parked the Alvis at the corner of the Green and was halfway across the road when he remembered that he had not locked it, and had to go back. As he approached the car he had the distinct impression, as he frequently had, that it was regarding him with a baleful and accusatory aspect. There was something about the set of the headlamps, their cold, alert, unblinking stare, that unnerved him and made him feel defensive. No matter how respectfully he treated the machine, no matter how diligently he strove to make himself familiar with its little ways — the slight yaw that it did on sharp right turns, the extra pressure on the accelerator it called for when going into third — the thing resisted him, maintaining what seemed to him a sullen obstinacy. Only on occasion, on certain open stretches of the road, did it forget itself and relinquish its hauteur and leap forward with eagerness, almost it seemed with joy, setting up that distinctive, muffled roar under the bonnet that made people's heads turn. Afterwards, however, when he pulled up at the garage in Herbert Lane, the idling engine seemed to him to be smouldering with renewed, pent-up rancour. He was not good enough to be an Alvis owner; he knew it, the car knew it, and there was nothing to do but gloomily acknowledge the fact and take care that the damned thing did not turn on him and kill him.

Could it be this evening that the car was aware he was in a more than usually vulnerable state of mind? It was the end of his first dried-out day back at work, and it had not been easy. Sinclair, his assistant, had been unable to hide his displeasure at his boss's return and the consequent eclipsing of the powers that he had wielded, and enjoyed wielding, in these past two months. Sinclair was a skilled professional, good at his job — brilliant, in some ways — but he was ambitious, and impatient for advancement. Quirke had felt like a general returning to the battlefield after an emergency spell of rest and recuperation who finds not only that his second-in-command has been running the campaign with ruthless efficiency but that the enemy has been thoroughly routed. He had walked in that morning confidently enough, but somehow his helmet no longer quite fitted him and his sword would not come out of its scabbard. There had been slips, vexations, avoidable misunderstandings. He had carried out a post-mortem — his first in many months — on a five-year-old girl and had failed to identify the cause of death as leptomeningitis, hardly a subtle killer. It was Sinclair who had spotted the error, and had stood by, coolly silent, examining his nails, while Quirke, swearing under his breath and sweating, had rewritten his report. Later he had shouted at one of the porters, who went into a sulk and had to be elaborately apologised to. Then he cut his thumb on a scalpel — a new one and unused, luckily — and had been compelled to suffer the smirks of the nurse who bandaged the wound for him. No, not a good day.

In the Russell Hotel as always a mysterious quiet reigned. Quirke liked it here, liked the stuffy, padded feel of the place, the air that seemed not to have been stirred for generations, the blandishing way the carpets deadened his footsteps, and, most of all, the somehow pubic texture of the flocked wallpaper when his fingers brushed against it accidentally. Before he had gone on the latest drinking bout, when he was supposed not to be taking alcohol in any form, he used to take Phoebe to dinner here on Tuesday nights and share a bottle of wine with her, his only tipple of the week. Now, in trepidation, he was going to see if he could take a glass or two of claret again without wanting more. He tried to tell himself he was here solely in the spirit of research, but that fizzing sensation under his breastbone was all too familiar. He wanted a drink, and he was going to have one.

He was glad to find himself the only customer in the bar, but no sooner had he got his glass of Médoc and settled himself at a table in one of the dimmer corners of the room — it was not, he told himself, that he was hiding, only that wine drunk in a shadowed, cool place somehow gained in depth — than a party of four came in, making a commotion. They had been drinking already, by the look and sound of them. There were three men and a woman. They gathered at the bar and began at once to call for gins and vodkas and Bloody Marys. Two of the men were the famous Hilton and

Mícheál, the queer couple who ran the Gate; the third was a handsome, hopeful youth with curls and a sulky mouth. The woman was smoking a cigarette in a long ebony holder, with which she made much ostentatious play. Quirke opened wide his newspaper and slid down behind it in his chair.

His mind soon drifted away from reports of the latest fears of an outbreak of foot-and-mouth disease and the horrors of foreign wars. Idly he pondered the distinction between solitude and loneliness. Solitude, he conjectured, is being alone, while loneliness is being alone amongst other people. Was that the case? No, something incomplete there. He had been solitary when the bar was empty, but was he lonely now that these others had appeared?

Had April Latimer been lonely? It did not seem probable, from everything he had heard of her so far. Had there been anyone with her when her child miscarried, or was aborted? Had there been one to hold her hand, wipe her brow, murmur words of solace in her ear? He did not know very much about women and their ways. That side of their lives especially, the having of babies and the rest of it, was a mystery into which he had no wish to be initiated. He could not understand how his brother-in-law had chosen to make a career amongst all that messy and transient melodrama — all that hysteria. Give me the dead, he thought, the dead whose brief scenes on the stage are done with, for whom the last act is over and the curtain brought down.

If the baby had been aborted, had April done it herself? She was a doctor; he supposed she would know how to do it. But would she have taken such a risk? It would depend on how anxious she was to conceal the fact that she had been pregnant. Surely she would have gone to someone for help, or at least to confide in. If she did, might that someone, he wondered, have been Phoebe? At the thought he sat upright suddenly in the chair and held the newspaper tighter, making the pages crackle. Was that why Phoebe was so sure her friend had come to harm? Were there things she knew that she had not told him and Hackett? Phoebe was a damaged soul astray in the world. How much of this he was responsible for he did not care to measure. He had not loved her when she needed to be loved. He was a bad father; there was no getting away from that sad, awkward and painful fact. If she was in trouble now, if she knew the truth about April Latimer and did not know whom to turn to, then it was his moment to help her. But how? He could feel himself beginning to sweat.

"I hope I'm not disturbing you."

He looked up from his paper, startled and at once wary. She stood before him, lightly smiling, with the cigarette holder in one hand and a gin and tonic in the other. She wore a clinging dress of red wool under an overcoat with a fur collar and fur trimming. Her face was narrow and wonderfully delicate and pale, and her dark-red hair had a rich metallic gleam. He felt a vague panic — was she someone he should know? She seemed faintly familiar. He was not good at remembering faces. He stood up, and the woman, suddenly loured over, gave a faint laugh and took a tottering step backwards. "I know you're Phoebe's father," she said. "I'm a friend of hers — Isabel Galloway."

Of course. The actress.

"Yes," he said. "Miss Galloway. Hello." He offered his hand but she glanced at the cigarette holder on one side and the gin glass on the other, amusedly pointing out her helplessness. "Phoebe often speaks of you," he said. "And of course I've seen your — I've seen you on the stage."

"Have you?" she said, opening wide her eyes in a simulacrum of surprise and pleasure. "I wouldn't have thought you were the theatre-going type."

She was slightly tipsy. Behind her, the others at the bar were making a point of not being in the least interested in who it was she was speaking to.

"Well, it's true," he said, "I don't go very often. But I've seen you in — in a number of things." She said nothing, only waited, pointedly, leaving him no choice but to invite her to join him. "Sit down, won't you?" he said, feeling the soft snap of something closing on him.

Later he would not remember if he saw, that first time, how lovely she was, in her sly, languid, feline way. He was too busy adjusting himself to the steady light of her candid regard; as she sat and gazed at him he felt like a slow old moose caught in the cross-hairs of a polished and very powerful rifle. Her self-possession alarmed him; it was the result, he imagined, of her actor's training. She seemed to be amused at something large and ongoing, a marvellously absurd cavalcade, of which, he suspected, he was just now a part.

They spoke of Phoebe. He asked her how long she had known his daughter and she waved the cigarette holder in a great circling gesture, like a magician twirling a flaming hoop. "Oh," she said, in that creamy voice of hers, "she's too young for me to have known her for long. But I'm very fond of her. Very fond." He drank his wine, she drank her gin. Smiling, she gazed at him. He felt as if he was being patted all over by someone searching for something hidden on his person. He put down his glass. He said he would have to go. She said it was time for her to go, too. She bent that gaze on him again, tilting her head a fraction to one side. He asked if he could give her a lift. She said, why, that would be wonderful. He frowned, and nodded. They paused as they were passing by the trio at the bar and she introduced Quirke.

"Oh, my dear fellow," the painted actor manager said, "by the size of you, I thought you must be a policeman at least."

When they came out into the street it was night, and raining.

"My God," Isabel Galloway said, "is that your car?"

Quirke sighed.

She lived in a tiny terraced house of pink and ochre bricks on the canal at Portobello. Inside, it was curiously impersonal, and reminded Quirke of a jewel box from which all the more intimate pieces had been removed. In the miniature living room almost the entire space was filled by two chintz-covered armchairs and a chintz-covered sofa that looked as if it had never been sat on. There were china and porcelain figurines on the mantelpiece, dogs and shepherdesses and a ballerina in a tutu hard and sharp-edged as coral. As soon as Isabel came in, and before she had even taken off her coat, she went and switched on the big wireless set that stood on a shelf beside the sofa; when after some moments it had warmed up it began at once to play dance music at a low volume, lush and swoony, though the signal was bad and there was static.

"Make yourself at home," Isabel said, with a faint, ironical flourish, and went off into another room, the kitchen, it must be, from the sounds that came out of clinking glasses and a running tap.

Quirke draped his rain-greyed overcoat on one of the armchairs and laid his hat on top of it. He considered the sofa but found it too intimidating and stood instead, waiting for her to return. The ceiling could not have been more than six inches higher than the crown of his head. He felt like Alice after she had eaten the magic cake and grown huge.

"I've only gin, I'm afraid," Isabel said, coming in with a tray of glasses and bottles and shutting the door behind her with a deft back kick of her heel. She set the tray on a low, rectangular table in front of the sofa and poured a generous splash of gin into one of the glasses, but Quirke put his hand over the mouth of the second one. "Just tonic for me," he said. "I don't drink."

She stared. "Yes, you do — you were drinking wine in the hotel, I saw you."

"That was by way of an experiment."

"Ah." She shrugged. "Yes. Phoebe told me you were — that you had a problem." He said nothing, and she poured the tonic into his glass. She was a little tipsy still, he could see. "There's no ice," she said, "since the bloody fridge stopped working. It does it every winter — I think it thinks it should be let have a holiday when the weather turns cold. Here you are." She handed him the glass, her cool fingers brushing against his hand. "It's a bit flat. Chin-chin." He was trying to place her accent. Had Phoebe said that she was English? "Think we might sit," she said, "or do you prefer to go on looming?"

The sofa felt as unsat-on as it looked; the cushion under Quirke was plump and hard, and perched on it he had the sense of being borne swayingly aloft, like a child on a merry-go-round, or a mahout on his elephant. He sipped the tonic water; she was right, it was flat.

The dance tune on the radio came to an end and the announcer said the next one would be a tango. "We could dance, if there was room," Isabel said. She looked askance at him. "Do you dance, Dr Quirke?"

"Not much."

"I thought so." She took a drink of her gin and laid her head back on the sofa, sighing. "God, I've been boozing all afternoon with those people. I'm sure I must be completely tiddly." Again she gave him that sideways glance. "Mind you, don't let that give you any ideas."

There was a silver cigarette box on the table, and now she leaned forward and took two cigarettes and put them both in her mouth and lit them and handed one to him. "Sorry," she said, "lipstick," and Quirke remembered another woman doing that, turning from a mantelpiece, in snow-light, and handing him a cigarette and saying those same words.

"How did you know me?" he asked. "At the hotel, I mean."

"I must have seen you, I suppose, with Phoebe." She narrowed her eyes, still smiling. "Or maybe I saw you in front of the footlights all those times when you came to see me act, and remembered you."

The tango music swirled, toffee-brown and smooth.

"Do you know Phoebe well?" he asked.

She heaved a sharp sigh, pretending to be vexed. "You keep asking me that. Does anyone know Phoebe well? Anyway, she's really April's friend — April Latimer?" Quirke nodded. "The rest of us I think she just tolerates."

"The rest of you?"

"We're a little band of friends, the Faubourg set, don't you know. We meet once a week and drink too much and talk behind other people's backs. Well, *I* drink too much, usually. You needn't worry about Phoebe, she's very careful."

"April Latimer, then," he said, "— how well did you know *her*?"

"Oh, I've known April for ever. She stole a man from me, once."

"Is that how you met her?"

"What? Oh, no. We'd known each other a long time when that happened."

"So you were able to forgive her."

She gave him a sharp look, suspecting mockery. "Well, of course. To tell the truth, he wasn't much of a catch in the first place, as April soon found out. We had many a laugh behind *his* back, April and I."

The tango ended and there was applause, tinny and remote, and the announcer came on to say that the news would be next. "Oh, turn that off, will you?" Isabel said. "Do you mind? I hate hearing of the day's disasters." She watched him get up and, craning her neck, followed him with her eyes as he went to the set to switch it off. "You really are very big," she said, putting on a lisping, little-girl voice. "I didn't quite realise it at the hotel, but in this dinky little house you look like Gulliver."

He returned to the sofa and sat down. "She was fond of men, was she, April?" he asked.

She gave him a wide-eyed stare. "You do come right out with it, don't you?" she said. She laid her head back on the sofa and rolled it slowly from side to side. "I notice you speak of her in the past tense. You must have been talking to Phoebe, who thinks April has been done away with by Jack the Ripper."

"And you — what do you think has become of her?"

"If her past behaviour is anything to go by, right now she'll be shacked up with some hunk in a nice cosy inn somewhere in — oh, let me see — in the Cotswolds, under the name of Mr and Mrs Smith, dining by candlelight and sporting a Woolworth's wedding ring. What do *you* think, Dr Quirke?"

He suggested she might call him by his first name. When she asked him what it was and he told her she gave a little shriek of delight and incredulity, and immediately put a hand over her mouth. "I'm sorry," she said, "I shouldn't laugh. But I think I'll stick to Quirke, if you don't mind — even Phoebe calls you that, doesn't she?"

"Yes," he said flatly. "Everyone does."

He finished his cigarette and was leaning forward to stub the end of it in the ash-tray on the table when he felt her fingers on the back of his neck. "You have such a nice little corkscrew curl just there where your hair ends," she said.

She allowed her hand to glide slowly down between his shoulder blades to his waist. He turned and put his hands on her shoulders — how delicate the bones were there! — and kissed her painted mouth. It was cool, and tasted of gin. She drew back an inch and laughed softly into his mouth. "Oh, Dr Quirke," she murmured, "I really must be drunk." But when Quirke put a hand on her breast she pushed him away. "Let's have another drink," she said, and sat up, touching her hair. She poured the gin and the last of the flat tonic water, and handed him his glass. She looked at him closely. "Now you're sulking," she said. "I can see you are. What do you expect? Don't you know what it's like for a girl, in this town?"

He cleared his throat. "I'm sorry," he said. "I made a mistake."

Her look hardened. "Yes, obviously you did. I'm an actress, therefore I must be a tart, right? Be honest — that's the mistake you think you made, isn't it?"

"I'm sorry," he said again, and stood up, brushing his hands down the front of his jacket. "I should go."

He took up his coat and hat. Isabel did not rise, but sat with her knees pressed together, gripping the gin glass tightly between her palms. He was stepping past her when she put out a hand and fumbled for one of his. "Oh, stop, you great lummox," she said. "Come here." She smiled up at him crookedly, pulling at his hand. "Maybe we can both get the wrong idea, and see where it leads us."

A church bell far off was tolling three o'clock when he slipped from the bed in the darkness and went and stood by the window. A crooked streetlamp was shedding a circle of light on the pavement outside. Behind him, Isabel, sleeping, was a tousle of dark hair on the pillow and one pale, gleaming arm flung across the sheet. The window was low and he had to stoop to see out of it. The rain had stopped, and the sky, amazingly, was clear — it seemed to him weeks, months, even, since there had been a clear sky. A silver of moon was suspended like a scimitar above the gleaming rooftops of the houses on the other side of the canal. A car sizzled past on this side, its headlights dimmed. It was cold, and he was naked, yet he lingered there, a stooped watcher of the night. He was calm, as if something, some perpetually turning motor in his head, had been switched to a lower, slower gear. How sweet it was for a little while not to think, merely to lean there, above the street, hearing the soft beating of his own heart, remembering the warmth of the bed that he would soon return to. Despite the stillness of the air the canal was moving, the water brimming at both banks and wrinkled like silver paper, and here came — look! — two swans, gliding sedately side by side, dipping their long necks as they moved, a pair of silent creatures, white as the moon and moving amidst the moon's shattered white reflections on the water.

In the morning, of course, it was not as easy as it had been in the night. Isabel had a hangover, though she tried to hide it behind a brightly brittle manner, and there was a knot of tension between her eyebrows and her skin had that grey, grainy pallor that was an unmistakable giveaway, as Quirke knew from many an ashen morning after a night before, glooming into the shaving mirror. She wore a silk tea-gown with a floral print in crimsons and yellows, the design so busy he wondered how she could bear it. They sat at the table in the cramped kitchen by a window that looked out on a yard with a dustbin in it; a weak winter sun was shining out there, doing its best but not making much impression on anything. Isabel smoked with almost a fierce concentration, as if it were a task that had been set her, hard and wearisome, but one that she must not shirk. She had made coffee in a percolator with a glass top; the coffee was black and bitter and had a tarry taste, and made Quirke think unpleasantly of a monkey's pelt. He wondered if he might tell her about the two swans on the canal in the moonlight but decided it would be better not to.

In the early hours they had lain awake and talked. Isabel had smoked then, too, and there had been something intimate in the way the red glare from the tip of her cigarette would burgeon in the darkness with each deep draw that she took and then fade again. She had been born in London, to an Irish mother and an English father — "Or did you think," she said, "I was born in a trunk?" Early on, her father had run off, and she had come to Ireland with her mother to live with her mother's parents. Isabel had loathed the elderly couple, her grandmother especially, who slapped her when her mother was not looking, and threatened to give her to the tinkers if she did not do as she was told. She had heard no more of her father, who might be dead for all she knew. She laughed softly in the darkness. "It all sounds so theatrical, when I hear myself tell it," she said. "Like a bad piece of social realism at the Abbey. But such is life, I suppose — much less colourful, darling, than at the Gate."

Then it was Quirke's turn to recount his story, though he did not want to. She pressed him, and turned on her side and leaned on an elbow, attending intently. He told her of the orphanage, the years at the industrial school at Carricklea, then rescue by Malachy Griffin's father. After a while he pretended to have fallen asleep, and soon she slept, too. She was a snorer. He lay awake in the dark, listening to her snufflings and snorkellings, and thought about the past, and how it never lets go its hold.

Now, at morning, they were awkward together. He wanted to be gone but did not know how to go.

"Did you know April Latimer was pregnant?" he asked.

She stared at him. "You're joking," she said. She threw herself back on the chair with a happy cry of laughter. "My God! I didn't think April would be so — so banal." Then she nodded. "Of course — that's where she is, then, gone to England to have it fixed."

Quirke shook his head. "No, she's not in England. Or if she is, it's not for that reason. She *was* pregnant, but not any more."

"She lost it?" He said nothing. "She got rid of it? — here?" A thought struck her and she looked at him more keenly, more searchingly. "How do you know these things?"

"I went to her flat — Phoebe and I."

"Oh, yes, of course. Phoebe told me. You had a detective with you. What clues did he find, your Sherlock Holmes?"

Quirke hesitated. "There was blood, on the floor, beside the bed."

"April's bed?"

"Yes,"

She looked down at the table. "Oh, God," she breathed, "how squalid. Poor April."

He waited, and then asked: "Would she have told you?"

She was shaking her head slowly, in dismay and disbelief, not listening to him, and now she looked up. "What?"

"What sort of terms are you on with April? I mean, would she talk to you about — about intimate things?"

"You mean, would she tell me she had got knocked up? God, I don't know. She's a funny one, our April. Acts extrovert and careless, a free spirit and all that, but she's secretive, more so than anyone I know." She thought for a moment, narrowing her eyes. "Yes, there's something hidden deep down, there, under layers and layers." She tapped her cigarette meditatively on the side of the tin ash-tray. "You think what Phoebe thinks, don't you? You think something has — something has happened to April."

He looked at her. Why did they have to be talking about April Latimer? Why could he not be allowed sit here at ease, in the glow of her fascinatingly tarnished beauty, watching the weak sunlight gilding the yard, drinking her awful coffee?

The morning was well advanced by the time he got to Mount Street. He should shave now and go to work, for which he was hours late already. Among the house post on the hall table there was a letter for him, delivered by courier; the brown envelope had a harp on it — who would be writing to him from the Government? One of the legacies of his childhood was a dread of all officialdom, a dread that he could never rid himself of. He carried the letter upstairs to his flat and laid it down, unopened, on the table in the living room and went to put away his coat and his hat. He lit the gas fire, too, and made himself a drink with hot water and honey and lemon juice from a lemon-shaped plastic container. He felt swollen and feverish, as if he were the one with the hangover; perhaps he was getting something, the flu, perhaps. He was distracted by images of Isabel lying naked in his arms, her skin so pale it was almost phosphorescent in the darkness. The word *Portobello* kept going round and round in his head, like the title of some song.

The letter, when at last he brought himself to open it, was from Dr William Latimer, TD, who addressed him as *A Chara*. The Minister requested Dr Quirke to call to the Minister's office in Kildare Street this morning at eleven o'clock — he looked at his watch and saw it was already thirty minutes past the hour — to discuss further the matter on which they had recently spoken. It closed by assuring him *Is mise le meas*, and was signed *pp* with an indecipherable signature with many accents on the vowels. He was about to pick up the telephone to call Leinster House when the machine suddenly exploded into an urgent shrilling. He flinched — a ringing telephone, even when it was his own, always alarmed him — then picked up the receiver gingerly.

"Hello," the voice said, in a familiar drawl. "It's Rose here — Rose Crawford. Is that you, Quirke? Yes, it's Rose! I'm back."

II

CHAPTER
ONE

Quirke arrived at noon at Government Buildings, where he was received by the Minister's private secretary, an oddly implausible person by the name of Ferriter, plump and shabby, with lank black hair and pendulous jowls. Quirke made his apologies for being late, and Ferriter said yes, that it had been necessary to reschedule two important meetings, his oily smile not faltering, which made the rebuke seem all the more pointed. He led Quirke into a cavernous room with two tall, grimed windows overlooking Leinster Lawn and left him there. Public buildings, their jaded atmosphere and brooding, somehow disapproving silences, always made Quirke uneasy; rooms such as this reminded him of the visitors' room at Carricklea. Why that institution needed a visitors' room was a puzzle, since no one came to visit except now and then one of the schools inspectors from Dublin, who hurried through the building with his head down and fled the place without a backward glance.

He squeezed the bridge of his nose between a thumb and forefinger; it was the second time today he had been forced to think of Carricklea.

Still in his overcoat he went and stood at a window and gazed out on the lawn. Ferriter, making unctuous small-talk, had claimed to detect a touch of spring in the air. If there was, it was lost on Quirke. Even the sunlight on the grass out there, pallid and uncertain, looked cold to his eye.

Presently Ferriter came back to fetch him. They walked along airless corridors where their footfalls made hardly a sound on the thick carpeting. The few other officials that they passed by either avoided Ferriter's eye or greeted him with obsequious smiles; he was clearly a man to be feared.

Latimer's office was panelled in dark wood and smelt of dust and mildewed papers. A tiny coal fire that was smouldering in an enormous grate was having little effect on the chilly, damp air. The window beside the desk looked out on a brick wall. Latimer sat behind his desk with his head bent over a document that he was pretending to read. Ferriter cleared his throat softly and Latimer looked up in feigned surprise and bustled to his feet, extending a hand. Quirke apologised again for his lateness. "Not at all, not at all," Latimer said distractedly. He seemed nervous, and there was a sickly tinge to his smile. "Sit down, please. Throw your coat on that chair." He glanced at Ferriter. "That'll be grand, Pierce," he said, and the secretary padded away, silently shutting the high white door behind him.

Latimer opened the lid of a lacquered box of fat, stubby cigarettes and turned the box towards Quirke. "The Turkish consulate sends them round," he said.

Quirke looked doubtfully at the cigarettes. "Yes, filthy things," Latimer said, "I can't stand the smell of them." Quirke produced his own silver case and offered it across the desk, and they lit up. "Well," the Minister said, leaning back in his chair, "this is a damned bad business, and getting worse."

"You spoke to Inspector Hackett?"

"He phoned me up, yes. That was a call I could have done without. I swear to God, I knew that girl would get us all into trouble some day."

Quirke studied the tip of his cigarette. "What did Hackett say?"

"That blood he found under her bed, it's hers, all right. They did tests — same blood type, type O, I think." He stood up from the desk with an almost violent twist of his body and went to a small wooden cabinet in a corner and brought out a bottle of Jameson Redbreast and two cut-glass tumblers. "Will you have a drop, early as it is?"

"No, thank you."

"Well, I hope you won't mind if I do. I need one, after that telephone call."

He set the glasses on the desk and filled one of them halfway and took a swallow of whiskey and grimaced. "Jesus," he said, shaking his head, "what a mess." He sat down again and set his glass on the blotter before him and glared at it for a moment in angry silence. Then he lifted his eyes and looked hard at Quirke. "You know what this could do to me, Dr Quirke, maybe even to the government?"

"I'm not sure that I know what 'this' is," Quirke said. "Have you news of April? Has she turned up? Have you heard from her?"

Latimer waved his cigarette dismissively. "No, no. There's no news of her. Christ knows where she is. And I'll tell you this, wherever it is she's gone to I hope she intends staying there for a good long while. Either stays there or comes back quietly and keeps her mouth shut. If this gets into the papers —" He broke off and cast a glance wildly about the room, as if he could read the headlines already, written in stark black capitals on the air.

"Has Hackett set up an official investigation?" Quirke asked.

"No, not yet — not official. I told him to hold off for a bit." He took another sip of his whiskey. "If it wasn't for that blood, God help us, I'd have made him lay off altogether." He fixed his angry gaze on the glass again. Quirke waited. "Will you tell me, Quirke," Latimer burst out, pained and angry, "why the hell did you bring a detective to her flat in the first place?"

"We were worried," Quirke said.

"'We'?"

"My daughter and I."

"Aye — and are you any less worried now, the two of you?"

Quirke had finished his cigarette and lit another. "Dr Latimer," he said, leaning forward in his chair, "I wonder if you've considered all the implications of what Inspector Hackett found in your niece's bedroom? Are you aware of the particular kind of blood it was?"

"Yes I know, I know — Hackett told me. I'm shocked, but I'm not surprised." He lifted his glass to drink again but instead set it back on the blotter and rose and went to the window and stood with one hand in a jacket pocket, looking out at the blank brick wall. "What does your daughter say about April?" he asked, without turning. "Does she know what sort of a girl she is?"

"I don't know. What sort of a girl *is* she?"

"Well, Dr Quirke, the sort, I suppose, that would leave blood like that on her bedroom floor. Oh, I don't claim she's bad all the way through. And, anyway, she didn't beg, borrow or steal it, for she's not the first wild one in the family." He returned to the desk and sat down, looking weary suddenly. He put his face in his hands for a moment, shaking his head, and then looked up again. "Her father was in the GPO in 1916," he said, "fought beside Pearse and Connolly."

"I know," Quirke said.

"Of course you do — doesn't everyone?" Quirke caught the note of bitterness in his voice. "Conor Latimer, the man they couldn't kill. And it was true — the British would have shot him but for who he was. Friend of Oliver Gogarty and George Bernard Shaw, Yeats and Lady Gregory — Lady Lavery, too, though we don't mention that particular connection too often, in the family, if you know what I mean. Were you aware that Bertrand Russell made a plea for clemency when the court martial found him guilty?"

"You were in the Rising too, weren't you?"

"Oh, I was, yes. I was no more than a lad, and hardly knew one end of a rifle from the other. Conor had been in training for months, up in the Dublin Mountains." He paused. "He was a hard man, Dr Quirke, a mad Fenian without respect for God or man. He was my older brother and I loved him, but by Jesus I was afraid of him, too. It was like being around some kind of half-tamed animal — you could never tell what he would do next. And it's from him that April got her wild streak. She's the dead spit of him, the dead spit." He drank off the last of the whiskey in the glass and helped himself to another splash. "And she never got over the loss of him, either. She adored him. When he died, although she was only a child at the time, something broke in her that was never healed." He sighed. "And now, God only knows what kind of trouble she's after getting herself into. And as for her poor mother —"

There was a light tap on the door and Ferriter entered. As he crossed the room he seemed to trot somehow on tiptoe, stealthily. He leaned down and spoke into the Minister's ear.

"My sister-in-law and her son are here," Latimer said to Quirke. "I asked them to come in, I hope you don't mind." He nodded to Ferriter, who once more withdrew, as silent as a shadow.

Celia Latimer was as meticulously groomed as she had been the last time that Quirke had seen her, in Dun Laoghaire, but today, behind the calmness of manner and the queenly smile, he detected something drawn and anxious. She wore a mink coat and a little hat the

154

size and blackness of a bat, held in place with a pearl pin. "Dr Quirke," she said, extending a gloved hand. "Very nice to see you again."

Quirke looked at the proffered hand; from the way she held it out to him, extended flat with the fingers dipped, it seemed she expected him to kiss it; instead he shook it briefly, feeling again that momentary, suggestive pressure. Oscar Latimer kept close behind his mother, bobbing busily from one side to the other, his face appearing now at her left shoulder, now at her right, as if she were a life-size doll that he was holding upright and walking along in front of him, as camouflage, or a shield. He nodded curtly to Quirke.

"I asked Dr Quirke to come along here today," Bill Latimer said, "to be with us because of his connection with April — I mean, his daughter's connection. He's as concerned as we are to know what's going on with April."

Oscar Latimer and his mother turned their heads and gazed at Quirke with blank enquiry. He returned their look, saying nothing. He wondered if they knew about the blood in April's bedroom. If they did it would account for those fan-shaped clusters of worry-lines at the outer edges of Celia Latimer's eyes, and for the rabbity twitching of her son's upper lip, where that ginger moustache, which surely must itch, looked more half-hearted and incongruous than ever. Oscar drew up a chair for his mother and placed another beside it and sat down. Now he and his mother and Quirke were sitting in a half-circle in front of the desk.

"Yes," Celia Latimer was saying to her brother-in-law, in an acid tone, "I've no doubt Dr Quirke is concerned." She was looking pointedly at the whiskey glass standing on the blotter, and Latimer snatched it up guiltily and carried it to the cabinet in the corner and put it away. His sister-in-law turned to Quirke again. "Have you heard something of April, Dr Quirke?"

Quirke suddenly found himself thinking about the smell of Isabel Galloway's skin. It was a warm, soft smell, with an undertone of what must be greasepaint; it had reminded him of something, and now he realised what it was. He saw himself as a boy, sitting cross-legged on a rug before a fireplace with sheets of paper strewn around him. The sheets were written on and he was using the back of them for drawing paper. He must have been in Judge Griffin's study, where often he was allowed to play while the Judge was working there; the sheets of paper he was drawing on must have been discarded drafts of judgments. The day outside was cold, a day like this one, in the depths of winter, but the fire was hot, and there were chilblain diamonds on his legs, and his forehead was burning in a way that he could just bear but that was pleasurable, too. Never such happiness since then, never such safety. He was drawing with crayons, and it was the waxen smell of them that he must have been remembering when in the bedroom in her little house by the canal Isabel Galloway put her face close to his, her face that seemed to be burning too, as his had burned that day, long ago, in front of the fire, in Judge Griffin's room.

He blinked. "What?" he said. "I'm sorry?"

"I said, have you heard something of April?" Celia Latimer asked again. "Has she been in touch with your daughter?"

He leaned forward to stub out his cigarette in the ashtray on the corner of Latimer's desk. "No," he said, "I'm afraid not."

She looked to her brother-in-law, returning to his chair. "And what do the Gardaí say, William?" she asked

Latimer did not look at her. "The Gardaí, as such, aren't involved, only this man Hackett, the detective you met at the house that day. In fact" — he glanced darkly in Quirke's direction — "I'm not sure why he was brought into it in the first place."

Quirke returned his look with a level stare. He disliked this large, truculent, stupid man. He wanted to be elsewhere. He thought of the sunlight outside, shining so wanly, so tentatively, on the greyed lawn. *Portobello.*

Oscar Latimer, who so far had been silent, now gave himself a sort of angry shake, clasping his hands on the wooden arms of his chair as if he were about to leap up and do something violent. "It's disgraceful," he said, his voice cracking. "First, strangers knowing our business, then the Guards! Next it'll be the newspapers — that will be a fine thing. And all because my sister couldn't be trusted to run her life in any sort of responsible fashion." His mother put a restraining hand on his arm and he stopped talking, and pressed his lips shut. There were spots of colour high on his cheekbones. He had,

157

Quirke thought, the striving, hindered air of a man elbowing his way through a seething mob.

Bill Latimer turned to his sister-in-law again. "I've told Hackett, the detective, that discretion is paramount. I presume" — he gave Quirke another hard glance — "we're all agreed on that?"

Quirke had been puzzled and now suddenly was not. He realised at last what was taking place here, and why he had been summoned to be part of it. A ceremony of banishment was being enacted. April Latimer was being tacitly but definitively thrust by her family out of its midst. She was being disowned. Her brother, her uncle, even her mother would no longer be held accountable for her actions, not even for her being. And Quirke was the neutral but necessary witness, the one whose seal, whether he offered it or not, would be put upon the covenant. And what, he asked himself, if she were dead? That possibility too, he realised, was to be incorporated in the anathema.

Rose Crawford was waiting for him in the back bar at Jammet's. There was a bottle of Bollinger in an ice bucket on the table before her. She had gone back to America before Christmas to attend to her financial affairs, and had returned on the *Queen Mary*, which had docked in Cobh that morning. She complained of the train from Cork, saying it was cold and dirty and without a dining car. "I had almost forgotten," she said, "what this country is like." She had brought him a box of Romeo y Julietas and a novelty tie with a half-naked blonde with an enormous bust and cherry-pink nipples painted on it. She was wearing a blue silk suit and a silk scarf loosely knotted at her throat. Her hair, in which she was letting some of the silver show, was done in a new style, parted in the centre and drawn back sweepingly at both sides. She appeared crisp and fresh, and her manner as usual was one of dark and sceptical amusement. "You look very well," she told Quirke, and signalled to the barman to open the champagne. "Certainly better than the last time I saw you."

"I've been away too," he said.

"Oh, yes?"

"I was in St John of the Cross."

"My — what's that?"

"A drying-out clinic."

"Yes, now that I think of it, Phoebe mentioned in one of her letters that you were in the bin. I thought she was exaggerating. What was it like?"

"All right."

She smiled. "I'm sure." The barman poured the champagne and set the sizzling glasses before them. Quirke looked at his, chewing his lip. "Do you dare?" Rose asked, smiling with sweet malice. "I don't want to be responsible for putting you back on the cross."

He picked up his glass and tipped the rim of it against hers. They drank. "Here's to sobriety," he said.

She had reserved her favourite table, in the corner with a banquette, from where they had a view of the rest of the dining room. They ordered poached salmon. Hilton and Mícheál from the Gate were at a nearby table, lunching in what seemed an angry silence; Mícheál's wig looked blacker and glossier than ever.

159

"Tell me the news," Rose said. "If there is any."

He sipped his champagne. It was a drink he did not care for, usually, finding even the best vintages too dry and acid; today, however, it tasted fine. He would drink one glass, he told himself, one glass only, and after that perhaps a glass of Chablis, and then would stop.

"I wondered if you would come back," he said. "I thought Boston might take you into its bosom and keep you there."

"Oh, Boston," she said dismissively. "In fact, I was in New York, mostly. Now, there's a town."

"But you returned nevertheless to dear, dirty Dublin."

"And you, Quirke, and you."

The waiter brought their fish, and Quirke ordered his glass of Chablis. Rose made no comment, only told the waiter she would keep to the champagne.

"Have you spoken to Phoebe yet?" Quirke asked. "Since you got back, that is."

"No, Quirke dear, you were my first port of call, as always. How is the darling girl?"

He told her about April Latimer, how she was missing and that no one knew where she was; he did not mention the blood that had been found beside her bed. Rose listened, watching him in her shrewd way. She was the second wife, now widow, of his father-in-law, Josh Crawford, Irish-American haulage giant, as the newspapers used to call him, and sometime crook. He had been much older than she, and had left her a rich woman. After he died she had moved to Ireland on a whim and bought a great house in Wicklow which she rarely visited, preferring what she called the cosiness of her suite at the Shelbourne, where she had her bedroom, two reception rooms, two bathrooms and a private dining room. Quirke and she had gone to bed together once, and once only, in turbulent times, a thing they never spoke of but which remained between them, something to be aware of, like a light shining uncertainly afar in a dark wood.

"And what do you think has become of her," she asked, "this young woman?"

"I don't know."

"But you have your suspicions."

He paused, setting down his knife and fork and gazing before him for some moments. "I have — fears," he said at length. "It doesn't look good. She's wild, her family tell me, though Phoebe insists they're exaggerating. I can't say. She worked at the hospital, but I never came across her."

"Does Malachy know her?"

"He must have had some dealings with her in the course of his days, but he says he can't remember. You know Mal — she would need to sprout feathers and a tail before he noticed her."

"Oh, yes, Malachy," she said. "How is he?"

Quirke's glass of Chablis seemed somehow to have become empty all by itself, without his noticing. He would not have another, no matter how loudly his blood clamoured for it; no, he would not. "He says he's going to retire."

"Retire? But he's so young."

"That's what I said."

"He should marry again, before it's too late."

"Who would he marry?"

"Isn't this country supposed to be thronged with women looking for a man?"

He called the waiter and asked for another glass of wine. Rose lifted an eyebrow, but made no remark.

"By the way," he said, "I bought a car."

"Well, you devil, you!"

"It was very expensive."

"I should hope so. I can't see you in a cheap jalopy."

When they finished their lunch he suggested they should go for a drive. Rose gave the Alvis barely a glance — Rose was not easily impressed, and when she was impressed she was careful not to show it — and when they had got in she would not let him drive off until he had put on the tie with the painted blonde on it. He laughed and said that if they were stopped by the Guards he would be arrested for causing a disturbance of the peace. "Add the fact that I have no driving licence and I'll probably end up in jail." His brain was fizzing pleasantly from the effects of the champagne and the two glasses of Chablis, and he felt almost skittish. He pulled down the mirror so he could see to knot the ridiculous tie. Rose sat sideways in the seat, watching him.

"You'd like that," she said.

"What would I like?"

"Being in jail. I can see you there, in your suit with the arrows on it, contentedly sewing mailbags and writing your memoirs in the evenings before lights-out."

He laughed. "You know me too well." He smoothed the tie and readjusted the mirror and started up the engine. "I'm glad you've come back," he said. "I missed you."

Now it was her turn to laugh. "No, you didn't. But it's nice of you to say so."

They went out by Rathfarnham and set off up into the mountains.

"You didn't drive, before," Rose said, "did you?"

"No. Mal taught me. It wasn't difficult to get the hang of it."

"And you've bought yourself a brand-new shiny car." She patted the polished dashboard. "Very smart. I imagine it impresses the girls?"

He did not answer that. The sunlight of earlier was gone now and the day had turned iron-grey. Between them, too, unaccountably, something had darkened a little, and for a number of miles they did not speak at all. The mountainsides, burned by frost, were ochre-coloured, and there was ice at the sides of the road and patches of snow lay in the lee of rocks and in the long, straight furrows where turf had been cut. Below, to their right, a circular volcanic lake appeared, the water black and motionless, unreal-seeming. Winding higher and higher on the narrow road they felt the air growing steadily thinner and colder, and Quirke turned the heater on full. At Glencree there was a sudden squall of sleet, and the windscreen wipers had a hard time coping with it.

"I used to come up here with Sarah," Quirke said. "It was here one day, somewhere around here, that she told

163

me Phoebe was my daughter, mine and Delia's, not hers and Mal's."

"But you knew that already."

"Yes. I'd always known, and never told her I knew. God knows why. Cowardice, of course, there's always cowardice."

Rose laughed again, softly. "Secrets and lies, Quirke, secrets and lies."

He gave her an account of his meeting that morning with the Latimers. She was fascinated. "He called you all together in his office, where the government is, this man — what's his name?"

"Bill Latimer. Minister of Health."

"Bizarre. What did he want you to do?"

"Me? Nothing."

"You mean, nothing nothing?"

"Exactly. He wants the fact of his niece's disappearance kept under wraps, at least for the time being, so he says. He's afraid of a scandal."

"Does he think he can keep it a secret for ever? What if she's dead?"

"You can do anything in this country, if you're powerful enough. You know that."

She nodded in grim amusement. "Secrets and lies," she said again, softly, in her Southern drawl, almost singing it.

The sleet shower passed and they drove down into a long, shallow valley. Distantly the sea was visible, a line of indelible-pencil blue on the horizon. There were blackish-green clumps of gorse, and thorn bushes raked by the wind into agonised, claw-like shapes; tatters of

164

sheep's wool fluttered on the barbed wire by the side of the road. "My God, Quirke," Rose said suddenly, "this is a terrible place you've brought me to."

He raised his eyebrows in surprise. "Up here? Terrible?"

"So barren. If there's a Hell, this is how I imagine it will be. No flames and all that, just ice and emptiness. Let's go back. I like to be around people. I'm no cowgirl, the wide open spaces frighten me."

He turned the car in a gateway and they set off back towards the city.

They were out of the mountains before Rose spoke again. "Maybe I should marry Malachy," she said. "It could be my mission in life, to cheer him up." She looked sideways at Quirke. "Aren't you lonely?" she asked.

"Yes, of course," he said simply. "Isn't everyone?"

She did not answer for a moment, and then chuckled. "You're nothing if not predictable, Quirke."

"Is that bad?"

"It's not bad or good. It's just you."

"A hopeless case, is that it?"

"Hopeless. Maybe Malachy isn't the one I should marry."

"Who, then?" Quirke asked lightly. Then the lightness drained from him and he frowned, and kept his eyes on the windscreen.

Rose laughed. "Oh, Quirke," she said. "You look like a little boy who's been told he may have to go and live with his grandmaw for the rest of his life. — By the way," she said, turning her head quickly to look back,

165

"aren't you supposed to stop when someone steps out on one of those — what do you call them? — those zebra crossings?"

He delivered her to the Shelbourne. She said she still had to unpack, and then rest a while. She suggested that he and Phoebe might join her for dinner. He was back in his flat before he realised that he was still wearing the lewd tie she had given him. He looked at himself in the mirror. There were shadows under his eyes. He wished he had not drunk that glass of champagne: he could taste its sourness still. He took off the tie and went into the kitchen and threw it in the waste-bin with the kitchen slops.

CHAPTER
TWO

Phoebe lay rigid, staring into the darkness. It was often like this: she would go to sleep and then after an hour or two would start awake from a nightmare not a single detail of which had stayed with her. Somehow this was what was most terrifying, the way the dream just vanished, like an animal scuttling down a hole and leaving nothing behind but an aura of horror and filth. So many dreadful things had happened in her life and surely they were what she dreamed of, yet how was it she forgot everything as soon as she woke? Were the visions in her dreams so terrible that her mind, feeling itself about to wake, whipped them away and hid them from her? If so, she was not glad of it; she would rather know than not know. She had woken lying on her back with her fists clenched against her throat and her teeth bared and her rib-cage heaving. It was as if she had been fleeing headlong from something and at last had made her escape, although the thing, whatever faceless thing it was, was still out there, hiding in the dark, waiting for another night to come creeping out again and terrorise her.

She switched on the bedside lamp and laid her head back on the damp, hot pillow and squeezed her eyes shut. She did not want to be awake but there would be no sleep now for a long time. Sighing, she got up and put on her silk dressing gown — *peignoir* was what it was properly called; she liked the word. It had belonged to the woman who for the first nineteen years of her life she had thought was her mother.

She went out to the kitchen. Night smells, she had often noticed, were different from day ones, were mustier, fainter, more insidious. She drew open the lapels of her silk gown and put her face into the hollow there and sniffed. Yes, her smell too was different, a babyish, secret staleness.

The thought came to her that she had never got used to being alive.

She took a half-full bottle of milk from the cupboard and shook it to make sure that it had not curdled — she had no refrigerator — and poured some into a blackened saucepan and set it on the gas ring to heat, adding a spoonful of raspberry jam. There was a slice of pound cake left from the piece she had bought two days ago to have after her dinner; it had gone hard and crumbly, but she needed to eat something. Behind her the milk began to seethe and she whipped it off the flame just as it was about to come to the boil. A wrinkled scum had formed, of course, and she had to lift it off as best she could with a teaspoon, trying not to let it break, a thing that always made her feel slightly sick. She poured the scalding, pink-tinged milk into a mug and unwrapped the cake from its greaseproof paper and put it on a plate and brought the mug and the plate to the table and sat down. She shut her eyes and sat motionless for a moment, then reopened them. She had not pulled down the blind — she hated blinds, they looked to her like unrolled sheets of pale-grey skin — and the window beside her was a tall rectangle of shining blackness. It was not very late, one o'clock, maybe, yet all outside was silent. She drank her milk with the jam in it and ate the morsel of dry, sweet cake. Her heartbeat even yet was uneven, from the stress of the forgotten dream.

Her thoughts turned, of course, to April, as they always did in sleepless hours such as these, although she thought of her in the daytime, too. It was strange, the sense of helplessness she had about her friend. Indeed, it was like being in a dream, one in which there is something of great importance to be done — a warning to be delivered, a secret revealed — yet everybody else is relaxed and indifferent and there is no one who will bother to listen to the dire news that only she is in possession of. Even though no one else seemed to be as worried as she was, she had thought that Quirke surely would appreciate the awfulness of April's disappearance — of her just being gone, without a word, without a trace left behind — for, after all, another young woman whom she had known had disappeared last summer and Quirke had discovered her to have been murdered. Yet when he went with her and the detective to April's flat, and then next day to see April's brother, he had said hardly a word and had seemed not to care about April or what had become of her. But perhaps he was right and she was wrong, perhaps she was being fanciful and melodramatic about the entire thing. Or maybe, simply, it was true that he did not care. Did any of them, really, Isabel, Patrick, Jimmy Minor? They did not seem to be very worried, or not as worried as she was, anyway. She was filled with dread, she could not rid herself of it.

Odd, how clear and sharp the mind can be at this time of night, she thought. Is it just that there are so few distractions in the small hours, or does the brain make use then of energy that normally it would be storing to fuel the next day's mental business? Thinking of April now, and the seemingly careless attitude of Quirke and the others, she, too, had a sense of estrangement, a sense of alienation, which, to her surprise, seemed to be allowing her to consider her friend's case with a new and calm dispassion. Somehow in her mind April became separated from all the things that together made up the image she had of her friend, and floated free, as sometimes in one's consciousness a word floats free of the thing it is attached to and becomes something else, not just a noise, exactly, not a meaningless grunt or bark, but a mysterious new entity, new and mysterious because it is itself only and not merely a means of signifying something.

Who *is* April? she asked herself. She had thought she knew her, but now she wondered if she had been wrong all along, if April was someone else entirely from the person she had always taken her to be. Instead of the frank and open friend that she had spoken to almost every day, had chatted and gossiped with, there appeared now in her mind a different creature altogether, secretive, guarded, one who hid her real self

170

from Phoebe and maybe from everyone else, too. Yes, guarded, that was how April was, not open at all, but concealed. And behind this figure there was something else again that was hidden too, or someone else, perhaps, always there in the background, some secret, all-pervasive presence. Yes. Someone there, always.

She had seen Jimmy Minor last evening. They had met in O'Neill's in Wicklow Street. The pub had been crowded and noisy — Trinity students were celebrating a win in some match or other — and they could hardly hear themselves speak. She had suggested they go somewhere that would be more quiet but of course someone only had to suggest something to Jimmy for him to dig his heels in and resist, and instead of agreeing to move to another pub he had ordered drink and lit up a cigarette. He was telling her something about April and his newspaper. She could not believe her ears the first time and made him say it again: he had gone to the Editor and told him that April was missing.

"Oh, Jimmy, you didn't!" she cried.

He looked at her in hurt surprise. "I'm a reporter," he said, holding up his miniature hands in a show of simple sincerity. "Someone is missing, I report it." Anyway, the Editor, it seemed, had not been interested in April Latimer, or had pretended not to be, and had told him to drop the story. "I said to him, 'Do you know who she is, who she's related to?' That only made him put on his stony-faced look — he doesn't like what my old fellow used to call back-chat. I kept on, mentioning the Minister her uncle and her brother the

Fitzwilliam Square consultant, but it was no good, there was no —"

A raucous cheer went up from the crowd of red-faced young men at the bar and she missed the rest of it. "But did he know something about it?" she asked. "Did he already know April was missing?"

"I told you, all I got was the stony face. But, yes, I had the impression someone had been on the blower to him, telling him to keep the lid on any stories about missing girls."

She stared at him, speechless for a moment. "Who would call him?" she asked, baffled. "Who would make that kind of phone call?"

"Oh, Phoebe," he said, with a pitying smile, shaking his head. "Don't you know anything about this town, how it works?"

"You mean her uncle, Mr Latimer, the Minister, would telephone the Editor of a newspaper and order him not to publish a story, not even to follow it up?"

"Listen, sweetheart, let me explain," he said, putting on his Jimmy Cagney voice. "The Minister wouldn't phone, and there would be no order. Someone from the Department would give a little tinkle, some flunkey of the Minister's, and super-Gael with a name like Maolseachlainn Mahoganygaspipe, and talk for ten minutes about the weather and the shocking price of spuds, and then, just as he was about to ring off, would say, *Oh, by the way, Séanie, the Minister's young one has gone off on a bit of a skite and the family is trying to get her to come home — there'd be no use in the paper running any kind of a story on it, don't you*

172

know, you'd only end up with egg on your face, or should I say printing ink? Ha ha ha. That's how it's done. The velvet word, the silken threat. Wise up, sister."

"And the Editor of a national newspaper would give in to a threat, just like that?"

This was greeted with a whinny of laughter. "Threat? — where's the threat? Friendly advice, a word to the wise, that's all. And then there's grace and favour — next time Séanie the Editor needs a bit of inside info he'll call up Mr Mahoganygaspipe and mention the little service he did for the Minister and his family by keeping his newshounds on the leash that time when the Minister's troublesome niece went off on her travels. See?"

Now Phoebe, sitting by the black window, went over again all that Jimmy had said, trying to decide if it could be true, if it could be what had happened. But what of it, she thought then, even if it was? If the Latimers were using their influence to stop the newspapers reporting April's disappearance, was that so terrible? Any family would do it, that had a wayward daughter and the power to keep stories about her out of the papers. Yet the thought of that pinched, insinuating voice on the telephone — Jimmy was a good mimic — whispering menaces into someone's ear gave her the shivers.

She must concentrate. Think. Remember. Summon up. *Who is April Latimer?*

The milk in the mug had gone tepid, but she drank it anyway, drank it to the dregs, and got a raspberry pip, sharp and hard, stuck in a gap between two molars, making her think of childhood.

Once, not very long ago, they had sat, she and April, on a bench by the pond in St Stephen's Green, watching the children and their mothers feeding the ducks. It was an afternoon in late summer: she remembered the trees soughing gently above them and the sunlight seeming to lift big flakes of gold from the surface of the water. April was smoking a cigarette in that way she did, holding it close in front of her face, leaning forward and hunched around herself as if she were cold. It was the way old women smoked, Phoebe remembered thinking, with a rush of fondness for her friend, a fondness both sweet and unsettling. She could not recall what it was they had been talking about, but at one point she realised that April had gone quiet, had retreated into herself, and was sitting there smoking and frowning and staring at the water with a strange, haunted look in her eyes. Phoebe too had fallen silent, instinctively respecting whatever private place it was that her friend had withdrawn into. At last April spoke.

"The thing about obsession," she said, still watching the spangled surface of the pond, "is that there's no pleasure in it. You think at the start, if there is a start, that it's the greatest delight you could know" — that word, *delight*, the way that she said it, had struck Phoebe as disturbing, almost indecent — "but after a while, when you're caught in it and can't get out, it's a prison cell." She had stopped then, for another interval of intent brooding and smoking, and then had described how, in this cell, you look up longingly at the

174

barred window that is too high to reach, at the sunlight and the patch of blue sky there, and realise that you do not know what life is like, on the outside, where others are free.

Phoebe had not known what to say, how to respond. She did not think of April as a person who would be obsessed — there was another dark and troubling word — and she felt as if a curtain had been flicked aside for a moment to allow her a glimpse down a long, dim passageway murmurous with unseen presences, where the air that pressed back into her face was damp and dank and sweetly heavy. She remembered the shudder that had gone through her, glimpsing that dark place, even as she sat there in the park in the bright sunlight, amidst that summer scene. A flock of seagulls appeared, thrashing their wings and shrieking, intent on seizing the crusts of bread that the children were throwing to the ducks, and she shrank back in sudden fright. April, though, had roused herself at the sight of the scavengers descending, and laughed. "Oh, look at those!" she cried, "— those *monsters*!" gazing at the ravening gulls with a smile of what seemed fierce approval, her small, white, even teeth bared a little and glistening and her eyes eagerly alight. That was a moment when Phoebe did not know her friend, did not recognise her. Had there been other such moments that she failed to notice as they went past, moments of awful insight she had forgotten, or had chosen to forget? What did she know about her friend? What did she know —?

She stood up from the table, and almost fell over because her legs had gone stiff from the cold. Wrapping herself tight in the thin silk robe she went into the living room and stood by the window there. She had not turned on the light. She did not mind the dark, had never been afraid of it, even as a child. The mist was down again, she saw, not dense enough to be called a fog, and the streetlamp below had a grey halo around it. The street was silent. A prostitute had recently taken up her beat here, a sad creature, young and skinny, who always seemed to be freezing; Phoebe spoke to her sometimes, about the weather, or an item in the news, and the girl would smile gratefully, glad not to be ogled or glared at, or called something filthy. She had even told Phoebe her name, which was Sadie. What must her life be like, Phoebe wondered, having to go with anyone who had a pound in his pocket? How would it feel to —?

She started. There was someone in the street, someone she had not noticed until now, a person standing just outside the streetlamp's ring of wettish light. She could not make out if it was a man or a woman, though she knew it was not Sadie. It was just a figure, standing there, quite still, looking up, it seemed, at this very window where she was looking down from. Whoever it was, would he see her, here in the dark? No. But what if she were to move forward, and stand right up against the glass, would she be visible then? She advanced a step, holding her breath. She put a hand to her throat. She was shivering, she did not know whether from the cold or from fright, or from something else. The figure did not stir — was it there at all or was she just imagining it? This had happened before, when she lived in Harcourt Street; she had thought then that she was being watched, and had told herself then, too, that it was her imagination, but as it turned out she had not imagined it. She realised she had left the light on in the kitchen, whoever it was would know she was here, and not sleeping, perhaps had even seen her sitting at the table with her milk and her cake — would it have been possible to have been seen at that angle, from the street, if she was sitting down? — and was waiting for her now to come back into the light, in her flimsy silk wrap, with her hair undone, unsleeping and restless, worrying about her vanished friend.

Abruptly she turned from the window and fairly raced to the kitchen and, without crossing the threshold, reached in and switched off the light. She waited a moment, then moved forward cautiously into the darkness, avoiding the outlines of the furniture yet managing to jar her hip on a corner of the stove, and peered down into the misty street. No one was there. Probably no one had been there in the first place, probably it had been only a shadow she had seen and thought it a person. Yet she did not believe that. There *had* been someone, standing in the darkness and the damp air, looking up, watching for her. But whoever it was that had been there was gone.

CHAPTER
THREE

Quirke could never quite account for his fondness of Inspector Hackett. After all, there were not many people he had a fondness for. Despite the many evident differences between them they seemed to have something in common. Perhaps what he appreciated was the policeman's amused, easy-going scepticism of the world in general. At one time Quirke had thought that Hackett, like him, must have spent his early years in an institution, but there was a pliancy to the detective's personality, an essential amiability, that would not have survived a place such as Carricklea. The Quirkes and the Harknesses of this world were a closed and unwilling fraternity, whose secret handshake betokened not trust or fellowship, but suspicion, fear, coldness, remembered misery, unflagging rancour. Fellowship and trust, these were among the good things behind the cold glass of the great shop window against which they pressed their faces half in longing and half in angry contempt. The thing to do was to hide the damage. That was what they expected of each other, what they asked of each other, the maimed ones; that was their token of honour. What was it Rose Crawford had said to him once, a long time ago? *A cold heart and a hot soul — that's us, Quirke.* And yet the fact remained that he was fond of Hackett — how was that?

Nevertheless, when the telephone rang and he picked it up and heard the detective's drawn-out Midlands vowels, his heart sank. April Latimer, again. Quirke was in his office at the hospital, in his white coat, leaning back in his chair with his feet on the desk. Through the big plate-glass window of the dissection room he could see his assistant Sinclair working on a cadaver, busy with saw and scalpel. "Is there something new, Inspector?" he asked wearily.

"Well, now," Hackett said, and Quirke pictured him, in his cubby-hole on the top floor of the barracks in Pearse Street, putting his head on one side and squinting up at the tobacco-coloured ceiling, "it's new, all right, but whether it's a thing or not I'm not so sure." Sinclair, Quirke noticed for the first time, had a peculiar way of approaching a corpse, sidewise, with his head tilted and his tongue stuck in a corner of his mouth, like a hunter stalking his prey. "I went around again to the house in Herbert Place," Hackett said. "There's a person there that lives in the top-floor flat, a very queer sort of a woman altogether. A Miss Helen St John Leetch, no less." He chuckled. "Isn't that a grand name?"

"What had she to say?"

"I'd venture she's a bit touched, the unfortunate creature, but she's watchful, too, in her way, and doesn't miss a thing."

"And what did she see, on her watch?"

There was a wheezing sound on the line, which after a moment or two of puzzlement Quirke recognised as laughter. "You're a very impatient man, Dr Quirke," the policeman said at last, "do you know that? I'll tell you what, why don't you jump in that grand new car of yours and drive down here and we'll go out for a bite to eat? What do you say?"

"I can't," Quirke lied. "I already have a lunch engagement."

"Ah, do you say — a lunch engagement?" He liked the sound of that, it seemed, and there was another interval of wheezing. "Well, could you spare me ten minutes before you repair to your luncheon? Would that be at all a possibility, do you think?"

Quirke grudgingly said yes, that he would call at the inspector's office, but that it was too late now, it would have to be after lunch.

He put the phone down and sat for a long time leaning back with his hands behind his head, looking at Sinclair at work, but not seeing him. Isabel Galloway was still haunting his thoughts. The image of her, the cool, long, pale length of her, preyed on him. She was not like the women he was accustomed to. After that night in her house at Portobello, with the two swans gliding on the moonlit waters of the canal, something in him that had been locked all his life had begun to loosen, grinding and groaning, like a glacier on the move, or an iceberg breaking.

Now when he phoned her and gave his name she let a silence hang, then said: "Well, if it isn't you. And I thought my one-night stand had been stood down."

"I wondered," he said cautiously, "if we might meet."

"What were you thinking of?"

"I thought we might have lunch."

"Yes, you like your lunch, don't you?"

He held the receiver to one side and frowned at it, then put it back to his ear. "What's that supposed to mean?"

"A rather large and painted bird — *two* rather large birds, in fact — told me they spotted you in Jammet's in the company of a *femme mystérieuse*, a lady *d'un certain âge* but handsome withal and, my two chickadees surmised, moneyed to boot."

Although he was in the basement of the building he knew that it was raining outside; he could sense rather than hear it, a sort of far-off, general, moist humming. "Her name," he said, "is Rose Crawford. She used to be married to my father-in-law."

"Ah. Complicated. So she would be your — what, your stepmother-in-law?" She laughed softly.

"She lives here now," he said. "In Wicklow. She has fallen for the romance of the place — the wind in the heather, the rain on the crag, that kind of thing." With his free hand he eased a cigarette out of the packet on the desk and fumbled in the pocket of his white coat for his lighter. "I'm angling for a mention in her will."

"From what my feathered friends had to say, she's far from on her last legs. In fact, dear Mícheál — who, surprisingly, has an eye for these things — remarked particularly on the shapeliness of the lady's ankle." She gave another low laugh. "You wouldn't try to deceive a

181

simple player-lass on the nature of your relations with this in-law, would you?"

"I probably would," he said.

"You don't have to be so frank, you know. Frankness is a much overrated quality, in my opinion."

"So what about it? — lunch, I mean."

"Yes. But not Jammet's, I think. Too many associations already."

She said she would meet him in the Gresham Hotel — "I'm rehearsing, darling, it'll be just a tripping step for me from here" — where now in the sombre, mock-grandeur of the place Quirke felt ill at ease. Some film star was expected from the airport and the place was abuzz with reporters and flash photographers and dozens of what must be fans milling outside on the pavement despite the wind and the scudding rain. Isabel was waiting for him in the bar. "It's Bing," she said, indicating the crowd outside. "They're mad for a crooner." She had her stage makeup on — "It's a full-dress rehearsal, Gawd help us" — and was wearing a mackintosh, which she had not unbuttoned. She had not had time to change out of her costume, she said, and made a pained face. "We're doing Maeterlinck, *The Blue Bird*. I'm afraid I'm a fairy."

She was drinking Campari and soda. He said he would settle for a soda by itself, and lit a cigarette. He must have been staring at her, for she blushed a little now, and lowered her long eyelashes. "You make me self-conscious," she murmured, smiling. "Imagine that, an actress, and self-conscious — have you ever heard of such a thing?"

He would have liked to be in bed with her, now, this minute, while she was like this, not brittle and smart, but shy, confused, almost defenceless.

"Do you know what his full name is, Maeterlinck's?" she said, looking into her drink and pretending to be busy stirring it with a plastic cocktail stick. "Maurice Polydore Marie Bernard, Count Maeterlinck." She looked at him from under those lowered lashes. "What do you think of that?"

He took the cocktail stick from her and put it on the bar. "You've been on my mind," he said. "I don't know what to — I don't know how to —" He shrugged. "I'm not good at this."

She leaned forward and kissed him, lightly, on the cheek. "As if," she whispered, "anyone is."

"Why don't you open your coat," he said, "and let me see your fairy costume?"

In the lobby there was cheering: Bing had arrived at last.

Sitting in Hackett's office Quirke might have been in the wheelhouse of a trawler battling its way through a stormy sea. The stunted window behind the detective's desk was grimy at the best of times but on this day of wind and driving rain the daylight itself had to fight its way through the streaming, misted panes. There was a coal fire burning in the grate, and the air in the room was hot and leaden. Now and then a backdraught would send a ball of smoke rolling across the threadbare carpet, to mingle with the general fug of cigarette smoke. Hackett was in his shirtsleeves, with his tie loosened and his collar-stud undone. The upper half of his forehead, usually hidden by his hat, was baby-pink and soft-looking, and his hair, pomaded with what seemed to be boot polish, was brushed fiercely back; it was, Quirke noted, beginning to go grey around the edges.

"That girl of yours," the policeman said, "seems to attract trouble."

For a giddy moment Quirke thought he meant Isabel Galloway, and wondered how he could possibly know about her; then he realised his mistake. "Oh, Phoebe," he said. "Trouble seems to find her, you mean — not quite the same thing."

Hackett nodded, doing his froggy grin. "Either way, she keeps herself busy — and keeps me busy, too. I suppose there's been no word of her friend?"

"Not that I know of. And I'm coming to believe there won't be."

This time Hackett sighed, and riffled through the papers that cluttered his desk, a sign of frustration, as Quirke well knew. "It's a fine old mess, so it is," the policeman said.

"Yes, that's what her uncle says."

"He'd know a mess when he sees one, all right."

Quirke watched the crowding raindrops on the window-panes shaking and shivering in the pummelling gusts of wind. "The woman in the flat above April's, what did she say?"

"Miss Helen St John Leetch," Hackett said, rolling it on his tongue. "I never knew before the right way to pronounce that name 'St John'. Queer."

"Did she know April?"

"She kept tabs on her, shall we say? Lonely people always make the best eye-witnesses."

"And what did she see, while she was keeping tabs?"

"Not much. By the way" — he leaned forward eagerly — "I'm coming up in the world. Look at this thing." It was an electric bell set in a Bakelite bulb that was fixed to the corner of his desk. "Watch this now." He pressed the bell and sat back and waited, a finger lifted in the air. After a few moments the door opened and a young Guard came in. He was tall and gangly with a shock of carroty hair and a pustular chin. "This is Garda Tomelty," Hackett announced, in a tone of pride, as if he had personally conjured the young man into existence. "Terence," he said to the Guard, "would you ever be so good as to bring us up a pot of tea and a few biscuits?"

"Right, sir," Garda Tomelty said, and withdrew.

The detective beamed at Quirke. "Isn't that impressive now, what?"

He had finished his cigarette, and he fished about on the desk again and came up with a packet of Player's and lit a new one. Outside, a swooping gust of wind struck so strongly it sent a tremor through the entire building.

"The woman in the flat," Quirke prompted. At lunch with Isabel he had drunk a glass of claret that had gone straight to his head, and even yet he was feeling the afterglow of it. Was it a good sign or a bad that a single glass would have so much of an effect?

"Aye, the woman in the flat," Hackett said. "Miss Leetch — Miss St John Leetch. But wait" — he cupped a hand behind his ear — "do I hear the dainty footsteps of the law?"

The door was opened again and Garda Tomelty came in bearing a small wooden tray on which were a teapot, a milk jug and sugar bowl and two large, blue-striped mugs. "Good lad," Hackett said, pushing to one side the jumble of papers on his desk. "Put it down there, now, and many thanks."

The young man set the tray on the desk and clattered out in his big black shoes and shut the door behind him.

Hackett slopped tea into the mugs and passed one of them to Quirke. "Milk? Sugar?"

"I'll take it black."

"Oh, of course," the detective murmured, smirking to himself. Into his own mug he poured a generous dollop of milk and added four heaped spoonfuls of sugar, then plunged the sugar spoon into the tea and began to stir. "Miss Helen St John Leetch," he said again softly, musingly. He watched with a slack eye the spoon going slowly round and round in the mug. "She saw her with a black man," he said.

"A what?"

"A black man. A Negro."

"Who — April?"

"Aye. So she says, Miss Leetch." He tossed the wet spoon back into the sugar bowl and heaved himself sideways in his chair and put one foot up on the desk. The weathered leather of his hobnailed boots was finely cracked all over like the surface of an old painting. "Hanging around, she says he was."

"Did she see them together, April and this fellow, whoever he is?"

The detective took a slurping drink of his tea and considered. "She wasn't the clearest, I have to say. I thought she was talking about one of the girl's relatives, but the lady laughed at me and said she hardly thought Miss Latimer would have a relative who was black." He paused, lifting his eyes and squinting at a corner of the ceiling. He smoked, he drank, he smoked. "And that was as much as I could get out of her." He swivelled his squinting eye in Quirke's direction. "Do you know of any black man she might know, Dr Quirke?"

Quirke put his mug back on the tray, the tea undrunk. "I know very little about her, except what my daughter tells me. And in fact I'm not sure how much my daughter knows, herself. April Latimer was — is — a very private person, so I gather."

Hackett nodded, pouting his lower lip. "That seems to be the case, all right. And so are the family — private sorts of persons. I'd say they wouldn't be too happy to hear of young April consorting with — a foreigner. Would you?"

"Would I say so, or would I be unhappy if it were so?"

"Well, think if it was your daughter we were talking about."

"I'm afraid I don't have much say, where my daughter is concerned. She lives her own life."

Hackett let fall a little cough; he knew of Quirke and Phoebe's troubled past and their still strained relations. "Aye, I've been wondering about my own lads," he said. "They're both over there in America now, you know, making a life for themselves. What if one of them came home one day in the company of a fine big black woman and said, *Da, this is the lady I'm going to marry?*"

"Well, what *would* you do?"

"I doubt there'd be anything I could do — none of us has much of a say, these days, where the youngsters are concerned." He finished his tea and heaved his foot off the desk and sat forward in his chair again and put aside the mug and planted his elbows on the desk and leaned on them. "But I'll tell you this," he said. "I can imagine what Mrs Celia Latimer and her brother-in-law the Minister, not to mention Mr Oscar Latimer of Fitzwilliam Square — I can well imagine what those folks would say if young Dr Latimer was to turn up with a big strapping black lad on her arm and introduce him all round as her intended."

"From the little that I know of her," Quirke said, "April Latimer wasn't the marrying kind."

They were silent, listening to the hollow drumming of the rain on the window.

"I wonder, though," Hackett said softly, "if the family did know about this coloured fellow, and, if they did, what they decided to do about it." He chuckled. "You and I, Dr Quirke, mightn't have much say in such matters but, by God, the Latimers would make it their business to say everything that was on their minds, and a good bit more."

Quirke considered this. "You think they may have got her out of the country? That they're putting on a show of not knowing where she is or what's become of her?" Hackett said nothing, only leaned there, toad-like, gazing stolidly across the desk. "It wouldn't be so easy, even for the Latimers," Quirke said thoughtfully. "I doubt April would have gone quietly, no matter how much pressure they put on her."

"But go she would, in the end — and go she seems to have gone. The Latimers of this world are not to be balked, wouldn't you say, Dr Quirke?"

They sat again in silence, gazing off in opposite directions, thinking.

"I'll talk to Phoebe," Quirke said at last. "I'll ask her about this black man, if she knows of him."

"She might not," Hackett said, "but that wouldn't mean he doesn't exist. Oh, and speaking of knowing people" — he had drained his mug and was peering into it now as if to read the runes of the tea leaves in the bottom — "did you ever hear your daughter talk of someone by the name of Ronnie?"

"No. Why?"

"Her ladyship, Miss Leetch, mentioned someone going by that name. I could get no sense out of her on the subject. It doesn't sound like what a black man would be called, does it." They looked at each other, and Hackett sighed. "The only Ronnie I've ever heard of is Ronnie Ronalde — the fellow on the wireless, you know, that whistles."

"No," Quirke said, "no, I don't think I know him. He *whistles*?"

"'Mockin' Bird Hill', that's one of his tunes. 'If I Were A Blackbird' is his best-known one, though. Amazing — you'd swear he was the bird itself."

Quirke stood up. "I think, Inspector," he said, "I'll be on my way."

Going down the stairs he heard behind him, from on high, the faint sound of Hackett's voice raised in warbling melody.

If I were a blackbird, I'd whistle and sing —!

CHAPTER
FOUR

The little band had not met since the night in the
Dolphin Hotel that seemed so long ago now, that night
when Phoebe had come home and telephoned Oscar
Latimer. Since then she had seen them all, but
separately, Patrick at his flat, Isabel in the Shakespeare,
and Jimmy Minor in O'Neill's when he told her how
his Editor had ordered him to stay away from the story
of April's disappearance. He told her something else,
too, that night, something that came back to her now,
as if there were one connection, one that she could not
at all make out, between what Jimmy had said and the
phantom figure in the street-light.

They had come out of O'Neill's and were standing
on the corner there while Jimmy finished his cigarette.
Rain was falling, the kind that was so fine it was barely
felt but that could wet through to the skin in a minute.
She was anxious to get away — the last buses were
already departing and she did not welcome the
prospect of having to walk home on such a night — but
Jimmy had drunk three pints of stout and was in an
even more loquacious mood than usual and would not
let her go. He began to talk about Patrick Ojukwu, as
he almost always did when he had drink taken.

"Of course," he said, and sniggered, "if you met him coming along here on a dark night like this you wouldn't be able to see him unless he was grinning." Phoebe did not understand. Jimmy put on a clownish grin. "The black skin, the white teeth? Get it, yes?"

"I wish you wouldn't talk about him like that, behind his back," Phoebe said. "You're supposed to be his friend. Why do you dislike him? Is it because he's black?"

Jimmy scowled and drew hard on the butt of his cigarette; he held it sheltered in the hollow of his hand, like, she thought, a corner boy. "I'm not the only one," he muttered, looking down towards the lights of Dame Street.

"Not the only one *what*?" she demanded. "Not the only one that hates him because of the colour of his skin?"

"It's nothing to do with colour," he snapped.

She sighed. "I don't know what you're talking about, Jimmy. And it's late, I've got to go for my bus."

He was giving her one of his pitying looks. "You never take notice of anything, do you?" he said. "You just sail on blithely as if everything was nice and comfy and uncomplicated."

She felt like stamping her foot. "Tell me what you mean, Jimmy, or let me go. The last bus will be passing the gates of Trinity down there in ten minutes. And *don't* light another cigarette, for Heaven's sake!"

He put the cigarette, unlit, into the top pocket of his tweed jacket and pulled the wings of the plastic coat around him. Even in the dark she could see how blue his lips were from the cold. He does not take care of himself, she thought; he could get pleurisy, or TB, even. He seemed to her suddenly so small, and frail, and unhappy. She took him by the arm and drew him with her back into the shelter of the doorway of the pub.

"You knew Bella and him were having it off," he said. "— You knew that much, didn't you?"

She said nothing; she would not give him the satisfaction of showing how pathetically little she did know. He was right: she did not care to see too deeply into other people's business, into other people's hearts. In that, at least, she was her father's daughter.

"What if they were?" she said. "What about it?"

"And did you know that April took him away from her?"

She looked down, to avoid his fiercely glaring, slightly drunken eye. "No," she said, surrendering, "no, I didn't know that."

"I thought you didn't," he said, in a tone of sour satisfaction. "There's an awful lot about April that you don't know — an awful lot."

She could hear from inside the pub the drunken students beginning to sing and the barmen shouting at them to stop, that the place would be raided if there was singing and they would all be arrested. It was the same every night, the fellows drunk and the girls wanting to go home, and then the place emptying, and fights in the street, and later on the fumbling in the back laneways and the front seats of motor cars. She was sick of this city, sick of it. Maybe Rose Crawford would offer to take her to America again. No place had ever seemed so far away as America seemed to her at that moment.

"And what about Isabel?" she asked. "Was she very upset?"

"What do you think? Isabel and the Prince, what a combination! She saw herself as Desdemona, without the smothering bit at the end. And then April crooked her finger and His Majesty was off, his tail-feathers twitching. I'd say it's a close thing as to which of them she hates the more, His Negritude or April the cruellest —"

She would not listen to any more of this, and stepped past him out of the doorway of the pub and walked rapidly down to the traffic lights and ran along Dame Street to the bus stop. The bus was just about to pull away and she had to jump on and grasp the rail to keep from falling backwards, and the conductor swore at her. It was only when she went inside and sat down that she felt the tears on her face, and realised that she had been crying since she walked away from Jimmy, and she could not stop.

Now, today, it was raining again, hard, and there was a gale blowing, tearing through the streets and shaking the bare trees along the canal. Despite the weather she had decided to walk to work. It was easier to think when she was walking. She had tried opening her umbrella but at once the wind had caught it and would have turned it inside-out if she had not let it down straight away. Anyway, she did not mind the rain. Even such stormy mornings as this were a presage of spring, for her. She was thinking of America again, of the rain

194

on Boston Common and the trees along Commonwealth Avenue thrashing in the wind; it was a way of trying not to think of April, of Isabel, of Patrick Ojukwu.

She could see from Mrs Cuffe-Wilkes's smile, all dentures and treacly sweetness, that she was furious at her — not only was she late, but she was wet and bedraggled and her shoes were muddy from the tow-paths.

"You really should be more careful, my dear," Mrs Cuffe-Wilkes said, in her steeliest voice. "You could catch your death walking in the rain like that."

"The bus was delayed and I thought it would be quicker if I walked."

"And was it?"

"No, Mrs Cuffe-Wilkes. I'm sorry."

The woman had stopped pretending to smile and her face was puffing up, her cheeks and forehead all pink and shiny, in the awful way that it did when she was about to lose her temper. Mrs Cuffe-Wilkes's anger fed on itself and could go on whipping itself up throughout a morning. Phoebe retreated to the back room and took off her wet coat and hung it on a chair and set it in front of the gas fire; at once it began to give off a strong smell of sheep. The soles of her stockings were soaked too, and she took them off, hoping her employer would not notice. At least the hood of her coat had kept her hair from getting wet — Mrs Cuffe-Wilkes would not have stood for wet hair in the shop.

The morning dragged. There were few customers, because of the weather. It would be nearly impossible to see in from the street, for the window was streaming with rain on the outside and was becoming steamed up on the inside. Mrs Cuffe-Wilkes, still in an angry sulk, kept to the cubby-hole she called her office, whence at intervals there issued long, trembling, put-upon sighs and faint, vexed mutterings. Phoebe tried not to watch the hands crawling over the face of the clock. She tried too not to think about her friends, her so-called friends, and all the things she was finding out she had not known about them. Was Jimmy telling the truth about April taking Patrick Ojukwu away from Isabel, and about Isabel hating the two of them for it? Because if he was, then Isabel had lied to her in the Shakespeare that night when she laughed at her for thinking April and Patrick were lovers. And Patrick, he would have been lying, too, in his flat that lunchtime when she asked him straight out about April and he denied that he was in love with her, or at least that he had been in love with her. Or had he denied it? She tried to remember what exactly he had said, how he had answered when she asked him, *Do you love her?* These lies, these pretences, these coverings-up — she hated all that. It had started, for her, when Jimmy told her so casually about the key that April left under the stone, the key that April had never told her about. What was she to believe, what was she to take as the truth of anything anyone said to her? Had not everyone lied to her, from the very first moments of her life?

The pinging of the little brass bell over the door roused her from these bitter thoughts. Rose Crawford had come into the shop.

196

Mrs Cuffe-Wilkes was at once surprised, charmed and suspicious. She had ignored the doorbell, thinking it was just some ordinary customer entering, but when she heard that languid American drawl, suggestive as it was of transatlantic gullibility and a Bergdorf Goodman bag bursting with dollars, she came hurrying out of her cubby-hole like a large, over-painted cuckoo popping out of its clock. Rich American visitors were only expected in the summertime, but here, in the depths of winter, was what was certainly an American, and obviously a rich one at that. Rose wore a Burberry raincoat that showed no more than a few light raindrops on the shoulders — not only had the taxi man walked her to the door of the shop, he had escorted her there under his own umbrella — and beneath it what Mrs Cuffe-Wilkes's practised eye saw at once was a Chanel suit in light-pink wool.

"My dear," Rose was saying to Phoebe, releasing her from a light, deft embrace, "look at you, all in black as usual, like a Mafia widow."

Phoebe introduced her employer, then hesitated — how was she supposed to explain her relationship to Rose? — but Rose immediately rescued her, putting on her most glittering smile and extending an expensively manicured hand. "Rose Crawford," she said. "Delighted, I'm sure."

Mrs Cuffe-Wilkes was uncertain how to proceed. Although she allowed Phoebe now and then to make a discount purchase for a family member or a pal, she had set it out clearly to her assistant that actual visits to the shop by friends or relatives would not be countenanced unless they were prepared to pay full retail prices — there were professional standards to be maintained, after all. Rose Crawford, whoever she might be, was no hard-up cousin trying to cadge a bargain or an old school acquaintance on the eve of her nuptials looking for something fancy to top off her going-away outfit; Rose was Money, possibly even Old Money, and that was all that Mrs Cuffe-Wilkes needed to know about her.

"I was on my way to Brown Thomas when I remembered where Phoebe worked," Rose said. "I need something to cope with your Irish weather" — a wry smile and eyes cast upwards — "but at the same time won't make me look like Mother Machree's older sister."

Why, of course, Mrs Cuffe-Wilkes said eagerly, and began plucking hats from all corners of the shop and strewing them along the counter like so many overblown lotus blossoms. Phoebe could see by the tightening of her nostrils that Rose found them all equally ugly; nevertheless she took up two models at random and went to the full-length mirror by the door and tried them on in turn. "Which is the least awful?" she asked of Phoebe, out of the side of her mouth.

Phoebe, standing close beside her, smiled. "You don't have to buy anything, you know," she murmured.

Mrs Cuffe-Wilkes, who was a little deaf, was watching them sharply.

In the end Rose decided on a rather severe black felt toque with a ruby pin. It looked very smart on her,

Phoebe saw. Rose asked if she could pay with a traveller's cheque, and Mrs Cuffe-Wilkes scuttled into her office to phone the bank to ask for guidance.

"So," Rose said to Phoebe, putting the hat carelessly aside, "how are you, my dear?"

"I'm very well."

"You've changed. You're older."

Phoebe laughed. "Not much older, I hope?"

"I worry about you."

"Do you? Why?"

Mrs Cuffe-Wilkes came back, wheezing in distress. "I'm so sorry, the young man at the bank seemed to think it wouldn't be —"

"It doesn't matter," Rose said. "I'll go and get some cash and come back." She smiled her toothed smile again. "Perhaps Miss Griffin here can show me the way to the American Express office?"

"Oh, it's just down there at the bottom of the —"

"I meant, she could take me there? I get lost so easily in these dinky little streets."

Mrs Cuffe-Wilkes began to make a further protest, but then retreated a step, seeming to deflate. "Oh, well, yes, of course."

The rain was stopping as Rose and Phoebe walked down Grafton Street. "I wanted," Rose said, "to consult you about something." She linked her arm in Phoebe's. "It's rather" — she gave a small, embarrassed laugh — "rather delicate, I suppose you'd say."

Phoebe waited, breathless with curiosity — what could it possibly be that would make Rose Crawford behave so awkwardly? They came to the American

Express office. "Here we are," Phoebe said. "Tell me before we go in."

Rose looked all about the street, as if fearing to be overheard, and bit her lip. For a moment she might have been half her age. "No," she said, "let's get my money first. I always feel more confident, somehow, with a wad of greenbacks in the back pocket of my blue-jeans."

It seemed to take for ever to get the cheque cashed. Phoebe waited near the door, looking at the travel posters and reading the brochures. At last the business was done, and Rose came back, shutting her handbag. "All right," she said. "Let's go and make your boss a happy woman."

But Phoebe would not budge. "I'm not moving until you tell me what it is you want to 'consult' me about."

Rose stood and gazed at her in smiling dismay. "Oh, Lordy!" she exclaimed. "Why did I start this?" She took Phoebe's arm again and led her determinedly into the street, and there they halted again. Rose took a deep breath. "I wanted to ask you, my dear, how you would feel if I were to — well, if I were to marry into the family again."

"Marry?"

Rose nodded, pressing her lips tightly together. Phoebe looked upwards. Between the rooftops the narrow strip of sky, flowing swiftly with grey and silver clouds, seemed for a moment a gorgeous, shining, inverted river.

"Of course," Rose went on quickly, "he may not say yes. In fact, I'll be — well, I'll be pretty surprised if he does."

"You mean, *he* hasn't asked *you*? — you're going to ask him?"

"I've dropped hints. But you know how it is with Irishmen and hints. And your father, well — he's the Irishman's Irishman, isn't he?"

"But but but —"

Rose put a finger to the girl's lips. "Ssh. Not another word, for now. I've embarrassed myself quite enough for one day. I need that hat to hide my blushes under."

And they set off up the street towards the Maison des Chapeaux and its expectant proprietress. Above their heads, Phoebe saw, that river of cloud flowed on in joyful spate.

When Rose had paid for her hat and left, still looking flustered, Phoebe asked Mrs Cuffe-Wilkes if she might use the telephone. This was a daring request, for the telephone was an object of reverence and some awe to its owner, and sat enshrined in state on the desk in the cubby-hole, making Phoebe think always of a pampered, pedigree cat. But the hat that Rose had bought was so costly that Mrs Cuffe-Wilkes had not even bothered to bring it down until Rose spotted it on a high shelf and asked to see it, and after such a lavish sale how could she refuse the girl a phone call? She was itching to know who exactly Rose was, but Phoebe offered no account of her and the moment to insist on being told seemed to have passed. Mustering what grace she could, therefore, Mrs Cuffe-Wilkes said of course, the phone was there, please feel free.

It was her father Phoebe called, inviting him to invite her to dinner. Like her employer, what could he say but yes?

CHAPTER
FIVE

Quirke himself had been about to make a telephone call, though he was not at all sure that he should. He was in his office, and had been thinking of April Latimer. He had never met the young woman, had never even seen her, as far as he knew, though he might have passed her by in a corridor of the hospital, yet the thought of her kept coming back to his mind. It was as if he had glimpsed a figure in the fog and were stumbling in pursuit of it, though it maintained a maddeningly constant distance in front of him and at times disappeared altogether amidst the deceptive grey billowings. The recollection of that day in Bill Latimer's office with Latimer and April's mother and her brother nagged at him; it had felt unreal, like an amateur theatrical performance put on just for him. Someone there knew something more than had been said.

Oscar Latimer answered the phone himself, on the first ring.

They had agreed to meet by the canal at Huband Bridge. Quirke was early, and went down to the tow-path and sat on the old iron bench there, huddled in his coat. The rain had stopped and it was damp and misty, with a great stillness everywhere, and when a drop fell from one of the branches of the plane tree above him and landed with a thwack on the brim of his hat it made him start. Ghosts lingered in this place, the ghost of Sarah, poor, lost Sarah, and even the ghost of himself, too, as he was then, when she was alive and they used to walk on days like this beside the water here. Today moorhens paddled among the reeds, as they had then, and that same willow trailed its fingertips in the shallows, and a double-decker bus that might have been the prototype of all green buses went past up there at Baggot Street, lumbering over the hump-backed bridge with the ungainly grace of some large, loping creature of the forest.

He should have married Sarah when he had the chance, should not have let her turn in her disappointment of him to Mal, who was not worthy of her. Vain thoughts, vain regrets.

He lit a cigarette. The smoke that he exhaled lingered in the moist air, vague and uncertain, with not a breath of breeze to disperse it. He held the match before his eyes and watched the flame burn steadily along the wood. Should he let it scorch his fingers? In his life he craved some strong, irresistible sensation, of pain, of anguish or of joy. It would take more than a match-flame to furnish that.

Oscar Latimer arrived from the direction Quirke was not looking in, from Lower Mount Street. Quirke heard his light, rapid footsteps and turned, and stood up from the bench and threw away his half-smoked cigarette and squared his shoulders. Why should he be nervous of this dapper, pent-up little man? Perhaps it was precisely because of what it was that was pent up in him, all that indignation, that anger, that sense he gave of an insulted self raging for release and never finding it. He wore a short, herringbone-tweed overcoat and a tweed cap. He kept his hands in his pockets and stood before Quirke and looked up at him with an expression of distaste and sour scepticism. "Well?" he said. "Here I am — what have you to say to me?"

"Let's walk along for a bit, shall we?" Quirke said.

Latimer shrugged, and they set off on the path. Quirke was thinking what a contrast they must make, the two of them, him so large and Latimer so little. A dun-coloured duck rose up out of the grass verge and waddled ahead of them for a little way along the path and then flopped into the water.

"I haven't been here since I was a child," Oscar Latimer said. "I had an aunt who lived in Baggot Street, she used to take us over here to fish for minnows. What was it we called them? — there was an Irish name, what was it?"

"Pinkeens?" Quirke said. "Or bardógs was another word."

"Bardógs? I don't remember that. We put them in jam jars. Horrible things, they were, just two big eyes with a tail attached, but we were thrilled to catch them. My aunt used to make handles for the jam jars out of string. She had a special knack, I could never see how she did it. She'd wrap the string tight under the neck of the jar and then tie a special knot that let the string loop over two or three times to form the handle." He shook his head wonderingly. "It seems so long ago. An age."

The fellow could be no more than thirty-five, Quirke was thinking. "Yes," he said, "the past wastes no time becoming the past, all right."

Latimer was not listening. "We were happy, April and I, here, with our fishing nets. Life was suddenly — simple, for a few hours."

A workman in shiny black waders was standing hip-deep in the canal, cutting reeds with a knife. They paused a moment to watch. The knife had a long, thin, hooked blade. The man eyed them warily. "That's a dirty old day," he said. Quirke wondered if he was a council worker or if he was gathering the reeds for himself, to fashion something from them. But what? Baskets? Mats? He made the cutting of the stiff, dry stalks seem effortless. Quirke felt a twinge of envy. How would it be, to live so simple a life?

They walked on.

"Where's your daughter today?" Latimer asked. "— I presume it's again about April you wanted to speak to me, yes?"

"And I suppose you're going to tell me again that it's none of my business."

Latimer gave a brief, dismissive laugh. "Do I need to?"

They came to Baggot Street Bridge and climbed the steps to the street. Across the way, the poet Kavanagh, in overcoat and cap, was sitting in the window of Parsons bookshop, among the books laid out there, with his elbows on his knees and the holes in the soles of his cracked shoes on display, intently reading. Passers-by took no heed of him, being accustomed to the sight.

"Have you had lunch?" Latimer asked. "We might get a sandwich somewhere." He looked doubtfully in the direction of the Crookit Bawbee.

"There's Searsons, down the way," Quirke said.

The place was crowded with lunchtime drinkers but they found two stools by the bar at the back. Quirke ordered a cheese sandwich, fearing the worst, and Latimer asked for a ham salad and a half-pint of Guinness. Quirke said he would take a glass of water. The barman, who knew him, gave him a quizzical look.

The sandwich was all that Quirke had expected; he opened it up and slathered Colman's mustard on the shiny slice of bright orange processed cheese. "You know about the blood on the floor beside April's bed," he said, "don't you?"

When he was at school at St Aidan's there was a boy, he could not remember his name, that he used to beat up regularly, an odd, fey little creature with slicked-down, dandruffy hair and an overlapping front tooth. Quirke had nothing in particular against him. It was just that nothing, not even repeated punchings, could ruffle the little twerp's composure and air of self-possession. He almost seemed to like being hit; it seemed, infuriatingly, to amuse him. Latimer was like that, detached and slyly smiling and mysteriously untouchable. For a time now he went on calmly eating, and might not have heard what Quirke had said. Then he spoke. "I don't find it appropriate to discuss this kind of thing with you, Quirke. It's a family matter, and you're not even a policeman."

"That's true," Quirke said, "I'm not. Only the police, too, have been told that your sister's disappearance is a family matter. And frankly, Mr Latimer, I don't think it is."

Latimer was smiling thinly to himself. He put a forkful of moist, pale-pink ham into his mouth and chewed thoughtfully for a minute, then took a delicate sip of his stout. "You keep saying she has disappeared. How do you know that?"

Quirke had bitten into his sandwich and now he put it back on the plate and pushed the plate aside and drank a deep draught of water from his glass; the water tasted faintly of tar. "Your sister hasn't been seen in three weeks," he said. "I'd say 'disappeared' is the right word."

"By whom?"

"What?"

"She hasn't been seen by whom, in three weeks?" He spoke as if to a child, or to one of his patients, spacing the words deliberately, giving each one an equal emphasis.

"Have *you* seen her?" Quirke asked. "Have *you* heard from her?"

Latimer touched a finger to his stubbly, sparse moustache and again smiled faintly. He ate his food and drank his drink with a contented air. His hands, freckled on the back, were tiny, pale and deft. He wiped his lips on a paper napkin and turned on the stool, putting an elbow on the bar, and gazed at Quirke for a long moment, as if measuring him. "I've asked around about you," he said. "About your background, where you come from."

"And what did you find out?"

"You come from nowhere, apparently. Some orphanage here in the city, then an industrial school over in the west, from where you were sprung — I think that's the right word? — by Judge Garret Griffin, who brought you up in his home as if you were his own son. You and Malachy Griffin, like brothers. All very colourful, I must say." He chuckled. "Like something you'd read in a cheap novelette."

Quirke rotated the water glass on its base, round and round, as if he were trying to screw it into the wood of the counter. "That about sums it up," he said. "As a matter of interest, who were your informants?"

"Oh, various people. You know what this town is like, everyone knows everyone else's business."

Malachy, Quirke was thinking — would Malachy have spoken to this vehement little man? What if he had? — none of what Latimer had said was a secret. He gazed along the length of the bar. The light indoors was brownish, dim, and outside it was grey. He felt he was in a cave, far at the back, crouched and watching.

"I mention all this," Latimer said, "to make the point that you can't possibly know anything about families. How could you? There are ties you wouldn't feel — blood ties."

"Blood ties? I thought we dispensed with stuff like that when we left the caves."

"Ah, but there, you see? The very fact that you say that shows your ignorance, your lack of experience in these things. The family is the unit of society, and has been since the very beginning, when we were still going on all fours — you know that much, at least, surely. Blood is blood. It binds" — he clenched one of those little hands into a fist and held it up before Quirke's face — "it *holds*."

Quirke signalled to the barman, and asked for a whiskey — Bushmills Black Label — slurring the words as if to pretend he was not really speaking them. The barman gave him another look, more knowing than the first one, more complicit.

Latimer was picking up crumbs from his plate rapidly with the wetted tip of a finger and putting them into his mouth. His head was small, too small even for that neat little body. A tom-tit, Quirke thought, that is what he is like, a tom-tit bird, quick, bright, hungry, watchful.

"Tell me the truth," Quirke said quietly. "Tell me where April is."

Latimer widened his eyes, putting on a look of large, mild innocence. "What makes you think I know?"

The barman brought the whiskey and Quirke drank off half of it in one swallow. The feeling of it spreading through his chest made him think of a small, many-branched tree bursting slowly into hot, bright flames.

"You sister disappears, vanishes without trace," he said, shifting his weight on the stool. "There's blood on the floor beside her bed that someone has cleaned up.

210

It's a very particular type of blood. Her family's reaction is to hush up the whole thing —"

"Hush up!" Latimer said, with an ugly laugh. "You make us sound like the Borgias."

Quirke said nothing to that. "I think you know where she is," he said, in a harsh undertone. "I think you all know — you, your mother, your uncle."

"They don't."

"What?" Quirke turned to look at him. "What do you mean, *they* don't? Does that mean that you do? Tell me."

Latimer calmly drank the last of his drink, then wiped a fringe of foam from his silly moustache with a busy finger, more like a cat now than a bird. "I mean," he said, "that none of us knows." He chuckled again, shaking his head as if at something childish. "You're quite wrong about all this, you know, Quirke. It's what I said earlier, you don't understand families, and especially you don't understand a family such as ours." Quirke too had finished his drink and Latimer signalled to the barman to bring him another one. "Tell me, what, really, do you know about the Latimers, Dr Quirke?"

Quirke was watching the barman reaching for the Bushmills. "I only know," he said, "what everyone else does." There is, he was thinking, something special about the way light congregates inside a whiskey bottle, the way it glows there, tawny and dense, as it does nowhere else; something almost sacramental.

"To belong to a family like mine," Latimer said, tapping the tip of an index finer on the bar for emphasis, "is like being a member of a secret society — no, a secret tribe, one that has accepted all that's demanded of it by the invading mercenaries and missionaries but on the quiet still keeps to its own ways, its own customs, its own gods — especially its own gods. Outside, in the world, we look like everyone else, we talk like everyone else, we might *be* everyone else — in other words, we blend in. But amongst ourselves we're a breed apart. It comes, I suppose, from being obsessed with ourselves — I mean with each other." He paused. Quirke's whiskey arrived. He had determined he would not touch it until a full minute had gone by. He looked at the blood-red second hand of his watch making its round, steadily and, so it seemed to him, smugly. "My father," Latimer said, "was a very proud man. Everybody knew him for a hell-raiser and all that, but it was only a front. Inside the house he was nothing like the image the world had of him."

The minute was up. In Quirke's breast another small tree flared and flamed.

"What *was* he like, then?" Quirke asked, taking a second sip of whiskey and holding it in his mouth, savouring the scald of it.

"He was a monster," Latimer said, without emphasis. "Oh, not in the conventional sense. A monster of pride and determination and — and *dauntlessness*. Do you know what I mean? No, you don't, of course. How I loved him, how we all did. I suppose I should have hated him. He was a big man, with a big heart, handsome, dashing, brave — all the things that I'm not."

He paused, gazing into the creamy dregs of his glass. Quirke's whiskey glass was almost empty again, and he was measuring off another minute on his watch. "You've made a success of your life," he said. "Look at the reputation you have, at — what age are you?"

"Anyone can become a physician," Latimer said dismissively, "but you have to be born a hero." He turned to Quirke again. "I suppose my uncle told you how he and my father fought side by side in the General Post Office in 1916? My father fought, all right, but Uncle Bill did nothing more than carry a few messages and was nowhere near the GPO that week. That didn't stop him getting elected on the patriotic ticket. My father despised him. *Little Willie*, he used to call him, *the man in the gap*."

The minute had fled and Quirke was gazing pensively at his re-emptied glass. "How did he and April get on?"

Latimer laughed. "You just won't let the subject of poor April alone, will you?" He shrugged. "She loved him as I did, of course. His death was a disaster in both our lives. It's as I say, Quirke, you wouldn't understand that kind of closeness. And then my mother erected the monument to her beloved, lost husband. It was more like a totem pole, but carved out of the living tree and set solidly in the middle of the living room floor. It kept growing all the time, sending its branches along the hall and up the stairs into the bedrooms, and under its shade we clung to each other. The leaves never fell off those limbs."

His voice had grown husky, and Quirke wondered uneasily if he were going to weep.

"Yes," Quirke said, "I suppose it would be hard, living in the shadow of a man like your father."

Latimer sat quiet for a long moment. Then, suddenly gone pale, he turned on Quirke a look of deep and furious scorn. "I don't want your pity, Quirke," he said. "Don't you dare."

Quirke said nothing, only signalled for another drink.

CHAPTER
SIX

The early dark had fallen by the time he got back to the hospital. He descended with careful steps the grand marble staircase that led to nothing but the dim lower regions of the building. The pathology department was empty — Sinclair must have decided to let himself go home early. He went into his office and sat down in his overcoat at his desk and lit a cigarette, encountering a difficulty in aligning the tip of it with the match flame. He could hear the heavy sound of his own breathing. He scowled. He could not remember what it was he was supposed to be thinking about. It might be best, he thought, to lie down for a while. He took off his coat — was there rain, had he been walking in it? — and curled up on the old buttoned-down green leather sofa in the corner and at once pitched headlong into riotous sleep, in which he dreamed of being lured along endless dark and winding corridors by something he could not see but only sense, a cat-like, purring presence retreating ahead of him, always around the next corner, and then the next. He woke with a muffled cry and did not know where he was. He had dribbled in his sleep and his spit had dried and made his cheek stick to the leather of the sofa. He sat up, gouging the heels of his hands into his eyes. His mouth felt as if it had been reamed of two or three layers of protective membrane. His innards, too, were burning. *Insult*: the word came to him, reverberant — *a gross insult to the system*. It was a judgement he had handed down himself on many a cadaver.

He fumbled with his sleeve, squinting at the face of his watch that refused to stay steady, but kept flicking sideways in a dizzy-making fashion. He had suddenly remembered his dinner date with Phoebe. He lowered his head, a throbbing gourd, into his cupped hands, and groaned.

They went to the Russell. The place was sombre and silent as it always was. After lunching with him here one day Rose Crawford had refused to return, saying the dining room reminded her of a funeral parlour. The waiter who showed him to his table was fascinatingly ugly, with a square blue jaw and deeply sunken eyes under a jutting brow. Quirke remembered that his name, improbably, was Rodney. He saw with relief that Phoebe had not arrived — he had forgotten what time they had agreed to meet and he had assumed he would be late. While Rodney was drawing back his chair for him he caught a glimpse of his own reflection in the gilt-framed looking-glass on the wall behind the table. Tousled and wild of eye, he was a dead ringer for the escaped convict in a Hollywood prison picture. "Now, sir," the waiter said, pronouncing it *surr*. Quirke sat down, turning his back on the mirror.

He had walked from the hospital in his still-damp, heavy overcoat and his droop-brimmed hat. The whiskey he had drunk with Oscar Latimer had left him with a hollowed-out, ashen sensation, and lingering fumes of alcohol swirled in a hot fog in his head. That sleep on the couch had not helped, either, and he was groggy. Would he drink a glass of wine with Phoebe — should he?

Phoebe when she arrived was wearing a dark-blue silk dress and a blue silk stole. As she walked across the room, making her way between the tables in Rodney's wake, she looked so like her mother that Quirke felt a catch in his heart. She had tied her hair back in the complicated way that Delia used to do, and carried a small black handbag pressed against her breast, and that, too, was Delia to the life.

"I'm sorry," she said, seating herself quickly, "have you been here long?"

"No, no, just arrived. You look very nice."

She set the velvet bag beside her plate. "Do I?" she said. Quirke was normally not one for compliments.

"Is that a new dress?"

"Oh, Quirke." She made a smiling grimace. "You've seen me in it a dozen times."

"Well, it looks different on you this time. *You* look different."

She did. Her face glowed, ivory with the faintest tinge of pink, and her eyes shone. Had she met someone? — was she in love? He longed for her to be happy; it would release him from so much.

"That waiter," she said in a whisper, indicating Rodney, where he stood just inside the door, blank-faced as a statue, with a napkin draped over his wrist, off in some idle dream of his own. "He's a dead ringer for Dick Tracy in the comics."

Quirke laughed. "You're right, he is."

They ate sole fried in butter. "Has it ever struck you," Phoebe said, "that you and I always order the same thing?"

"It's simple. I wait to see what you're having and then ask for the same."

"Do you really?"

"Yes."

She gazed at him, and something happened to her smile, a sort of crimpling at the edges of it, and her eyes grew liquid. He lowered his gaze hastily to the tablecloth.

The wine waiter arrived. Quirke had ordered a bottle of Chablis. It was good they were having fish, since white wine was hardly a drink at all, and so he would be safe. The waiter, a sleek-haired, acned youth, poured out a sip for Quirke to taste and, while he waited, let his pale eye wander appreciatively over Phoebe, all ivory glow in her night-blue frock. She smiled up at him. She was happy; she had been absurdly happy all afternoon, since that moment with Rose Crawford outside the American Express office. She had read somewhere that there are insects that travel from continent to continent suspended individually in tiny bubbles of ice borne along by air currents at an immense height; that was how she had been, sailing aloft in a frozen cocoon, and now the ice was melting, and soon she would come sailing down happily to earth. Quirke and Rose; Mr and Mrs Quirke; the Quirkes. She saw them, the three of them, standing at the rail of a white ship cleaving its way through waters as blue as summer, the sea wind soft in their faces, on their way to a new world.

What age was Rose? she wondered. Older than Quirke, certainly; it would not matter; nothing would matter.

"Tell me about Delia," she said.

Quirke looked at her over the rim of his wine glass in startlement and alarm. "Delia?" he said, and licked his lips. "What — what do you want me to tell you?"

"Anything. What she was like. What you did together. I know so little about her. You've never told me anything, really." She was smiling. "Was she very beautiful?"

In panic he fingered his napkin. The steaming fish lay almost menacingly on the plate before him. His headache was suddenly worse. "Yes," he said, hesitantly, "she was — she was very beautiful. She looked like you." Phoebe blushed, and dipped her head. "Elegant, of course," Quirke went on desperately. "She could have been a model, everybody said so."

"Yes, but what was she *like*? I mean as a person."

What she was like? — how was he to tell her that? "She was kind," he said, casting down his gaze again and fixing anew on the napkin, somehow accusing in its whiteness, its mundane purity. "She took care of me." She was not kind, he was thinking; she did not take care of me. Yet he had loved her. "We were young," he said, "— or at least I was."

"And did you hate me," she asked, "— did you hate me when she died?"

"Oh, no," he said. He forced himself to smile; his cheeks felt as if they were made of glass. "Why would I hate you?"

"Because I was born and Delia died, and you gave me to Sarah."

She was still smiling. He sat and gazed at her helplessly, clutching his knife and fork, not knowing what to say. She reached across the table and touched his hand. "I don't blame you, any more," she said. "I don't know that I ever did, only I felt I should. I was angry at you. I'm not now."

They sat in silence for a minute. Quirke filled their glasses; his hand, he saw, was a little shaky. They ate. The fish was cold.

"I saw Inspector Hackett today," Quirke said. He looked at the empty wine bottle lolling in its bucket of half-melted ice. Would he order another? No, he would not. Definitely not. He turned and signalled to the pimpled waiter. "I talked to her brother, too."

"Why?"

"What?"

"Why did you want to talk to him again?"

"I don't know."

"You're like me — you can't let it go."

The waiter came with the second bottle, but before he could begin again the tasting ritual Quirke motioned him impatiently to pour. Phoebe put a hand over her glass, smiling again at the waiter. When he had filled Quirke's glass and gone, she said: "You think what I do, don't you, that April is dead?" Quirke did not reply, and would not look at her. "What did he say, Oscar Latimer?"

Quirke drank his wine. "He talked about families. And obsession."

She looked at him quickly. "April talked about that too, one day, about being obsessed."

"What did she mean?"

"I don't know. I couldn't understand her. April was — was strange, sometimes. I've come to think I didn't know her at all. Why do people make life so difficult, Quirke?"

Quirke had emptied his glass and was filling it again for himself, drops of ice-water falling from the bottle on to the tablecloth and forming grey stains the size of florins. He was making himself drunk, she could see. She thought she should say something. He planted his elbows on the table and rolled the glass between his palms.

"Hackett went to see the woman in the flat above April's," he said. "A Miss St John Somebody — did you ever meet her?"

She shook her head. "I saw her once or twice, lurking on the stairs. April sometimes brought things up to her, a bowl of soup, biscuits, things like that. What did she say to Inspector Hackett?"

"He couldn't get much out of her."

"That doesn't surprise me."

"Mind you, she seems to have kept a watch on things. Saw people come and go."

"What sort of people?" Blue-jawed Rodney approached and enquired if they wished to see the dessert menu. They shook their heads, and he withdrew. As he padded away Phoebe noticed how shiny the seat of his trousers was; she always felt sorry for waiters, they had such a disappointed and melancholy air. She looked back at Quirke. His steadily blearing gaze was fixed on the wine glowing in the bottom of his glass. "What sort of people did she see?" she asked again.

"Oh, people who came to see her. Visitors. Gentlemen callers, I suppose."

"Such as?" She felt a tingling at the base of her spine. She did not want to hear his answer.

"One of them, it seems, one of the gentlemen callers, was black. Or so Miss Whatsit claims. Does April know any black men?"

She was holding on tightly to the stem of her empty glass, pressing and pressing. The tingle in her spine ran all the way up, and for a second, absurdly, she had an image of one of those fairground test-your-strength machines, the sledge-hammer striking on the pad and the weight shooting up along its groove and banging into the bell. Oh, no, she was thinking; oh, no.

She shook her head, and a strand of her hair came loose and fell across her cheek and she pushed it quickly away again. "I don't think so," she said, trying to keep the wobble out of her voice.

Quirke was looking round for the waiter, to order a glass of brandy.

222

Phoebe put a hand on the velvet bag beside her plate, feeling the soft black fabric. She was thinking of the skin on the backs of Patrick's hands, the ripple and gleam of it.

Oh, no.

She had to help Quirke to a taxi. The sky had cleared and a hard frost was falling, she could see it in the air: an almost dry, grey, grainy mist. He had said he would walk home, that it was no distance, that they could go together and he would see her over to Haddington Road and then return across the canal to his flat. "You're not walking anywhere," she said. "There's ice on the ground already, look." She had an image of him on a bridge, and then a great dark plummeting form, and then the splash. The doorman blew his whistle and the cab came rattling up, but still Quirke resisted, and in the end she had almost to shove him inside. He scrabbled at the door, trying to get out again, then rolled down the window and began to protest. "Go home, Quirke," she said, reaching in and patting his hand. "Go home now, and sleep." She told the driver the address and the taxi pulled away from the kerb and she saw Quirke in the rear seat topple backwards in his overcoat like a huge, jointless manikin, and then she could see him no more. She gave the doorman a shilling and he thanked her and pocketed the coin and tipped a finger to the brim of his cap, and turned back into the yellow-lighted lobby, rubbing his hands. The night's icy silence settled about her.

She set off to walk. She could have gone in the taxi and delivered Quirke to Mount Street and then taken it on to her own place in Haddington Road, but it had not occurred to her. It seemed she was not going home. She thought of her room, the cheerless cold of it, the emptiness, waiting for her.

At York Street she turned left. It was very dark in this steep, narrow defile, and the sound of her own footsteps on the pavement seemed unnaturally loud. The tenement houses were all unlighted and there was no one abroad. A cat on a window-sill watched her with narrow-eyed surmise. Before her, low in the velvet darkness of the sky, a star was suspended, a sparkling silver sword of icy light. In Golden Lane a tramp slouching in a doorway croaked something at her and she hurried on. She supposed she should be frightened, all alone in the empty city in the hour before midnight, but she was not.

At the corner of Werburgh Street, opposite the cathedral, clandestine, late drinkers were being let out through the side door of a pub. They loitered on the pavement, befuddled and muttering. One of them went and stood in a doorway to urinate, another began to sing in a hoarse, quavering voice.

I dreamt that I dwe-elt in ma-arble halls . . .

She hung back in the darkness, waiting for them to disperse. She thought of Quirke again, lolling helplessly in the taxi, looking back at her, wild-eyed. He always seemed frightened when he was drunk. Soon he would

224

be drinking again in earnest, she knew the signs. But Rose would put a stop to that.

She walked forward quickly and passed by the drunks, telling herself not look at them. They took no notice of her. She turned into Castle Street.

— *That you loved me, you lo-oved me*
still the same!

There was a light on in the window of the upstairs flat, printing on the glass the pattern of the lace curtain inside. The cathedral bell began to toll, unnervingly loud, making the air shake around her. She stood and gazed up at the glowing window. Her toes and the tips of her fingers were going numb from the cold. Her breath flared before her in the frosted air. What would she say to him, how would she form the questions that were crowding in her mind? How was she even to let him know she was here? — if she knocked on the door she would alert his landlady. The bell finished tolling and the last beats of sound faded on the air. *Go!* a voice inside her head urged her, *go now!* Instead she dug into her purse and found a ha'penny and, taking careful aim, flung it up at the window. She missed the first time, and the second — what a ringing noise the coins made when they fell back on the road! — then she had no more ha'pennies left and had to use a penny. This time she hit the target. There was such a sharp *pang!* of copper on glass that she thought everyone in the houses round about must hear it. She waited. Perhaps he was not there, perhaps he had gone out and forgotten to

225

turn off the light. A courting couple, their arms linked, went past. The fellow gave her a speculative look from under the peak of his cap, but his girl only said goodnight. She looked up at the window again. The curtain had been pulled back and Patrick was there, peering down into the street. She moved quickly into a circle of lamplight so that she would be more clearly visible. She could not make out his expression. Would he recognise her — could he even see her? He let the curtain fall back into place, and a minute later the front door opened a little way and a hand beckoned her in.

He had not switched on the light in the hall. When she came forward he caught her by the wrist and put a finger urgently to his lips. "*Ssh!*" he hissed. "*She'll wake up!*" He drew her into the dark hall, and she smelt again the dank smell that she remembered from the last time. They crept up the stairs. He was leading her by the wrist. He eased open the door of the flat and motioned her inside and then closed the door silently behind them. "*Poh!*" he said, letting go his breath in an exaggerated gasp of relief, and smiled at her. "Well, Miss Phoebe Griffin! To what do I owe this pleasure?"

All the way down here from the hotel, and then standing outside in the dark, trying to attract his attention, she had not stopped to consider what she would say to him, what reason she would offer for appearing under his window at dead of night like this.

"I —" she said "— I — I wanted to talk to you."

He wrinkled his brow, still smiling. "Oh, yes? It must be very urgent."

"No, not urgent. I just —" She stopped, and stood helplessly, looking at him.

"Well, now that you are here, will you join me in some tea?"

He took her coat, and again put it on the bed, the bed that she again tried not to see. When they came in he had switched off the overhead light, but she remembered everything in detail from the last time, the armchair draped with the red blanket, the green typewriter on the card-table by the window, the photograph of the smiling couple in native costume, the jumbled stacks of books. Her eye fell on the little wooden milking stool, and she smiled.

He poured her a cup of tea. "Camomile," he said. "I hope you like it."

The tea was pale and had the fragrance of warm straw. "It's lovely," she said. "It's perfect."

He led her to the armchair, bringing the milking stool for himself. "You're cold," he said.

"Yes, it's icy outside."

"Would you like to put the blanket over your knees?"

"No, no, thank you. The tea will warm me."

He nodded. She looked about the room again. There was a green paraffin heater by the window; the air felt rubbery with its fumes. She must not let the silence draw out or she would lose her nerve altogether, would put down the cup and jump up and run from the place, back out into the night. "Were you working?" she asked.

He gestured towards the table and the stacked books. "Studying a little, yes."

"And now I'm interrupting."

"No, not at all, I was about to stop and go to — I was about to stop."

He was dressed in an old pair of corduroy trousers and a hand-knitted woollen jumper. He wore no shirt, and his neck was bare and she could see the top part of his broad, smooth, gleaming chest. His feet were bare, too. "Aren't *you* cold?" she said. "Without socks, even!"

"I like to be cool, a little." He smiled, showing her his shining teeth. "For me it's a luxury, you know."

"Is it very hot, where you come from, in Nigeria?"

"Yes, very hot, very humid." He was watching her, nodding faintly as if to a slow, steady rhythm in his head. That awful silence began to stretch again between them, and it was as if the air were expanding. "Is the tea all right?" he asked. "I think you do not like it. I could make some coffee."

Kiss me — please, kiss me. The words had leaped into her mind with such sudden force that for a moment she was not sure she had not spoken them out loud. She looked at his hands where he held them clasped between his knees. He is so beautiful, she thought; so beautiful.

"I had dinner with my father," she said, sitting upright in the chair and squaring her shoulders. "At the Russell. Do you know it — the Russell Hotel?"

"I have been there, yes." He laughed softly. "It's a little expensive, for me."

"I'm afraid he got a bit — a bit tipsy, my father. He has a problem with drink."

"Yes, you told me he was in St John's."

228

"Did I? I forgot. I put him in a taxi and sent him home. I hope he'll be all right." He took the cup and saucer from her and set them on the floor. "I feel guilty. I shouldn't have let him drink so much. I —"

He took her hands in his, and when he spoke her name it was somehow as if she had never heard it before, or had never taken notice of it, at least, this strange, soft sound. She began to say something about this, she did not know what, but he drew her to her feet and released her hands and held her by the shoulders instead, and kissed her. After a moment she turned her face aside; she fancied she could hear her heart, it was pounding so. "Is Patrick really your name?" she said, still looking away. "Haven't you a — a tribal name?"

He was smiling, and moved his head so that he could see into her eyes. "I was educated by the Holy Ghost Fathers," he said. "My mother called me Patrick in honour of them."

"Oh. I see."

They were whispering. He laid his hands now on her shoulder-blades. The silk of her dress crackled a little under his fingers. He put his face to her hair at the side. "Is this why you came here?" he murmured.

"I don't know." It was true. "I wanted to talk to you about —"

He touched the tips of his fingers to her lips. "Ssh." He said again, softly, "Ssh."

The only light in the room was from the little reading lamp on the desk, and now he reached past her and switched it off. At first all was blackness, then a faint, ghostly, ice-blue radiance began to spread slowly from the window. Her coat slid from the bed on to the floor and neither bent to pick it up. She caught a finger-nail on her stocking. As she leaned down to take it off he cupped the side of her face in one of his great, square hands, and again spoke her name. She stood up and he embraced her again. She felt the ribbed pattern of his jumper and wondered who had knitted it for him; when he crossed his arms and grasped it at both sides and drew it quickly over his head she smelt his sweat, a sharp, oniony odour. The sheets were cold against her back, and she shivered, and he pressed her more closely to him, giving her his warmth. His skin had a curiously stippled texture, like soft sandpaper; it felt exactly as she had known it would. The bed-springs set up a faint tinkling, like the sounds of a distant orchestra beginning to tune up. She put her face into the hollow of his shoulder and laughed a stifled laugh. "Oh, Lord," she whispered, "Mrs Gilligan will hear us!"

She woke with a cry. Something about — about what? — about an animal, some kind of animal, was it? She kept her eyes shut tight, grasping at the dream as it poured out of her mind like water. An animal, and — ? No: it was gone. She turned on to her side. The lamp was burning again and Patrick was sitting at the card-table, bent over a book, his back a broad, strong curve. She put a hand flat under her cheek on the pillow and watched him, smiling to herself. The paraffin heater was still on — she could taste the fumes, an oily film on her lips — and the warmth in the room made her think of a lair underground, a place of safety and calm.

"I was dreaming about a lion," she said. Yes, a lion, that was what it was.

Patrick looked at her over his shoulder. "What kind of a lion?"

"What kinds are there?"

He stood up from the table and came to the bed and sat down on the edge of it. He was wearing his jumper again and the baggy corduroys; it was, she thought, as if some wonderfully fashioned thing, a piece in ebony or gleaming bronze by one of the masters of Benin, had been put into an old sack to protect it. She brought out her hand from under her cheek and gave it to him to hold between both of his brick-pink palms.

"I've never seen a lion," he said.

"Aren't there any, in Nigeria?"

"There may be some left, in the bush. It's not the jungle, you know." He smiled. "We live in towns and cities, just like you."

She sat up. "My hair must be a haystack — is it?"

"It is very beautiful," he said.

She lowered her eyes quickly. "Were you studying?" she asked.

"Yes, but only to pass the time. Since you were sleeping."

"I'm sorry, I didn't mean to fall asleep. What time is it? It must be late."

"Yes, it's late."

This made them feel suddenly shy of each other. She withdrew her hand from his, and was startled to feel tears welling up hotly in her eyes.

"What is the matter?" he asked, alarmed.

"Nothing, nothing." She laughed at herself, brushing at her eyes. "I'm just — happy, I suppose."

He held her head between his hands and drew her to him and kissed her solemnly on the forehead. "My Irish girl," he whispered. "My wild Irish girl."

"Come," she said, "lie down again, just for a little while."

He stretched himself beside her on top of the blankets. "You remember," she said, "when I was here that day, that first day, I asked you about — about April and — and you?" He had closed his eyes and was lying very still, his hands folded on his chest. He said nothing. "It wasn't any business of mine, of course, but I had to ask. Jimmy had said something, and then I asked Bella. They seemed to think —"

He waited, still with his eyes closed. "Yes? What did they seem to think?" She had an urge to touch his eyelids, to feel with her fingertips their delicate, silken texture.

"Oh, nothing, really." She could hear him breathing through those broad, carven nostrils. His skin fascinated her, she could not stop looking at it. Yes, ebony, she was thinking, only not smooth, not polished, but with that wonderful, soft roughness. "It's just that someone went round to April's and talked to the old lady who lives on the top floor. She's half cracked, of course, and terribly sad." She hesitated. She was not worried, not really, not as she had been when Quirke told her what Miss Leetch had said. So much had happened to her life in the past hour — how could she be worried? "She said that she had seen someone with April, in the house." She looked at him more closely. His breathing had become regular and deep — was he asleep? "She said this person was — was black."

Slowly he opened his eyes and gazed straight upwards, at the shadows under the ceiling. "Who was it?" he asked.

"She didn't know, I think. She just said he was —"

"I meant, who was it that went to question her."

"Oh. A policeman. A detective."

For a long time he lay very still and did not speak. Then, abruptly, he rose up and swung his legs off the bed and sat there a moment, with his hands to his face. She had a trickling sensation between her shoulder-blades, as if a drop of ice-cold liquid were sliding down inside her spine, through the very marrow.

"You must go home now," he said. "Please — get dressed."

"But —"

"*Please.*"

He put on his shoes and an overcoat and walked with her across to the cathedral, where the streetlights were brightest. The pavements sparkled with hoar-frost. There was hardly any traffic, and they had to wait a long time before they saw a taxi coming, with its light on. For all that time he did not speak to her, only stood hunched in his coat; his broad face greyed from the cold. She tried to think of something to say, some question to ask, but could not. He was angry, she could feel it. She was furious at herself for telling him what the old woman had said — how could she have been so stupid, to say it just like that, as if it were the weather she was talking about? What did it matter if he was at April's, if it was he the woman had seen — and who else, after all, could it have been? — what did any of that matter, now? They all came and went at the house, Jimmy, Isabel, she, too, all of them had been there at one time or other — why not Patrick? April had probably told him about the key under the stone, why would she not?

She got into the taxi. Patrick stood over her, holding the door open for a moment. "I'm sorry," he said, his voice distant. He shut the door. She was still looking up into his eyes through the window as the taxi pulled away and set off over the crest of the cathedral hill.

It was cold in her flat. She switched on the light in the living room and lit the gas fire, then went into the kitchen and put on a saucepan of milk to heat, and opened the biscuit tin. She had not turned on the kitchen light, since the glow coming in from the streetlamp was enough for her to see by. She was still wearing her overcoat. She waited, listening to the low hiss and occasional splutter of the gas jets. She tried not to think about Patrick, about all that had happened tonight. Fool! she told herself. Fool!

When the milk was heated she poured it into a glass and went to the table for the biscuit tin and as she did so she glanced down through the window to the street.

Something moved down there. It was that shadow again at the edge of the lamplight. How was it she was not surprised? She stepped back as far as she could from the window while still able to see down to the pavement. The glass was too hot to hold but she held it anyway. Someone was there, she was sure of it this time, someone she could not so much see as sense, a motionless figure standing outside the circle of light, looking up at the window. Her fingers of their own accord relaxed and the glass dropped and shattered at her feet and she felt the hot milk splash on her ankles. Before she went into the living room she reached around the door and switched off the light, then crossed to the window. She tried to tell herself the secret watcher was not real, that she was imagining it, as she had imagined it, surely, on that other night, too. But she knew it was not so, that the watcher was real. She tried to think, to reason, to decide what she should do, but her mind had gone sluggish.

She hurried down the stairs, carrying her shoes, trying not to make a sound. The forty-watt bulb in the hall seemed to shed not light but a sort of sullen dimness. Her hands shook, and she was hardly able to get the pennies into the slot. She dialled Quirke's number and stood with the receiver pressed under her cheek, breathing into the hollow of the mouthpiece and staring at the front door. How strong was the lock there? If someone pushed hard against it would it hold? The ringing tones went on and on — *brring! brring!* — a dull, measured rhythm, making her think of someone pacing a floor, back and forth, back and forth, with short, rapid steps. She could not take her eyes off the door. It was locked with only a Yale lock. She would ask the landlord to put in a deadbolt. She considered the matter with a kind of crazy calmness. Yale, lock, deadbolt lock — and what about the hinges — would they hold, if the person pushing against the door were strong enough? At last the ringing tone stopped and was replaced by rapid pips. Either Quirke was so deeply asleep he had not heard the phone, or he was not there. But where would he have gone to? Had he got the taxi man to take him to a shebeen where he could go on drinking? She put down the heavy black receiver — it had the heft and chill smoothness of a weapon — and went to the foot of the stairs. Instead of going back up to the flat, however, she sat down on the lowest step and put her arms around her knees and hugged them against her breast. She watched the door, unblinking.

He had to think. It was important now to think clearly and calmly. It was only a matter of time, surely, before they would come and question him. He did not know what he would say, what he could say. Somehow he had managed to make himself believe that this moment would never arrive. There were periods, long periods, when it was as if what had happened was a dream, one of those dreams that feels so real it lodges in the mind for months, for years, even, a dark patch of terror and vague, unassuageable guilt. There had been a place like that on Odoni Street down behind the Holy Rosary secondary school in Port Harcourt, when he was little. A track there ran along by the creek and at a certain place, where a big clump of weeds leaned out over the muddy, purplish water, his heart would clench up like a fist every time that he passed by. Something must have happened there, he must have seen something, something he had forgotten but the aura of which had remained in his mind for all these years. This, now, was worse, of course; this was something he would never be allowed to forget, though he had pushed it so far back into his mind he managed at times to think it was not real at all.

When Phoebe's taxi drove away he stood on the hill by the cathedral in the light of the streetlamp for a long time, turning this way and that, not knowing what to do. It was bitterly cold, and the frosty air when he breathed it in sliced at his throat like a cold flame. Should he hide? — should he run away? Yet where could he go to? It was not as if he could melt into the crowd, not in this city. London, perhaps? But he knew no one there, and besides, he had no money, or not money enough to keep himself in a place like London. And would they be watching the mail boats, the airport?

He knew so little about this country, about the people in it. They were strange. They took such a grave view of some things, while other, apparently serious, matters they ignored, or laughed about. You could get so much done here for nothing just by asking, not like at home where every smallest service had to be bought with *dash*, that nice term for a bribe. Here they would not take your money but neither would they take you seriously. That was what puzzled him most of all, the

237

way they mocked and jeered at everything and everyone, themselves included. Yet the laughter could stop without warning, when you least expected. Then suddenly you would find yourself alone in the midst of a circle of them, all of them looking at you, blank-eyed and silently accusing, even though you did not know what it was you were being accused of.

He crossed the street and let himself into the house, pausing with the key in his hand and glancing back both ways over his shoulders, just like a real felon. It was three o'clock in the morning and not a soul was to be seen. He eased the key out of the lock silently, and silently closed the door behind him and crept along the pitch-black hall — above all he must not disturb Mrs Gilligan, who would surely call the Guards if she heard someone down here at this time of the morning. He crept up the stairs.

In the room a hint of Phoebe's fragrance lingered, though it was hard to smell anything over the sticky reek of paraffin from the stove. That was another thing about this country — how was it that people had never tried to cope with the climate? In winter they were content to huddle over tiny fires of evil-smelling coke or smouldering turf, while at the first hint of summer they began immediately to complain of the heat.

Mechanically he set about making the bed, then realised he would have to change the sheets, for he knew Mrs Gilligan often came up and poked around during the day when he was out. He was suddenly assailed by the memory of Phoebe not half an hour ago lying here in his arms. Would it ever happen again? —

238

would he ever see her again? He sat down on the bed and stared at the floor, trying to think and yet not to think.

But this was no good: he could not allow himself to lose his nerve and feel sorry for himself like this. Wearily he lay down on the bed, stretching out his limbs. Yes, he was tired, very tired. His mind began to drift. A thought came to him, a thought of where he might go, of who might help him, but all at once he was too sleepy and could not hold on to what the thought was trying urgently to tell him.

CHAPTER
SEVEN

It was eight o'clock and still not fully light when Quirke woke, enveloped in a hot and muggy haze of alcohol fumes and his own stale stink. At first he could not tell where he was. The bedroom and the bed he was lying on were not his, and yet not entirely unfamiliar. He remained some moments without stirring, wary even of lifting his head, which felt at once leaden and as breakable as a globe of crystal. He tried to summon up the previous night's events. Dinner with Phoebe, wine, too much wine, and then — ? He had been in a taxi; he remembered it driving him away from the Russell. Following that there was a blank, and the next thing he recalled, indistinctly, was being in another hotel. The Central, was it? No, Jury's, in Dame Street, he remembered the stained-glass windows of the bar there. Then he had been in one of the rooms upstairs, where a party was going on. People had kept giving him drinks — who were they? He saw shiny red faces pressing forward, four or five of them bristling at him as if they shared only one neck, and heard booming laughter, and a woman's voice saying something to him over and over. Then he was outside again, in another taxi — no, not a taxi, for he was driving this time, driving along the canal, with the window open, the air in his face as cold and sharp as a blade.

He got out of bed, sliding himself sideways from under the sheet and straightening up cautiously. He was in his shirt and underpants, and was wearing his socks, too. He went to the window and drew back the curtain at one side. A grey dawn was breaking on the canal. It was cold, down there, with a whitish coating of frost on the roadway and floatings of ice on the unmoving surface of the water. The Alvis was parked at a sharp angle to the pavement. He heard a sudden loud beating in the air and flinched instinctively, and two swans like intent and vehement ghosts went flying past, low and straight, their great wings thrashing on the air. He had seen them before, those birds.

The bedroom door behind him opened. "Ah. Sleeping Beauty has awoken at last." Today Isabel Galloway wore not her silk wrap but an outsized pink wool dressing-gown. She was smoking a cigarette. She leaned in the doorway and folded one arm into the crook of the other and regarded him with a faint, sardonic smile. "How do you feel, or need I ask?"

"About as bad as I imagine I deserve to feel. Where are my trousers?"

She pointed. "On the chair, behind you." He pulled them on, then sat down on the edge of the bed. He was dizzy. Isabel came forward and put a hand on top of his head, pushing her fingers into his hair. "Poor you."

He looked up at her out of suffering eyes. "I'm sorry, I don't remember much," he said. "Was I very drunk?"

"I'm not sure what you'd consider *very* drunk."

"Did I — did I disgrace myself?"

"You tried to get me into bed, if that's what you mean. But then you toppled over, very slowly, rather like a tree being felled, and so my honour was preserved."

"I'm sorry."

She heaved an exaggerated sigh and grasped a fistful of hair and tugged it. "I hope you're not going to keep on apologising, are you? Nothing as annoying for a girl as a man in the morning saying sorry. Come down, there's coffee on."

When she had gone he went into the tiny bathroom at the end of the hall and peered at himself in the mirror. It seemed for a moment that he was about to be sick but then the nausea passed. He bathed his face in ice-cold water, gasping softly.

In the kitchen Isabel was standing by the stove, waiting for the percolator to come to the boil. She saw him looking at her dressing-gown. "The silk one was for effect," she said. "My bottom was blue as a baboon's by the time you left." He looked at her socks, too; they were thick and grey. "My mother knits them for me," she said. She turned back to the stove. "Yes, I have a grey-haired old mother, who knits for me. It's all terribly banal, my little life."

He sat down at the table, bracing a hand on the back of the chair and easing himself down slowly. He was about to apologise again but stopped himself in time.

She brought the coffee to the table and poured out cups for both of them. "The toast is cold," she said. "Shall I make more?"

"No, thank you, coffee will do. I don't think I could eat anything."

She stood over him with the percolator in her hand, regarding him with a look of wry compassion. "Where were you drinking?"

"A number of places, as far as I recall. I had dinner with Phoebe."

"Surely she didn't let you get that drunk?"

"No, I went on afterwards. Jury's, I think. There was a party that I got invited to. Don't ask me who the people were."

"All right, I won't." She sat down opposite him, setting the coffee pot on a cork mat. She folded her arms, sliding her hands into the sleeves of the dressing-gown as if into a muff, and leaned there, studying him. "What a sorry mess you are, Quirke."

"Yes." The grey light was strengthening in the window behind the sink. He felt cold and hot at the same time, and there was a rippling sensation in his innards, as a wave of something slow and foul and warm flowed through them. "I shouldn't have come to you," he said. "You shouldn't have let me in."

"You were very insistent. And I didn't want to give scandal to the neighbours. It was three o'clock in the morning. You can be very loud, you know, Quirke."

"Oh, God."

"Let me make some toast for you."

"No. The coffee is working. I'll be all right. It's only a hangover, I'm used to it."

She leaned back on the chair, still with her arms folded and her hands hidden. "So you were with Phoebe," she said. "How is she?"

"All right. Better than all right, in fact. Has she got a new boyfriend, or something?"

"I don't know. What made you think she might?"

"She seemed — happy."

"Ah." She nodded sagely. "That would be an indication, all right. Why didn't you ask her?"

"What? — if she has a boyfriend?"

"Would it be such a strange thing to do? She is your daughter, after all."

He frowned, and flexed his shoulders, dipping one and lifting the other. "We don't — we don't talk about things like that."

"No," she said flatly, "I don't suppose you do." She refilled his cup. "I'm going to take a bath, and then get dressed. I have a rehearsal this morning. Maeterlinck and fairyland await me." She stood up, drawing the dressing-gown around her. As she was going past she paused and leaned down and kissed him quickly on the crown of his head. "What about you?"

"What about me?"

"Won't you have to go to work, and so on?"

"Yes, I suppose so."

"Don't leave before I come down."

When she was gone he sat at the table for a long time, watching the wan light struggling to establish itself in the window. He was thinking about Phoebe. At

244

dinner last night she had lied to him. When he told her what the woman in the flat had said to Hackett, about April and the black man, she had lied. He did not know it at the time but he did now. She was a bad liar, always had been.

He got to his feet and pushed back the chair, making its legs squeal on the tiled floor. The wave rippling through his insides had suddenly broken. He made for the back door and wrenched it open and stumbled into the yard and leaned over the drain there as the coffee he had drunk came gushing back up his throat and spilled out in a hot cascade, spattering his trousers. He waited, panting, then retched again, but this time there was nothing to come up; he had vomited up the sole already, during the party in the hotel, he remembered now. He straightened, and leaned against the pebble-dashed wall. The cold air was like a hand laid comfortingly against his forehead. He put his head back and gazed up at a sky as flat and dully white as pipeclay. The cold was striking through his shirt and gripping at his throat. He went inside and rinsed his mouth at the sink with water from the tap that tasted of metal. Then he climbed the narrow stairs, and knocked at the bathroom door, and went in.

Isabel was lying full-length in the bath, reading a magazine. It was a worn bath, yellowed with age, and there were brownish streaks in the enamel behind the taps. Fine wreaths of steam moved in the air, billowing in the draught from the doorway. "Do come in," she said, glancing up at him. "I'd ask you to join me but I'm afraid you'd swamp the house." She wore a plastic cap over her hair, which made her face seem all the more slender, narrowing to the delicately cleft point of her chin. Her nakedness glimmered under the greenish water. A cigarette was smoking in an ash-tray beside her head, and now she reached up to it with one dry hand and took a draw of it and set it down again. She tossed the magazine over the side of the bath and it flopped on the floor, the pages splaying in a multicoloured fan. "I used to read good books," she said, "but they always got so soggy I gave up. What do you do in the bath, Quirke? I suppose you don't do anything. I suppose you're like all men, you dive in and have a quick sluice and then out again. Women are true sybarites when it comes to bathing, don't you find? It's one of our only real self-indulgences, despite what people say. I can quite see myself in ancient Egypt, up to my neck in asses' milk, with dusky handmaids fanning me with palms." She stopped, and made a face, twisting her mouth upwards at one side. "What is it, Quirke?" she asked. "Tell me."

"I was sick," he said. "— It's all right, I got to the yard in time. It was just the coffee, anyway." She waited, watching him. He sat down on the edge of the bath. "I wanted to say — I wanted to ask —" He rolled his shoulders again helplessly. "I don't know."

"Ask," she said.

"You could — I feel you could — save me. From myself, I mean." He turned his face away from her. In a small round mirror on a shelf behind the sink he saw himself, one eye and an ear. He noticed the stains on the knees of his trousers; he must have fallen, somewhere, last night. "A doctor in St John's told me I drink to get away from myself. It wasn't exactly news, but still." Now he turned back and looked at her. "What shall we do," he asked, "you and I?"

She thought a moment. "More or less what everybody else does, I suppose," she said. "What do you think we'll do?"

"What everybody else does — make each other unhappy."

She found her cigarette and this time did not put it back on the ash-tray, but lay there smoking, one eye half shut, looking at him. He could not tell what she was thinking. "Oh, Quirke," she said.

He nodded, as if he were agreeing with some proposition she had offered. He took the limp cigarette from her fingers and took a drag on it and gave it back to her.

"You know that feeling that you have in dreams," he said, exhaling smoke, "that something is happening and you can't do anything to stop it, only stand by and watch as it goes on happening? That's how I feel all the time."

"Yes," she said. "I know."

She sat up, making the water around her sway wildly, and stubbed out the cigarette in the ash-tray. "Give me that towel," she said. She stood. Palely gleaming there, with bath water running down between her breasts and along her legs, she seemed for a moment very young, a child, almost, skinny and vulnerable. He handed her the towel, and she wrapped herself in it, shuddering. "Dear God," she said, "how I hate the fucking winter."

She led him by the hand to the bedroom. When they lay down together he pressed her in his arms and she was still damp. She put her mouth to his ear. "Warm me up, Quirke," she said, with a low laugh. "Warm me up, there's a dear."

CHAPTER
EIGHT

The telephone was ringing in the flat: Quirke could hear it as he came up the stairs. The sound provoked in him its usual vague dread. He did not quicken his step; whoever it was could wait, or call back. He plodded; he was tired. The phone was still ringing when he walked into the living room. He took off his overcoat and hung it up, and hung up his hat, too. He thought of going into the bedroom and crawling under the blankets. Still the thing went on, shrilling and shrilling, and there was nothing for it but to pick up the receiver. It was Phoebe. "What's the matter?" he asked. "Are you all right?" She said she had called him earlier, much earlier, in the middle of the night, in fact, and that she had been worried when he did not answer. Had he got home from the Russell all right? He said he had. He did not tell her about going out again, about the party at Jury's; he did not tell her about Isabel Galloway.

"Are *you* all right?" she asked. He put up a hand and rubbed his eyes. Then she told him about the watcher in the street.

He might have walked to Haddington Road — it was ten minutes away, across the canal — but he drove

249

instead, the car seeming to him even more sullen and obstinate than usual. Phoebe was wearing the silk dressing-gown that had once belonged to Sarah. She said she had probably imagined it, that shadowy presence in the lamplight.

"When was this?" he asked.

"I told you, in the middle of the night. It must have been — I don't know — three o'clock, four?"

"Why were you up so late?"

She went to the fireplace and took a packet of cigarettes and a lighter from the mantelpiece. "I couldn't sleep," she said. She blew a quick stream of smoke at the ceiling. "I often can't sleep."

He took off his overcoat and put it on the back of a chair. "I see you're smoking again," he said.

She held the cigarette away from her and looked at it as if she had not noticed it until then. "Not really," she said. "Just once in a while. Good for the nerves, they say."

He came to her and took the packet from her hand and looked at it. "Passing Clouds," he said. "Your old brand."

She puffed again and grimaced. "They're so old they're stale."

He helped himself to one and lit it with her lighter. The gas fire was muttering in the grate; they sat down on either side of it.

"So," Quirke said, "tell me."

"Tell you what?"

She was smoothing the silk drape of the dressing-gown over her knee. Not a dressing-gown — what was it called? A tea-gown? Sarah used to go and put it on after dinner, even when there were guests. He pictured her leaning back in the chair by the fireplace in the house in Rathgar, while the talk went on and Mal fussed with the drinks. Everything had seemed simpler, then.

He thought of Isabel Galloway, in her *peignoir*.

Phoebe was pale and her temples seemed sunken, as if something had been pressing on them.

"You're frightened," Quirke said. "Tell me exactly what you saw."

She picked up an ash-tray from the grate and rolled the tip of the cigarette on it, sharpening it, like a pencil. "Do you want anything?" she asked. "Tea? Coffee?" He did not reply, only sat watching her. She gave a vexed shrug. "I just thought there was somebody down there, standing by the streetlamp."

"Who do you think it was?"

"I don't know. I told you, I'm not even sure there was anyone — I may have imagined it."

"But it's not the first time, is it?"

She compressed her lips and looked down into her lap. After a moment she gave a rapid shake of her head. "No," she said, so quietly he could hardly hear her. "I thought there was someone there before, in the same place."

"When was that?"

"I don't know — the other night."

"You didn't call the Guards?"

"No. What would I have told them? You know what they're like, they never believe anything."

He thought for a moment, then said: "I'll talk to Hackett."

"Oh, no, Quirke, please don't," she said wearily. "I don't want him poking about here."

"He can put someone on the street, a plainclothes man, to keep watch, for a night or two. If there's anyone, they can collar him."

She laughed. "Oh, yes, the way they did with —"

She looked away. That other nightwalker who had watched her window, no one had collared him, until it was too late. He reached for the ash-tray and she handed it to him and he stubbed out the half-smoked cigarette. "You're right," he said, "they are stale."

She stood up and went out to the kitchen, where he heard her filling a kettle. "I'm going to make a cup of Bovril," she called to him. "Do you want some?"

Bovril. That brown taste, the very taste of Carricklea Industrial School. "No," he called back. "I suppose you wouldn't have a drink, would you?" She pretended not to hear.

When she returned, carrying her mug, he had risen from the chair and was standing by the window, looking out. The air in the street was grey with frost-smoke and there was ice on the windscreens of the cars parked on the other side of the road. The dusty smell of the cretonne curtain was a smell from the far past. "Have you settled in here?" he asked.

"I suppose so," she said. "It's not as nice as Harcourt Street, but it will do." She was thinking how in any room Quirke always, eventually, headed for the window, looking for a way out. She sat down by the fireplace again, her knees pressed together and her shoulders hunched, clutching the steaming mug in both her hands. She was cold.

"You could come and live with me, you know," Quirke said.

He turned from the window. She was staring at him. "In Mount Street?"

"I don't think there'd be room there. I could buy a house."

Still she stared. Had Rose spoken to him? Was the thing decided already — was this what he meant, that he would buy a house and the three of them would live in it together? "I don't know," she said. "I mean, I don't know what to say. It would be lovely, of course, but —"

"But?"

She stood up, holding the mug; everything seemed to be happening at half speed. "You can't just ask me something like that and expect me to answer straight away," she said, "as if it was nothing more than — than — I don't know. I have to think. I'd have to — I don't know."

He turned to the window again. "Well," he said, "it was just a thought."

"A *thought*?" she cried. "Just a *thought*?" She put the mug down on the mantelpiece with a bang. "I don't know why I drink this stuff," she said. "It's disgusting."

Quirke crossed the room and took up his coat and his hat. "I've got to go," he said.

"Yes, all right. Thank you for coming."

He nodded, pinching the dents on either side of the crown of his hat. "I'll always come," he said. "You know that."

"Yes, I know. But please, Quirke" — she lifted a hand — "please don't talk to Hackett. I really don't want you to."

"All right. But the next time there's someone there you'll call me straight away, won't you?"

She did not reply. She had called him straight away, and he had not been there. She wanted him to go, now, and yet did not. She would have to tell him. He walked to the door. "Quirke," she said, "wait. I lied to you."

He stopped, turned. "Yes? About what?"

She swallowed. She felt colder now in her thin silk wrap. "When you asked me about April, if she knew anyone who was — who was black." He waited. "There's a friend, a friend we all have, he's Nigerian. A student at the College of Surgeons."

"What's his name?"

"Patrick Ojukwu."

"I see."

"I suppose he might be the one that the old woman saw with April, in the house. It's possible." She was watching him. "You don't seem surprised."

"Do I not?" He stood there, looking at her, fingering his hat. "This fellow — what did you say he's called?"

"Patrick. Patrick Ojukwu."

"What was he to April?"

"What I said, a friend, that's all." He turned again to the door. "You're going to go to Hackett, aren't you?" she said. "You're going to tell him about Patrick."

Again he stopped, again he turned and looked at her. "If there's someone watching the house we'll have to find out who it is."

"I'm sure there's no one — I'm sure I imagined it." She went to the mantelpiece and took another cigarette from the packet and lit it. "Don't go to Hackett," she said, looking at the fireplace. "Please."

"It was you who came to me about April Latimer," he said. "You can't expect me to give it up now."

On the way to the hospital he stopped at the police station in Pearse Street and asked at the desk to see Inspector Hackett, but he was not there. The carrot-haired young Guard — what was his name? — said the inspector would not be back until the afternoon. Quirke's headache was beating a slow drum between his temples. Outside the station a Guard was standing in front of the Alvis and writing in a notebook with the stub of a pencil. He was large and not young, and had a bony, mottled face. He pointed a finger at the windscreen. "You've no tax or insurance showing there," he said.

Quirke told him the car was new, that it was taxed and insured and that the papers were on their way, which was not true: he had got the forms but had not yet filled them out. "I'm a doctor," he said.

"Are you?" the Guard said, looking him up and down. "Well, I'm a Garda sergeant and I'm telling you to get your insurance and your tax discs and display them on your windscreen." He shut his notebook and put it into the top pocket of his tunic and sauntered away.

When Quirke got to the hospital there was a message waiting for him at Reception. Celia Latimer had telephoned. She wished to speak to him, and asked if he would come out to Dun Laoghaire. He crumpled the note and put it into the pocket of his overcoat. He felt bad; he was raw all over, his skin crawled, and there was a sour burning in his belly. Yet it was strange: he never seemed more surely himself than when he was hung-over like this. It brought out a side of him, the Carricklea side, splenetic and vindictive, that he did not like but had a sneaking admiration for. He wanted to know who it was that had been spying on his daughter. He was in the mood to crack someone's head.

In the office the telephone rang. It was someone whose voice he did not recognise. "I'm a friend of your daughter, a friend of Phoebe's." The line was bad and Quirke had to ask him twice to repeat what he had said. "I'm just round the corner, I can be there in a minute."

He was tiny, an intricate scale-model of someone much larger. He had red hair and a stark-white freckled face, sharp and thin, like the face of an Arthur Rackham fairy. "Jimmy Minor," he said, coming forward with a hand extended. His plastic coat crackled and squeaked and gave off a faint, sharp, rubbery stink.

"Yes," Quirke said, "Phoebe has mentioned you."

"Has she?" He seemed surprised, and a little suspicious.

256

Quirke searched on the desk and came up with a packet of Senior Service, but Minor had already produced his own Woodbines. The top joints of the first and second fingers of his right hand were the colour of fumed oak.

"So," Quirke said, "what can I do for you, Mr Minor?"

What a name.

"I'm a reporter," Minor said. "*Evening Mail*." Quirke would not have needed to be told, the cheap fags and the plastic coat were as telling as a press badge in his hatband. "I knew — I mean, I *know* April Latimer."

"Yes?" There was a faint tremor in his hands. He reminded Quirke of someone, though for the moment he could not think who.

"I know you know she's missing."

"Well, I know no one has heard from her for two or three weeks. She's sick, isn't she? She sent in a sick cert, here, to the hospital."

The little man pounced. "Have you seen it?"

"The cert? No. But I know she sent it."

"Did she sign it? Is her handwriting on it?"

"I told you, I didn't see it." He did not care for this doll-like little fellow; there was something too vehement about him; he was too pushy, and sly, too. He realised who it was he reminded him of — Oscar Latimer, of course. "Tell me — Jimmy, is it? Tell me, Jimmy, what do you think is going on with April?"

Instead of answering, Minor stood up and in his bantam strut walked with his cigarette to the window of the dissecting room. Beyond the glass the light was a baleful, ice-white glare, and a porter in a dirty green house-coat was half-heartedly dragging a mop back and forth over the grey-tiled floor. Minor was staring at the dissection table; there was a cadaver there, covered with a plastic sheet. He glanced back over his shoulder at Quirke. "You keep them here, just like this, the bodies?"

"Where do you think we should keep them? This is the pathology department."

"I thought — I don't know. In cold storage, or something?"

"There is a cold-room. But that one" — he nodded towards the cadaver — "is waiting for a post-mortem."

Minor came back and sat down again. "Dr Quirke," he said, "I know you've spoken to the family, to April's uncle and her mother, to her brother, too. They won't see me, needless to say, and I —"

"See you about what?"

Minor glanced at him quickly, startled. "Well, about April."

"Are you planning to write something, something in the newspaper, about April's disappearance?"

The fellow's look became evasive. "I don't know. I'm just — I'm just trying to gather the facts, such as they are."

"And when you've gathered these facts, will you write a story then?"

Minor was squirming now. "Look, Dr Quirke, as I said, I'm a friend of April's —"

"No, you said you were a friend of Phoebe's. You said you knew, or know, April." He paused. "What I'm wondering, Jimmy" — he laid a menacing emphasis on the name — "is what exactly your interest is in this business. Are you being a friend, or a reporter?"

"Why not both?"

Quirke leaned far back in his chair. There was, he suddenly remembered, a bottle of whiskey in one of the desk drawers. "I don't think it works that way. I think you'd better decide which to be. There are facts and facts, and some of them might call for a friendly interpretation."

Jimmy Minor smiled, and for a second Quirke was taken aback, so sweet a smile it was, so sudden, so open and unguarded. "Even newshounds have friends, Dr Quirke." Along with the smile had come a movie-actor's accent — *nooshounds* — and now he too sat back, and lit another Woodbine, and dropped the spent match into the ash-tray with a finical little flourish. He had decided, Quirke saw, to give charm a try.

"Tell me what you want from me, Mr Minor," Quirke said. "Time moves on and there's a cadaver out there that's not getting any fresher."

"It's simple," Minor said, cocksure now and still with that winning smile. "I'm hoping you'll help me to find out what happened to April. I like her. What's more, I admire her. She's her own woman. She may have a funny taste in men but that doesn't mean that she —" He stopped.

"That she what?"

Minor examined his smoke-stained fingers and the cigarette they were holding. "Phoebe thinks something happened to her — to April. Do you?"

"I don't know — do *you?*"

"There must be some reason for her disappearing like this."

"Maybe she went off somewhere. Maybe she needed a break."

"You don't believe that any more than I do, or than Phoebe does. April would have told us she was going."

"So you do think something happened to her."

"It's not what I think that matters. You've spoken to the family. What do *they* think?"

"They think she's wild, and disreputable, and they don't want to have anything to do with her. So they say, and I've no reason not to believe them."

It came to him suddenly, with something of a mild shock, that he did not know what April Latimer looked like, that he had not even seen a photograph of her. All along she had been someone that other people talked about, worried about, someone that other people loved and, perhaps, hated, too. Now, though, suddenly, talking to this peculiar and unappetising little man, it was as if the wraith he had been following through the fog had stepped out into the clear light of day, but still at such a distance that he could make out the form of it only, not the features. How far and for how long would he have to press on before he saw April Latimer clear?

"Tell me," he said, "do you know this other friend of April's, the Nigerian, Patrick Ojukwu?"

The young man's expression altered, grew dark and sullen. "Of course," he said shortly. "We all know him."

"What can you tell me about him?"

"We call him the Prince. His father is some kind of headman of his tribe. They have their version of aristocrats, it seems." He snickered. "Big shots in the jungle."

"Were they more than friends, he and April?"

"You mean, did they have an affair? I wouldn't be surprised." He gave his mouth a sour twist. "As I say, April had strange tastes in men. She liked a bit of spice, if you know what I mean."

He was jealous, Quirke saw. "Was she promiscuous?"

Jimmy Minor laughed again nastily. "How would I know? She was never promiscuous in my direction, if that's what you're thinking."

Quirke gazed at him. "Where does he live, this Nigerian chap?" he asked.

"He has a flat in Castle Street. Phoebe, I'm sure, can tell you where." He smiled again, this time showing the point of a sharp tooth.

Quirke stood up. "I'm sorry," he said, "I have a busy afternoon ahead of me."

Minor, surprised, stubbed out his cigarette and slowly got to his feet. "Thanks for your time," he said, with smiling sarcasm. Quirke steered him towards the door. At the dissecting-room window Minor paused and glanced in again at the draped corpse on the slab. "I've never seen a post-mortem," he said, a little sulkily, as if it were a treat that had been wilfully denied him.

"Come round some day," Quirke said. "We're always happy to accommodate the gentlemen of the press."

When Minor had gone Quirke sat down again and looked at the telephone for a while, tapping out a tattoo with his fingers on the desk-top. He saw Sinclair come into the dissecting room — they gave each other the usual, faintly derisory wave through the glass — then he picked up the phone and dialled Celia Latimer's number. The maid answered, and said that Mrs Latimer was not available at the moment. "Tell her it's Dr Quirke," he said. "She's expecting a call from me." It occurred to him to wonder if Sinclair might have known April Latimer. The younger doctors in the hospital that he had asked had said that April kept herself to herself, and it seemed she did not socialise much, amongst the staff, anyway. He had the impression she was disliked, or resented at least, for her standoffishness. She might have made common cause with the cynical and jadedly laconic Sinclair, if their paths had crossed.

"Thank you for calling, Dr Quirke," Celia Latimer's cold, sharp voice said in his ear. "As I told you, I'd like to have a word. Do you think you could come out to the house?"

"Yes," he said. "I can come out. I have to see someone this afternoon."

"Shall we say five o'clock, would that suit you?"

Her voice was tense and tremulous, as if she were having difficulty holding something back. He did not want to go out to that house, but knew he would.

262

"Yes," he said, "five o'clock. I'll be there."

He put down the phone slowly, thinking, then rose and went into the next room. Sinclair had drawn back the sheet from the corpse — an emaciated young man with sunken cheeks and a stubbled chin — and was gazing down on it in his usual stony manner. "The Guards stumbled on him in the early hours in a lane behind Parnell Street," he said. "Hypothermia, by the look of it." He sniffed, nodding. "Somebody's son."

Quirke leaned against the stainless-steel sink and lit a cigarette. "April Latimer," he said. "A junior here. Do you know her?"

Sinclair was still eyeing the corpse, measuring it up. "I've seen her about," he said. "Not recently, though."

"No, she's been out sick." He tapped his cigarette over the sink and heard the tiny hiss as the flakes of ash tumbled into the drain. "What's she like?"

Sinclair turned and leaned in a slouch against the dissecting table and pushed back the wings of his white coat and put his hands in the pockets of his trousers. "No idea. I don't think I've spoken to her more than once or twice."

"What's the word on her?"

"The word?"

"You know what I mean. What do the other juniors — the men — what do they say about her?"

Sinclair studied his shoes, then shrugged. "Not much, that I've heard. Is she supposed to — is she supposed to have a reputation?"

"That's what I was hoping *you* would tell *me*. She's a niece of Bill Latimer."

"Is she? I didn't know that."

Quirke could see him wanting to ask what was his interest in April but not quite knowing if he should. Quirke said: "It seems she may not be so much sick as — well, missing."

"Oh?" Sinclair prided himself on never showing surprise. "Missing how? As in, presumed dead?"

"No, no one is presuming that. She hasn't been seen or heard from for a few weeks." He waited, then asked: "Patrick Ojukwu — know him?"

Sinclair frowned, a triangular knot forming above the dark promontory of his nose. "Patrick *who*?"

"African. Studying at the College of Surgeons."

"Ah." The young man took on a look of faint, sardonic amusement. "Is he the reason she's missing?"

Quirke was trying to press the spent butt of his cigarette through the grating in the sink drain. "Not so far as I know," he said. "Why do you think that?"

"The black boys up there at Surgeons, *they* have a reputation."

"There can't be many of them."

"Probably just as well."

"It seems he's a friend of hers, of April Latimer's."

"Which kind of friend?"

"A friend friend, so I'm told. My daughter knows them both."

Sinclair was still looking at his shoes. In the years they had worked together they had never allowed themselves to develop anything like a regard for each other, and would not, now. Quirke knew his assistant did not trust him, and Quirke was wary of him, in

264

return. Sinclair wanted his job, and would get it, sooner or later.

The fluorescent lamps in the ceiling were shedding a harsh glare on the corpse on the table, and the dry, grey skin seemed to shimmer and seethe, as if the light were picking out the very molecules of which it was made.

"And your daughter," Sinclair said, "what does she think has become of her friend?"

"She's worried about her. Which is more, it seems, than her family are."

"The Minister, that is?"

"And her mother. Her brother, too — Oscar Latimer."

"The Holy Father?" Sinclair laughed coldly. "He'll be offering Masses for her safe return."

"Is that what they call him, the Holy Father?" Quirke was thinking again of that bottle of whiskey in his desk. His hangover began to drum again in his head. He thought of Isabel Galloway. "Do you know him?" he asked.

"His Holiness?" Sinclair said. He produced a packet of Gold Flake and put a cigarette between his lips but did not light it. "I went to one or two of his lectures," he said.

"And? What would you say he's like?"

The young man considered. He took the unlighted cigarette from his mouth. "Obsessed," he said.

CHAPTER
NINE

Quirke picked up Isabel at the corner of Parnell Street and they drove down to the quays and turned right for the Park. The short-lived day had begun to wane already, and the sky above the river was clear and of a deep violet shade, and, lower down, the frost-laden air was tinged a delicate pink. She said again how much she hated this time of year, these awful winter days that seemed to be over before they had properly begun. He said he liked the winter, when it was frosty and the nights were long. She asked if it reminded him of his childhood, and after waiting in vain for an answer she turned away and looked out at the quayside passing by. He glanced at her sidelong; her expression in profile was sombre; he supposed she was angry. But he did not want to talk to her about his childhood, not her. The past had poison in it. He asked if she was all right and after a second or two she said yes, that the morning's rehearsal had been long and she was tired, and besides, she thought she might be starting a cold. "What a beautiful car this is," she said, but it was plain she was thinking of something else.

He asked if she would like to stop at Ryan's of Parkgate Street for a drink but she said no, that it was too early, and that she would prefer they should go for their walk while the daylight lasted. He drove in at the gate on to Chesterfield Avenue.

"This is where I learned to drive," he said.

"Oh? When was that?"

"Last week."

She looked at him. "My God — you only learned to drive a week ago?"

"There's nothing to it, just pressing pedals and turning the wheel." He drew the car to the side of the road and stopped. "Which reminds me," he said, "I must get a driving licence."

He sat for a moment looking blankly through the windscreen.

"How's the hangover?" she asked.

"Oh," he said, "weakening."

"You mean it's getting weak, or it's weakening you?"

"It's getting weaker and I'm getting better. That's the thing about a hangover, no matter how bad it is, it ends."

"I suppose you must be dying for a drink now — did you want to stop at Ryan's?"

"Not really."

"Phoebe worries about your drinking, you know."

He was still looking out at the winter afternoon. "Yes," he said. "So do I."

"What'll we do, to keep you out of the pub?" She laid a hand lightly on his thigh. "We shall just have to think of something, shan't we?"

They got out and set off walking through the misty air. Deer in a herd were grazing among the trees off to their left; an antlered stag watched them, chewing with that busy, sideways motion of its lower jaw. The animals' pelts were the same colour as the bark of the trees amongst which they stood.

"April's mother called me," Quirke said.

Isabel's arm was linked in his and as they walked she pressed up close against him for warmth. "What did she say?"

"She asked me to come out and see her."

"Has she had word of April?"

"I don't know. I don't think so. I said I'd come out at five."

"It's nearly four, now."

"I know. Will you come with me?"

"Oh, crikey," she said, in a quailing voice, "I don't know. The widow Latimer is rather a daunting prospect, you know."

A cyclist went past, crouched low over the dropped handlebars of his sports bike and shedding behind him comical puffs of breath, like the smoke of a train. An elderly couple sat on a bench, swathed in mufflers and wearing identical woollen hats with bobbles on them. Their dog, a snappish King Charles spaniel, ran over the grass in a complicated pattern of straight lines and angles, taking no notice of the deer.

"Do you know her, Mrs Latimer?" Quirke asked.

"Only by reputation. Which is formidable."

"Yes. She's a bit of an ogress, all right. Though I feel sorry for her."

"Because of April?"

268

"That, and the fact that it can't be easy being the widow of Conor Latimer."

"What was he?"

"Heart surgeon, and a national hero — fought in the War of Independence."

She laughed. "All the more reason for me to steer clear of her." She squeezed his arm and smiled up at him. "I am half English, after all."

"How could I forget it?"

"Why — because you got me into bed so easily?" She grimaced. "Sorry, that just popped out."

They walked on.

"Didn't April ever mention her father?" Quirke asked.

"She tended not to talk about her family. A delicate subject." She laughed, not quite steadily. "A bit like the subject we're not talking about now, I suppose."

After a dozen paces Quirke cleared his throat and said: "I'm sorry about this morning, walking in like that when you were in the bath."

"I didn't mind. Quite the opposite, in fact. I felt like — oh, I don't know, Helen, or Leda, or somebody, being swooped down upon by a god disguised as a bull. You do look quite bullish, you know, in a confined space."

"Yes," he said, "and the world is my china shop."

She squeezed his arm again, pressing it to her side, and through her coat he felt her warmth and the delicate curve of her ribs. They were silent again, and he could feel something gathering in her. Then, in a tight, small voice, she said: "Quirke, where are we going?"

"Where are we going? Well, we've passed the Wellington Monument and the Zoo is over there."

"Do you think this is funny?"

"I think we're both grown-up people and we should behave accordingly." He had not meant it to sound so harsh. She let go of his arm and strode on quickly, her hands thrust into the pockets of her coat and her head down. He quickened his pace and caught up with her and took her by the elbow, making her stop. She tried to pull her arm away from him but his grip was too strong. "I told you before," he said, "I'm no good at this kind of thing."

She looked up into his face; tears stood on the lower rims of her eyelids, quivering and shiny, like beads of quicksilver. "*What* kind of thing?"

"*This* kind. You, me, swans in the moonlight —"

"Swans in the —?"

"I mean I don't know how to behave, that's all. I never learned, there was no one to teach me. People, women" — he made a chopping motion with the side of his hand — "it's impossible."

She stood there, close in front of him, gazing up, and he had to force himself not to look away.

"Listen to me," she said, in a new voice, rapid and sharp-edged. "I haven't asked anything of you, no promises, no vows, no commitments. I thought you understood that, I thought you accepted that. Don't start taking fright already, when there's nothing to be frightened of. Do me that courtesy, will you?"

270

"I'm sor —"

"And *please*, no apologies. I told you, few things are as dispiriting as a man mumbling about how *sorry* he is." Suddenly she lifted herself up on her toes and seized his face between her hands and kissed him hard on the mouth. "You idiot," she said, drawing back. "You hopeless idiot — don't you realise you could be *happy*?"

It was dark by the time they got to Dun Laoghaire and a three-quarters moon, white as lightning, had hoisted itself over the harbour. It was not so cold out here by the sea and the road was blackly agleam with thawed frost. When they stopped at Albion Terrace they did not get out of the car at once but sat side by side listening to the engine ticking as it cooled. Quirke lit a cigarette and rolled down the window beside him an inch and flicked the spent match through the opening. "I shouldn't have asked you to come," he said. "I could bring you to the hotel back there and you could wait for me, if you like?"

Isabel was looking at the moon. "I'm glad you did ask me," she said, without turning. "You should ask for things more often. People like it. It makes them feel needed." She reached out blindly and took his hand. "Oh, Lor'," she said, with a quivery little laugh, "I think I feel another tear coming on."

"What? Why?"

"I don't know — isn't it awful, the way we cry for no reason?" Now she did turn, and he saw her eyes, how large they were and shining. "I can't imagine you weep much, do you, Quirke?" He said nothing, and she gripped his hand more tightly, giving it a rueful shake. "Big strong man, no cry, eh?" A shaft of moonlight shone on her hand holding his. Out in the darkness unseen seabirds were calling and crying. "I'm as lost as you are, you know," she said. "Couldn't we just — help each other a little along this hard way we've been set on?"

He took her awkwardly in his arms — the steering-wheel was in the way — and kissed her. He kept his eyes open, and saw, beyond the pale concavity of her temple, one of those birds come swooping suddenly out of the darkness, swift and startlingly white.

They walked up the pathway between glimmering lawns, the damp gravel squeaking under their tread. She had taken his hand again. "You've met before, haven't you, April's mother?" she said. "You know we're all afraid of her, of course?"

"Who is 'all'?"

"April's friends."

"Right," he said. "April's friends. I met one of them this afternoon. A reporter."

"Jimmy Minor?" She was surprised. "Where did you meet him?"

"He came to see me at the hospital, asking about April."

"Did he? What did he say?"

"He was poking about, looking for information, the way they do."

"I hope he's not thinking of writing something about her in the paper?" They came to the front door. A light was burning in the porch. "What did you tell him?"

"Nothing. What is there to tell?"

He rang the doorbell, they heard its distant chime. Isabel was looking out over the blackness of the garden, thinking. "I wonder what he's up to," she murmured. "He can be mischievous, can our Jimmy."

Marie the red-haired maid opened the door to them. Quirke she remembered, and said yes, that he was expected. She gave Isabel a look; he did not introduce her.

They were led along the hall to a small, square room at the rear of the house. There was an antique desk with many drawers, and two armchairs and a small sofa upholstered in worn red velvet. Dim, sepia photographs of bearded gentlemen and ladies in lace crowded the walls, and in pride of place above the desk there was hung a framed copy of the 1916 Proclamation. "As you can probably guess, this was my husband's room," Celia Latimer said, indicating another photograph in a silver frame standing on the desk, a studio portrait of the late Conor Latimer, looking impossibly smooth, with his head inclined and holding a cigarette beside his face; he had the smile of a film star, arch and knowing. "His den, he called it," his widow said. Her hair was drawn back from her forehead and she was wearing a tartan skirt and a grey wool jumper and a grey cardigan and pearls; she looked at once frumpish and vaguely regal, more the Queen Mother than the Queen. She had risen from her chair to greet them. Quirke introduced Isabel Galloway and she smiled frostily and said: "Yes, I saw you in that French play at the Gate. You were the — the young woman. I must say I was surprised by some of the lines they gave you to say."

"Oh, well," Isabel said, "you know what the French are like."

The smile grew frostier still. "No, I'm afraid I don't."

Isabel glanced at Quirke. He said: "Isabel is a friend of April's."

"Yes? I don't think I heard her mention you. But, then, there are many things that April doesn't mention."

She gestured for them to sit down, Quirke in an armchair and Isabel on the sofa. There was a fire burning and the air in the room was close and hot. As they were settling themselves the maid came in bearing a tray with tea things on it and set it on a corner of the desk. Mrs Latimer poured the tea and sat down again, balancing a cup and saucer on her knee.

"I'll come straight to the point, Dr Quirke," she said. "My son tells me you're still asking questions about April's whereabouts. I want you to stop. I want you to leave us alone, to leave us in peace. When she's ready, April will come back from wherever she is, I have no doubt of that. In the meantime it does no one any good to keep on harassing my son and me in the way that you've been doing." She glanced at Isabel, sitting very straight on the sofa with the teacup and saucer in her lap, then turned her attention on Quirke again. "I'm sorry to be so blunt, but I always think it's best to come straight out and say a thing rather than hemming and

274

hawing." Before Quirke could answer her she turned again to Isabel. "I take it, Miss Galloway, *you* haven't heard from April?"

"No," Isabel said, "I haven't. But I'm not as worried as — as other people seem to be. It's not the first time April has gone off."

"Gone off?" Mrs Latimer said, with a look of large distaste. "I'm not sure what you mean by that."

Isabel's smile tightened, and two pink spots appeared on her cheekbones, a deeper colour than the dabs of rouge there.

Quirke put his cup and saucer on the floor beside his chair; he could not drink china tea. "Mrs Latimer," he said, "I know that what your daughter does or doesn't do is no business of mine. As I told you already, my only interest in all this — this business, is that my daughter came to me because she was worried, and I —"

"But you brought the Guards in," Mrs Latimer said. "You spoke to that detective, what's his name — you even took him into April's flat. You certainly had no business doing that."

He looked at the photograph of Conor Latimer on the desk. The man's smile seemed more a smirk now.

"I'm sorry you feel this way, Mrs Latimer. It's just —" He paused, and glanced at Isabel. She was fixed on him, the teacup forgotten in her lap. "It's just that it's possible that something has happened to your daughter."

"Something," Celia Latimer repeated tonelessly. She too was looking off to one side of him, as if there were

275

someone standing there. Quirke turned his head; it was the photograph of her husband that had drawn her, of course.

"I know," he said, "how important your family is to you."

With a visible effort she transferred her gaze to him. "Do you?" she said, in an odd, almost playful tone, and for a second he had the notion that she was going to laugh. She stood up and crossed to the desk and set her cup and saucer down on the tray. She turned to Isabel. "Would you like some more tea, Miss Galloway?" she asked. She seemed weary suddenly, her shoulders indrawn and her mouth set tight in a crooked line.

"No, thank you," Isabel said.

She, too, rose, and brought her cup, also with the tea untouched in it, and put it on the tray. Quirke watched the two women standing there, not saying anything to each other and yet, it seemed to him, communicating in some fashion. Women; he could not fathom them.

Mrs Latimer turned and walked to the fireplace and lifted from the mantelpiece yet another photograph, this one framed in gilt, and held it out for Quirke to see. It was of a smiling girl of eight or nine, in a garden, kneeling on one knee on the grass, with her arm around the neck of a large, grinning dog sitting on its haunches beside her. The girl was pale, with a small, pointed face surrounded by a tumble of fair curls and a saddle of dark freckles on the bridge of her nose. "I took that myself," Mrs Latimer said, turning the photo to look at it. "A summer day, it was, here in the garden, I remember it as if it were yesterday — you see the

276

summerhouse there, in the background? And that's April's dog, Toby. How she loved her Toby, and how he loved her, they were inseparable. She was a real tomboy, you know, never happier than out rambling the roads looking for frogs, or lizards, or conkers — The things she brought home!" She handed the photograph to Quirke and went back to her chair and sat down again, folding her hands in her lap. She looked old, suddenly, careworn and old. "She wasn't born in April, you know," she said, to no one in particular. "Her birthday is the second of May, but she was due a week earlier, and I had already chosen the name April, and so I kept it, even when she was late, because it seemed to suit her. Her father had wanted a girl, so had I, and we were delighted." She gazed into the burning coals in the fireplace. "Such a quiet baby, just lying there, taking everything in, with those big eyes of hers. It proved what I always believed, that we're born with our personalities already in place. When I think of her in her crib it's the same April as the one I sent off to school on her first day at St Mary's, the same one who came and told me she wanted to be a doctor, the same one who — who said such awful things to me that day when she left the house and never came back. Oh, God." She closed her eyes and passed a hand slowly over her face. "Oh, God," she said again, this time in a whisper, "what have we done?"

Quirke and Isabel looked at each other, and Isabel made a restraining gesture and went to the woman sitting slumped in the chair and put a hand on her shoulder. "Mrs Latimer," she said, "can I get you anything?"

Mrs Latimer shook her head.

"Do you know where April is, Mrs Latimer?" Quirke asked, and Isabel glared at him, shaking her head.

For a long time the woman said nothing, then she took her hand away from her face and let it fall into her lap. "My poor child," she whispered. "My poor only girl." She was looking into the fire again. "They were so close, you know," she said, in a firmer voice this time, in almost a conversational tone. "I should have — I should have done something, but what? If he had lived —" She heaved a sigh that sounded more like a sob. "If her father had lived, everything would have been different, I know it would. I know it."

They waited, Quirke and Isabel, but the woman said nothing more. She sat as if exhausted now, her head hanging and the nape of her neck bared and defenceless, with the lamplight shining full on it. Quirke stood up, and replaced the photograph of the little girl and her dog on the mantelpiece.

"I think we should be going, Mrs Latimer," he said. He picked up his cup from the floor beside the chair and brought it to the desk, and stood there a moment, looking again at the photograph of Conor Latimer. What was that look in his eyes? — mockery, disdain, cruelty? All of these.

The maid led them along the hall and gave them their coats. When she had shown them out she held the door open so that the lamp in the hall would light their way along the path. They did not speak. The air in the car was acrid with the smell of cigarette smoke. Quirke started up the engine.

"Well," Isabel said, "what do you think?"

"What do I think about what?"

"Do you think she knows where April is?"

"Oh, for God's sake," he said, "what does it matter whether she knows or not?"

He steered the car into the road and turned its nose in the direction of the city. The moon had risen higher, and seemed smaller and shone less brightly now. When they stopped outside the house in Portobello there was a light on already in one of the upstairs rooms. Isabel kissed him quickly and slid out of the seat and hurried to her door, from where she turned and gave him the briefest of waves, and was gone.

CHAPTER
TEN

Inspector Hackett often thought that he had never been happier than he was when he was a young Guard on the beat. This was not a thing he would allow himself to express to anyone, not even Mrs Hackett. After all, he was a great deal better paid now, he had his own office, and the respect of those under him on the Force, and even of some of those above him, too. There was no comparison between his present conditions and what they had been in those early days when he came up first to Dublin from the Garda Training College at Templemore and was handed his badge and truncheon and sent out into the streets. Yet later, when he got a promotion, he found that it seemed to him not so much advancement as something else, a sort of dilution of his proper role and duty. The man on the beat, he came to believe then, was truly what a policeman was supposed to be, a guardian of the peace. This was so at all times of the day, but especially at night, when law-abiding citizens were abed and all manner of peril and menace might be let loose upon the city. This was not Chicago, of course, or old Shanghai: most of the crime committed here was petty, and the miscreants who committed it were in the main a shabby and meagre lot. All the same, the poor old flatfoot pounding the pavement through the long, dark hours was the only guarantee of safety and a peaceful sleep that the citizenry had. Without him there would be mayhem, robbery and rapine, blood in the streets. Even a rookie Guard, just by being there, was a deterrent to malefactors great and puny alike. It was a solemn duty, the duty of care with which the policeman was entrusted. This was what he believed, and took pride in, secretly.

After supper he had put on his coat and hat and his woollen scarf and told his missus that he had a thing to do and that she should not to wait up. She had stared at him, but made no comment; she was used to his peculiarities by now, though sauntering off into the night like this was a new one. She stopped him in the hall, and asked if he was likely to be outside, on such an icy night, and when he said yes, maybe, probably, she told him to sit down on the chair beside the hat-stand and wait there, and went off to the kitchen and came back a few minutes later with a flask of tea and a handful of biscuits in a brown-paper bag. She stood in the doorway and watched him walk down the short path to the gate and then turn right towards the river.

He had promised himself he would take a taxi if the cold was really bad, but it was a fine, sharp night, the kind of night he remembered from when he was a boy, the air clear and the sky sparkling with stars, and the moon greying the houses and throwing sharp-edged shadows across front gardens. The last buses had gone and there was little traffic, only the odd car, its dimmed lamps lighting up dense scatterings of diamonds on the frosty roadway, and, when he got to the canal, a fleet of newspaper vans on the way down the country with the first editions. He hummed to himself as he walked along. The flask of tea in the right-hand pocket of his overcoat kept banging against his knee, but he did not mind — it was good of her to think of it. He crossed a hump-backed bridge and turned left. He thought of taking the tow-path, but despite the moonlight it was too dark down there — a fine thing it would be if he lost his footing and went into the water arse over tip — and he kept to the upper concrete path instead, under the trees, the bare branches of which made a faint, restless clicking, although there was not a breath of wind to stir them. He stopped, and stood to listen, looking upwards into the dark tracery of twigs. Was it the cold, the frost falling on them, that made them move and tap against each other? The sound was like the sound of someone knitting while half asleep. He ambled on.

He had no plan, no specific action in mind. When Dr Quirke telephoned him to say his daughter had seen someone outside her flat he had thought he would get the duty sergeant to put someone from the squad on it, maybe that young fellow he had been given as an assistant, red-haired Tomelty, who chafed at office work and could not wait to get out on the streets and start apprehending wrongdoers. A four-hour stint on a winter night quartering the same fifty-yard stretch of pavement would cool his ardour nicely. But he had not asked for Tomelty, he was not sure why. He would be thought mad, of course, if anyone knew he had taken on the job himself, but he did not care; anyway, most of them at the station considered him already part-way cracked. The truth was he was savouring a sweet, intense nostalgia for former days, when he was young, like young Tomelty, and probably just as irritatingly eager.

Quirke had told him too about the black man, Ojukway or whatever he was called, that his daughter in turn had told Quirke about. So the old woman in the flat had been right, after all. He had got one of the squad-car men to drive him round to the house in Castle Street, but the fellow was not there, and the woman in the house, a queer one with a fag in the corner of her mouth and a head of yellow curls that would have looked too young on someone half her age, had said she had not seen him since the day before, though his bed had been slept in — oh, it certainly had, she said with a sniff and a significant look. She thought she had heard noises in the night — "*those* sort of noises, you know?" — but she could not be sure, and normally he was a quiet young fellow and kept himself to himself, though of course with *them* you could never tell what they might get up to. He had asked to see the room, but there was nothing there of interest, on a cursory glance, at least. He asked Goldilocks if she knew where he might have gone to but she did not. Like April Latimer, the black man had left without taking any of the necessities with him, so probably, unlike April, he would soon return. Hackett hoped so: he looked forward to having a word with Mr Ojakewu.

Just before Baggot Street Bridge he spotted a dim shape huddled on a bench beside the lock, and stopped to have a look. It was a tramp, cocooned in a bundle of rags, peacefully sleeping, and he decided not to disturb him. How did they survive, these poor creatures, out all night in any weather? It must be a couple of degrees below freezing tonight. Should he have roused him, and given him a few shillings to find shelter and a bed for himself somewhere? He would probably only be cursed for his trouble, and likely the money would be kept and spent on drink in the first pub to open in the morning. He sighed, thinking how hard a station life is for some, and how little there is to be done for the world's unfortunates.

The young trees on Haddington Road made no sounds, unlike their older cousins along the canal. He counted off the houses on the other side of the street until he came to the one where the Quirke girl lived — no, he remembered, she was not called Quirke, but Griffin. That was all a strange and painful business, Dr Quirke discovered to have given away his baby to his sister-in-law and her husband, the man who was as good as a brother to him. What got into folk, at all, to do such things? He supposed he was not much of a policeman if he was still capable of being surprised by the waywardness of human beings.

There were no lights to be seen in the house, save a faint glow in the transom over the front door, which would be the hall light. He stood on the opposite footpath, under one of the young trees, in a shadowed place midway between two streetlamps, looking up at the shining black windows of what he knew to be Phoebe's flat. His thoughts turned once more to Quirke, that difficult, troubled man. They had so little in common, the two of them, and yet he felt a closeness between them, a bond, almost. Strangely, the person Quirke most reminded him of was his sister, who had died. Poor Winnie. Like Quirke, she could not escape from the past. She had been a sickly child, and, as she grew older, something had happened to her mind, she became prey to nightmares and all kinds of waking horrors, and there was no helping her. She lived with her head turned away from everyone and everything in the present; she was like a person stumbling over stony ground and always looking backwards, terrified of losing sight of the place where she had set out from, however sad and painful a place it had been. And then one day she tripped, and fell. They found her in her bed with her rosary beads in one hand and the empty pill bottle in the other. "Now she's where she always wanted to be," their father said. That was Quirke, looking back longingly to a past where he had been so unhappy.

He heard a sound. Or not a sound, not exactly, more a feeling, a sensation. What first alerted him was his hearing making an adjustment by itself. It was as if a waveband had been changed and he was listening now on a higher, more finely tuned frequency. There was someone nearby in the street, he was sure of it. He looked to his left, barely moving his head. He was attending so hard now that he seemed to hear the frost itself falling, a faint ringing, needle-sharp, all around him in the darkness of the air. He could see no one. There was the line of trees, evenly spaced, and in every third space a lamppost, shedding its circle of chalky radiance. What should he do? — should he move, step into the light, call out a challenge? Slowly, slowly, he took a step backwards, paused, took another step, until he felt the cold hardness of garden railings at his back. He was still looking to the left. Then he saw it, the person-shaped shadow, a good fifty yards off, next to the trunk of a tree, just out of the lamplight. He began to edge sideways in that direction, putting his hands behind him and feeling his way along the railings to guide and steady himself. As he advanced into the light of the first lamp he shrank back but all the same he knew he could be seen, if the watcher were to turn in this direction. On he went at his crabwise pace, slowly, steadily, and then, when there were no more than twenty yards between him and his quarry, he came without realising it to an open gateway, and reaching his hands back into the sudden emptiness behind him he felt himself swaying sideways, and the Thermos in his pocket struck the metal gate-post with a dull, metallic *thunk*. He swore under his breath. The shadow turned, crouched, and then sprinted away into the darkness and in a moment was gone. He cursed himself again, leaning in the gateway. Tomelty, he thought, young Tomelty would have given chase, as he could not, on his middle-aged legs, with that damned flask banging against his knees.

He listened, and heard an engine starting up, and ran out into the street and saw the car speeding away in the direction of Ringsend. He stood there for a moment, fuming and sighing. What had he seen? Nothing. A crouched figure, fleeing — had he even heard the sound of those running feet? He could not swear that he had. If it had not been for the car he might have thought he had imagined there was someone there. And could he be sure the car was not someone else's, someone who had come out of a house farther down the street, a law-abiding citizen, going off to a night-shift, maybe? He was getting old, too old, certainly, for this kind of thing. What was that in his other pocket? — the bag of biscuits. Without taking it out of his pocket he clawed the bag open and brought out a biscuit and peered at it. Rich Tea. Not his favourite. He turned, gloomily munching his dry rations, and walked away.

Quirke was dreaming that there was a fire. He was in a tiny room inside what he knew was a large house. It was night-time and there was a window that looked out on a broad, deserted street where the streetlamps were making a dull gleam on the tarmac. He could see no sign of flames yet he knew that there was a conflagration somewhere very close by. A fire engine was on the way, or was here, indeed, was under the very window where he stood peering out, although he could not see it, either, in spite of the fact that its bell was ringing so loudly and so insistently that it seemed it must be in the room with him. He felt frightened, or at least felt that he should be frightened, because he was in grave danger, for all that there was no sign of the fire. Then he saw a dog loping along the street, and someone running after it. The two figures, the dog and its owner, seemed not to be fleeing, as he felt they should be, on the contrary seemed to be happily playing a game, a game of chase, perhaps. They came closer, and he saw that the one in pursuit was a girl, or a young woman. She was carrying something in one hand, he could see it fluttering madly as she ran; it was a paper, or a parchment, with scalloped edges, and it was on fire at one corner, he could see the flame blown back by the air rushing against it, and he knew that the girl or young woman was trying to put it out, and although she was having no success she was laughing, as if there were no danger, no danger at all.

It was the telephone. He struggled out of sleep, rising off his side and flailing one arm wildly to find the machine and stop the awful noise. He found the switch of the bedside lamp. It always seemed to him a ringing telephone should be hopping, but there it sat on the little locker by the bed, quite motionless, squat as a frog, yet making such a racket. He snatched up the receiver.

"I know, I know," Hackett's voice said, "I know it's late, and you were asleep. But I thought you'd want me to call you."

Quirke was sitting on the side of the bed now, rubbing at his eyes. "Where are you?" he asked. "What's going on?"

"I'm in a phone box, in Baggot Street. I was down on Haddington Road —"

"What? Why were you there? What's happened?"

"Nothing, nothing. I went round to have a look, after what you told me about your daughter, thinking she'd seen someone in the street."

Quirke could not take it in. "You went to Haddington Road, tonight?"

"Aye. It's a grand night, and I took a stroll."

Quirke looked to the bedroom window, rimed outside with frost. "You realise," he said, "it's — what time is it?"

"It's late, it's late. Anyway, I went and had a look. Your daughter wasn't seeing things. There was someone there, right enough, across the road from the house. At least I think there was."

"Someone there?"

"Aye."

"Doing what?"

"Just — watching."

"And what happened?"

There was a pause. Quirke thought he could hear the detective making a humming noise under his breath, or perhaps it was some buzzing on the line.

"Nothing happened," Hackett said, and chuckled ruefully. "I'm afraid I'm not the sleuth I used to be. I tried to get close to have a look but whoever it was heard me and took off."

"Did you see anything?"

"No."

"But you must have made out something?"

"If it was anyone, it was a very slight person, light on the feet. Coat, some kind of cap, I think. Had a car down the road, got in it and was gone."

"Slight, you say — what do you mean?"

The pips began and Hackett could be heard fumbling for coins, and then there was the crash of the pennies going into the slot and his voice again. "Hello, hello, are you there?"

"I'm here."

"Bloody phones," the detective said. "What were you asking me?"

"A slight person, you said — slight in what way?"

"Well, I don't know how else I can say it. Small. A bantam-weight. Fast on the pins."

A slow spasm was making its way slantwise down Quirke's back; it was as if a cold hand were brushing against his skin. "Could it have been — could it have been a female? A woman?"

This time there was a longer pause. Hackett was humming again, it was definitely he who was making that soft, nasal sound. "A woman?" he said. "I didn't think of that but, yes, I suppose so, I suppose it could have been. A young woman. If, as I say, there was anyone — the mind plays tricks at this hour of the night."

Quirke was looking up at the window again. The moon was gone and all beyond the glass was blackness. "Come round," he said. "Don't ring the bell, the bugger on the ground floor will complain. I'll watch for you, and let you in."

"Right. And, Dr Quirke —"

"Yes?"

"Whoever it was, it was no black man, I can tell you that."

They sat in the kitchen drinking tea and smoking. Quirke made the detective tell him again what had happened, little though it was, and after he had finished they had lapsed again into silence. The gas stove was turned full on but still the room was cold, and Quirke pulled his dressing-gown more snugly around him. Hackett had not taken off his woollen scarf, or his hat. He was wearing that shiny coat again, with the toggles and straps and epaulettes. He sighed, and said it was frustrating, but the more he tried to remember what he had seen of the fleeing figure the less certain he felt. It might have been a woman, he said, but somehow he thought that run was not a woman's run. "They tend to turn their toes out," he said. "Have you ever noticed that? They haven't got that — that co-ordination that men have." He shook his head, gazing into the mug of tea that by now was no more than lukewarm. "Mind you, with the young ones that are going about today you never know. Half of them are hard to tell from fellows."

Quirke rose and carried his mug to the sink and rinsed it under the tap and set it upside down on the draining-board. He turned, leaning back against the sink, and put his hands into the deep pockets of the dressing-gown. "What if it was her?" he said.

"What?"

"Hasn't it occurred to you? It could have been her, it could have been April Latimer. What if it was?"

Hackett with one finger pushed his hat to the back of his head and with the same finger scratched himself thoughtfully along his hairline. "Why would she be standing in the street on a freezing night like this, looking up at your daughter's window?"

"I know," Quirke said. "It makes no sense. And yet —"

"Well?" The detective waited.

"I don't know."

"As you say," Hackett said. "It makes no sense."

CHAPTER
ELEVEN

In the morning, at something before eight, the phone rang again. Quirke was shaving, and came into the bedroom with half his face still lathered. He thought it would be Hackett, to say he had remembered something about the figure in the street. He had offered to drive him home the night before, but then remembered that the Alvis was up at Perry Otway's place, locked in its garage, and he did not relish the thought of getting it out of there. He said he would call him a taxi, and asked him for his address, but Hackett had waved him away, saying he would walk home, that the exercise would do him good. Quirke was disappointed: he had hoped finally to find out where it was that Hackett lived. They went down to the front door together, Quirke still in his dressing-gown, and the detective strolled off into the night, trailing a ghostly flaw of cigarette smoke behind him. In the flat again, Quirke had been unable to get back to sleep, and sat in an armchair in front of the hissing gas fire for a long time. In the end the warmth of the fire sent him into a doze, where he dreamed once more of alarms, and things on fire, and people running. When he woke again it was still dark, and his limbs were stiff from huddling in the armchair and there was a vile taste in his mouth. And now the phone was going again, and he wished he did not have to answer it.

"Hello," Isabel Galloway said, sounding tense and guarded. "It's me."

"Yes," he said drily. "I recognised your voice, believe it or not."

"What? Oh, yes. Good." She paused. "How are you?"

"I'm all right. Something of a sleepless night."

"Why was that?"

"I'll tell you another time."

"Listen, Quirke —" Again she stopped, and he had the impression of her taking a deep breath. "There's someone here who needs to talk to you."

"Where are you?"

"At home, of course."

"Who is it — who's there with you?"

"Just — someone."

The lather drying on his face gave his skin an unpleasant, crawling sensation. "Is *she* there?"

"What?"

"April — is she with you?"

"Just come, Quirke, will you? Come now."

She hung up, and he stood for a moment looking at the receiver; there was a smear of shaving soap on the earpiece.

He was not sure that Perry Otway would be at the garage yet so he killed ten minutes by going round to the Q and L for cigarettes. The morning was frosty and the air seemed draped with transparent sheets of muslin, and his footsteps rang as if the pavement were made of iron. In Baggot Street the old tinker woman in her tartan shawl was out already, waylaying passers-by. Quirke gave her a sixpenny piece and she moaned her thanks, calling down on him the blessings of God and His Holy Mother and all the saints. The Q and L had just opened, the shopman was still putting away the shutters. He seemed in almost a fever of good cheer this morning. His eyes shone with a peculiar light, and his cheeks and chin were scraped to a polished gleam, as if he had shaved himself at least twice. The check pattern of his jacket looked even louder than usual, and he sported a Liberty tie with parrots on it. His mother, he confided, had died the previous night. He beamed as if from pride at the old woman's achievement. "She was ninety-three," he said, in a tone of malicious satisfaction.

Perry Otway, too, had just opened for business. He was at the back of the workshop, where he had hung up his sheepskin coat and was pulling on his oil-caked overalls. "Brass-monkey weather, eh?" he said, blowing into his cupped hands. They walked together up the lane to the lock-up garage where the Alvis waited in the darkness like a great black cat in its cage. Quirke had little trouble getting the car into the garage but he needed Perry to manoeuvre it out again, for he had not yet mastered the art of reversing in confined spaces and feared scraping the paintwork or putting a dent in one of the wings, for which, he vaguely feared, some severe penalty would be exacted. Perry treated the machine with a kind of solicitous delicacy and tenderness. He pulled out neatly into the street and stopped there, and left the engine running. "Nothing like it, is there," he said, swinging himself out from behind the wheel, "the smell of petrol fumes on a cold winter morning?"

Quirke was lighting a cigarette. He was in no hurry to get to the house on the canal, where he knew there could only be trouble waiting for him, though he did not know what it would be. The thought of April Latimer being there, at Isabel's, filled him with a peculiar sense of panic. What would he say to her, what would they talk about? In these past weeks she had become for him almost a mythical figure, and now he was prey to what he could only think was an attack of crippling, monumental shyness.

He drove around the Pepper Canister and turned right on the canal. As he was passing by the house on Herbert Place he slowed down and peered up at the windows of April's flat. In one of them a curtain rod had come away on one side and the lace curtain hung down at a crooked angle. He drove on, staying in third gear.

Outside Isabel's little house there were floatings of ice on the canal again, and water-hens were fussing and splashing among the reeds. The morning had a raw edge. He was lifting his hand to the knocker when the door opened. Isabel was already dressed. She wore a dark skirt and a dark-blue cardigan. Her bronze-coloured hair was tied back with a dark ribbon. She did not smile, only stood aside and gestured for him to come in.

He thought of that curtain in the window, hanging at a crazy angle on its broken rod.

The house had a stuffy, morning smell of bedclothes and bath soap and milky tea and bread that had been toasted under a gas flame. He paused, and Isabel went ahead, leading him along the short hall, through the living room and into the kitchen. How slim she was, how slim and intense.

The first person he saw was Phoebe, standing by the stove in her overcoat. He realised he was holding his breath and seemed unable to release it. When he came in she, too, did not smile, and gave no greeting. A young man was sitting at the table. He was black, with a large, smooth-browed head and a flattened nose and eyes that swivelled like the eyes of a nervous horse, their whites flashing. He was wearing a loose jumper and no shirt, and a pair of baggy corduroy trousers; he looked cold and exhausted, sitting there with his shoulders drooping and his clasped hands pressed between his knees.

"This is Patrick Ojukwu," Isabel said.

The young man regarded him warily. He did not stand up, and they did not shake hands. Quirke put his hat down on the table, where there were cups and smeared plates and a teapot under a woollen cosy. He looked from Isabel to Phoebe and back again. "Well?" he said. He was remembering the light that had been on in the window upstairs when he had brought Isabel back here last night, and of Isabel hurrying from the car, and waving to him in that tense way before going inside.

"Would you like something?" she asked now. "The tea is probably cold but I could —"

"No, nothing." His eyes shied from hers. He could not make out what he was feeling, things were so jumbled up in him. Anger? Yes, anger, certainly, but something else, too, a hot thrill that seemed to be jealousy. He turned to Ojukwu — had he spent the night here? In a recess of his mind an image moved, of black skin on white. "Where's April?" he asked.

The young man looked quickly at Phoebe and then at Isabel.

"He doesn't know," Isabel said.

Quirke gave a curt sigh and pulled back one of the chairs at the table and sat down. So far Phoebe had said nothing. "Why are you here?" he asked her.

"We're all friends," Phoebe said. "I told you."

"So where's the other one, then, the reporter?"

She said nothing, and looked away.

"We're all tired, Quirke," Isabel said. "We've been up half the night, talking."

Quirke was growing hot inside his overcoat but for some reason he did not want to take it off. Isabel had gone to stand beside Phoebe, as if in solidarity. He turned back to Ojukwu. "So," he said. "Tell me."

The black man, still with his hands pressed between his knees, began to rock back and forth on the chair, staring at the floor in front of him with those huge eyes. He cleared his throat. "April telephoned me that day," he said. "I was in college, they called me down to the reception place. She said she was in trouble, that she needed my help. I went to the flat. She did not come to the door but I let myself in with the key. She was in the bedroom."

He stopped. Quirke, on the other side of the table, watched him. There were marks of some kind in the skin over his cheekbones, small incisions the shape of slender arrow-heads, made a long time ago — tribal markings, he supposed, made at birth with a knife. His close-cropped hair was a mass of tightly wound curls, like so many tiny metal springs, or metal shavings. "Were you and April — were you her lover?"

Ojukwu shook his head, still with his eyes fixed on the floor. "No," he said, and Quirke saw the faint, brief start that Phoebe gave. "No," Ojukwu said again, "not really."

"What was she doing, in the bedroom?"

The silence in the room seemed to contract. The two women were fixed on Ojukwu, waiting for what would come next; they had heard it before and now would have to hear it again.

"She was in a bad state," he said. "I thought at first she was unconscious. There was blood."

"What kind of blood?" Quirke asked. As if he did not know already.

Ojukwu turned slowly and looked up at him. "She had — she had done something to herself. I did not know, I had not known, that she was" — he gave himself a shake, as he would shake someone in anger, accusingly — "that she was expecting a child."

Isabel stirred suddenly. She snatched a cup from the table and brought it to the sink and rinsed it quickly and filled it with water and drank, her head back and her throat pulsing.

"She had aborted the child, yes?" Quirke said. He was furious, furious, he did not know at what, exactly, this fellow, yes, but other things too indistinct for him to identify. "Tell me," he said, "had she aborted it?"

Ojukwu nodded, his shoulders sagging. "Yes," he said.

"Not you — she did it herself."

"I told you, yes."

Don't snarl like that at me, Quirke wanted to say. "And now she was bleeding."

"Yes. It was bad, she had lost a lot of blood. I did not know what to do. I — I could not help her." He frowned suddenly, remembering. "She laughed. It was so strange. I had helped her up and she was sitting on the side of the bed, the blood still coming out of her and her face so white — so white! — and still she laughed. *Oh, Patrick*, she said, *you were my second-best chance!*" He looked up at Quirke again, with a frown of bewilderment. "Why was that funny? *My second-best chance.* I did not know what she meant." He shook his head. "She was such a strange person, I never understood her. And now I was afraid she would die, and I could not think what to do."

There was a pause then, and the room seemed to relax with an almost audible creak, as if a wheel tensed on a spring had been released a notch. Quirke leaned back on the chair and lit a cigarette, and Isabel, having drunk another cup of water, filled the coffee percolator and set it on the stove. Phoebe came forward to the table and pointed to the packet of Senior Service that Quirke had put there, and asked if she could have one.

300

When she had taken the cigarette and he had held up the lighter for her she walked back to the window and stood looking out, with her back to the room, smoking. Only Ojukwu remained as he had been, crouched and tense as if he were nursing an internal ache.

"If you weren't lovers, you and April," Quirke asked, "then what were you?"

"We were friends."

Quirke sighed. "Then you must have been very intimate friends."

Isabel came and set down a coffee cup and saucer in front of Quirke and brusquely said: "He's lying — they were lovers. She took him away from me." She did not look at Ojukwu but went back to the stove and stood, like Phoebe, with her back turned. Quirke could see her fury in the set of her shoulders.

"Tell me the rest," he said to Ojukwu. "What happened?"

"When she saw I could not help her, that I did not have the training, she asked me to call someone — someone else."

"Who?" The young man shook his head, leaning more deeply forward on the chair and swaying slowly again, this time from side to side. "Who was it?" Quirke asked again, in a louder, harsher voice. "Who did she want you to call?"

"I cannot say. She made me swear."

Quirke had a sudden strong urge to hit him — he even saw himself stand up and stride around the table and lift high a fist and bring it down smash on the fellow's invitingly bowed neck. "She aborted your child," he said. "She was haemorrhaging. She was probably dying. And she *made you swear?*"

Ojukwu was shaking his head again, still huddled around himself as if that ache in his guts were steadily worsening. Phoebe turned from the window and, tossing the unsmoked half of her cigarette behind her into the sink, came forward and put a hand on the young man's shoulder. She looked coldly at Quirke. "Can't you leave him alone?" she said.

And then, all at once, Quirke saw it. How simple, and obvious. Why had it taken him so long? "Not Ronnie," he said, in a sort of wonderment, talking to himself. "Not a name — a *moustache.*" It was almost funny; he almost laughed.

Obsessed: he remembered Sinclair saying it, standing beside the cadaver that day.

Ojukwu stood up. He was not as tall as Quirke had expected, but his chest was broad and his arms were thick. The two men stood face to face, their eyes locked. Then Ojukwu took a small, almost balletic step backwards, and passed his tongue over his large lips. "The baby was not mine," he said.

There was a silence, and then Quirke said: "How do you know?"

Ojukwu looked away. "It could not be. I told you, we were not — we were not lovers." With a quick, twisting movement he sat down on the chair again and laid out his fists in front of him on the table as if to measure something between them. "I loved her, yes, I think she loved me, too. But April — she could not love, not in that way. *I am sorry, Patrick*, she said to me, *but I cannot.*"

"What did she mean?" Phoebe asked.

Isabel, too, had turned now and was watching Ojukwu. Her eyes were dry but the lids were inflamed.

"I don't know what she meant," Ojukwu said. "She would lie down on the bed with me, and let me hold her, but that was all. I asked her if there was someone else and she only laughed. She always laughed." He looked up at Phoebe standing beside him. "But it was not really laughter, you know? It was more like — I don't know. Something else, but not laughter."

Isabel strode forward, pushing Phoebe aside, and stood over Ojukwu, glaring down at him. "Is it true?" she demanded. "Tell me — is it true, that you and she — that you never —?"

He did not raise his eyes, but went on staring at his fists on the table, and nodded. "It's true."

There was silence again, and no one stirred. Then Isabel drew back her hand as if to strike the young man, but did not, and let her hand fall and turned away again.

Quirke stood and took up his hat. "I have to go," he said.

Phoebe stared at him. "Where are you going?" He had already turned towards the door. "Wait!" She made her way hastily around the table, bumping against the chair that Quirke had been sitting in and almost knocking it over, and put her hand on his arm. "Wait," she said again, "I'm coming with you."

He walked ahead of her along the hall to the front door. Two small boys had stopped to inspect the Alvis. "That's some motor car, Mister," one of them said. "Was it dear?"

Phoebe got in at the passenger side and slammed the door and sat staring through the windscreen. Quirke had started the engine when Isabel came quickly from the house. He opened the window on his side and she leaned down to look at him, bracing both hands on the door. "Will I see you again?" she asked. "I need to know."

She stood back and Quirke got out of the car, and they walked together back to the doorway. He put a hand on her arm. "Go in," he said, "it's cold."

She drew her arm away from him. "Answer me," she said, not looking at him. "Will I see you again?"

"I don't know," he said. "Maybe. Yes, I think so. Now go in."

She did not speak, only nodded. In his mind he saw her standing in the bath, naked, the water flowing down over her stomach and her thighs. She went inside and shut the door behind her.

CHAPTER
TWELVE

Quirke said he would bring Phoebe to Haddington Road, or to Grafton Street, if she liked — did she not have to work today? She said she did not want to go home, and not to the shop, either. She asked him where he was going, and he said he had to see someone. "Let me stay with you," she said. "I don't want to be on my own." They drove down to Leeson Street and turned left at the bridge, then right into Fitzwilliam Street. There was traffic now, the cars and buses going cautiously on the roads that were dusted still with frost. They did not speak. Quirke wanted her to tell him if she had known about Ojukwu and April, about Ojukwu and Isabel, and the unasked questions hung in the air between them. "I feel such a fool," Phoebe said. "— Such a fool."

He steered the car left into Fitzwilliam Square and drew it to the kerb and stopped. Phoebe turned to him. "Here?" she said. "Why?" He did not answer, only sat with his hands still braced on the steering-wheel, looking out at the black, dripping trees behind the railings of the square. "What's going on, Quirke — what do you know? Is April dead?"

"Yes," he said, "I think so."

"How? Did Patrick let her die?"

"No. But someone else did, I think. Let her die, or —" He stopped. There were coatings of white frost on the branches of the black trees. "Wait here," he said, and opened the door and got out.

She watched him cross the street and climb the steps to the house and ring the bell. Then the door was opened and he stepped inside. The nurse put her head out and looked across the road to where Phoebe was sitting in the car, then she followed Quirke inside and shut the door. It was some minutes before it opened again, and Quirke came out, putting on his hat. The nurse glared after him and this time slammed the door.

He got in behind the wheel again.

"What's happening?" Phoebe asked.

"We'll wait."

"For what?"

"To find out what happened to April."

The door of the house across the street opened again and Oscar Latimer came out, with the nurse behind him helping him into his overcoat. He looked about, and saw the Alvis, and came down the steps. "Sit in the back," Quirke told Phoebe, and got out and opened the rear door for her.

Latimer waited for a bread van to go past, then crossed the street. He got in at the passenger side, taking off his tweed cap, and Quirke once more got in behind the wheel. Latimer turned to Phoebe. "So," he said, "it's to be a family outing."

Quirke started up the engine. "Where are we going?"

"Just drive," Latimer said. "North, along the coast." He seemed in high good humour, and looked about him happily as they went down Fitzwilliam Street to Merrion Square and then on down to Pearse Street. "How are you today, Miss Quirke?" he asked. "— Or Miss Griffin, I should say. I keep getting that wrong." Phoebe did not reply. She realised that she was frightened. Latimer was looking back at her over his shoulder and smiling. "Quirke and daughter," he said. "That's a thing you never see over a shop, 'Such-and-such and Daughter'. 'And Son', yes, but never 'Daughter'. Odd." For a moment he looked to her so like April, with that pale, sharp, freckled face, that smile.

"Tell me where we're going, Latimer," Quirke said.

Latimer ignored him. He turned to face the windscreen again, and folded his arms. "Fathers and daughters, Quirke, eh? Fathers and daughters, fathers and sons. So many difficulties, so many pains." He glanced behind him again. "What do you think, Phoebe? You must have some thoughts on that subject."

She looked back into his eyes, which were regarding her so merrily. He was, she saw now, quite mad. Why had she not realised it before? "Do you know where April is?" she asked him.

He put a hand on the back of his seat and leaned his chin on it, pulling his mouth far down at the corners, making a show of weighing up the question. "It's hard to answer that," he said. "There are too many variables, as the mathematicians say."

"Latimer, I can't just keep driving," Quirke said. "— Tell me where it is we're going."

"To — Howth," Latimer said. He nodded. "Yes, good old Howth Head — Oops! Didn't you see that man on the bicycle, Quirke?" He twisted about to look out of the back window. "He's shaking his fist at you." He laughed. "Yes, Howth," he said again, resettling himself comfortably, "that's where we're bound. My father used to take us out there, April and me, on the tram. In fact, we could have taken the tram today, I suppose, made a jaunt of it — it's the last line still operating, after all — but it might have made for awkwardness in the end. Imagine how the other passengers would have stared when I produced" — he reached inside his overcoat and brought out a large, black pistol with a long barrel — "this." He held it upright by the butt, turning it this way and that as if for them to admire it. "It's a Webley," he said. "Service revolver. Bit of a blunderbuss, I'll grant you, but effective, I'm sure. I have it from my father, who took it off a dying British officer on Easter Monday 1916, or so he always said. He used to let me play with it when I was a lad, and would tell me about all the Black and Tans he had plugged with it. Then he had to go and turn it on himself." He paused, and looked at Quirke, and turned his head and glanced at Phoebe, too, smiling again, almost mischievously. "Oh, yes," he said lightly, "that's another strand of the Latimer Legend that my mother and my uncle between them have managed to keep secret all these years. A heart-attack, they said, and somehow got the coroner to back them up. Not such a large lie, when you think of it, seeing that he shot himself in the chest. Yes, anyone else would have put the gun to his temple, or even in his mouth, but not my Pa — too vain, didn't want to spoil his broth-of-a-boy good looks." He chuckled. "You're lucky to be a foundling, Quirke. I'm sure you feel terribly sorry for yourself, having no daddy that you know of, but you're lucky, take it from me."

They were in North Strand now, and before they came to the bridge they had to stop at traffic lights. Latimer laid the gun across his lap, with his finger crooked around the trigger and the barrel pointed in the general direction of Quirke's liver. "For God's sake, Latimer," Quirke said under his breath.

Phoebe's palms were damp. She tried not to look at the little man with the gun, tried not to see him, feeling like an infant hiding its eyes and thinking itself invisible.

"I've no doubt," Latimer said, "that you're both feverishly scheming in your minds to think of some way of getting out of here, maybe at traffic lights like this, or maybe if you see a Guard on the road and pull over and shout, *Officer, officer, he's got a gun!* I hope, I really do hope, that you won't attempt anything like that. — Ah, there's the green light. On, James, and don't spare the horses!"

Quirke caught Phoebe's eye in the driving mirror. They both looked away quickly, as if in embarrassment.

They passed through Clontarf and then they were on the coast road. The tide was out and wading birds were picking their way about the mud-flats under a low, mauve sky that threatened snow; a cormorant was perched on a rock, its wings spread wide to dry. On Bull Island the sand-grass was a vivid green. Everything is perfectly normal, Phoebe thought, the world out there just going about its ordinary business, while I am here.

"You couldn't leave it alone, Quirke, could you?" Latimer said. "You had to interfere, you had to bring in that detective and all the rest of it. And now here you are, you and your inconvenient daughter, trapped in this very expensive car by a madman with a gun. The things that happen, eh?"

"What did happen, Latimer?" Quirke said. "Tell us. It was you that she got Ojukwu to call, wasn't it, that night, when she was bleeding and knew she was dying? What did you do? Did you go round there? Did you try to help her?"

Latimer, the gun still resting negligently in his lap, had turned sideways in the seat now in order to look out past Quirke at the seascape going by. He seemed not to have been listening. "How did you know?" he asked. "How did you know it was me?"

"You were seen at the flat," Quirke said. "The old lady there, the one who lives upstairs."

"Ah."

"She remembered your moustache."

"Not so unusual for a brother to call on his sister now and then, surely?"

"Perhaps she didn't know you were her brother."

Latimer nodded. He seemed calm, reflective. "Yes," he said, taking up Quirke's earlier question, "Mr

Ojukwu telephoned to tell me that my sister had performed an abortion on herself and was haemorrhaging badly. What she was thinking of I don't know. She was a doctor, after all, she should have had more sense. And why didn't she call me in the first place? It's not as if we had any secrets from each other. Although I suppose she would have felt a certain reluctance, sitting there in that house of shame in a swamp of her own blood with her black lover-boy in attendance."

"What did you do?" Quirke asked again.

Latimer, with one hand on the pistol, slipped the other inside the breast-flap of his coat and put on a Napoleonic frown, pretending to work hard at remembering. "First of all, I told Sambo to make himself scarce, if he knew what was good for him. He didn't need telling twice, believe me. Gone like a shadow into the night, he was. I should have brought Big Bertha here" — he hefted the gun — "and shot the fellow, as my father would have done, but I missed that opportunity. Anyway, I was distracted, trying to patch up my unfortunate sister. She was very poorly, as you can imagine. She'd made a surprisingly awful hash of things, given her training and experience. But there you are, people will dabble in specialisms they know nothing about."

"When did she die?" Quirke asked, keeping his eyes on the road ahead.

There was a pause. Latimer, still looking out at the sea, frowned, and twisted up his mouth at one side, still making a pretence of racking his memory. "We made a great effort, both of us. A wonderful girl, April.

Wonderfully strong. In the end, though, not strong enough. I think perhaps she wanted not to be saved. I can understand that." He shifted on the seat, grimacing, as if something had suddenly begun to pain him mildly. "I told you, didn't I, Quirke, that you knew nothing about families? I said it to you, I said, *You've no experience of such things*. The closeness of people in a family. April and I were close, you know. Oh, very close. When we were little we used to say that we'd marry each other when we grew up. Yes, we'd marry, we agreed, and get away from Pa." He sighed, almost dreamily, and laid his head back on the seat. "Fathers and sons, Quirke," he said again, "fathers and daughters. He loved us very much, our pa, first me, and then April. What games he used to play with us, under the sheets. He was so handsome, so — dashing, as the English say. He was pleased as Punch when April came along — he had so wanted a girl, and now he had one. He was growing tired of me, you see, I knew that. I tried to warn April, when I thought she was old enough to understand. I said to her: *He's fed up with me, and besides, you're a girl, he'll go for you, now*. But she was too young, too innocent. She was six, or seven, I think, when Pa turned his affections on her." He paused. When he spoke again his voice had changed, had become distant. "I used to hear her in the night, crying, waiting for him to come creeping along and slide into bed with her. She was so small, so young." Latimer started up. "Really, Quirke, for heaven's sake!" he cried. "That light was red! You'll kill the lot of us if you keep on like this — where did you learn to drive?"

Phoebe closed her eyes. She thought of April sitting on the bench in Stephen's Green that day, smoking, remembering, and then the way she had laughed when the gulls came swooping down, flailing and screeching.

"I tried to tell our dear ma what was going on. Of course, she couldn't take it in. I don't blame her, it was simply beyond her comprehension." He nodded to himself. "Yes, beyond her. So then, since there was no help there, I had to take action myself. What age was I? I must have been — what? — fifteen? Why did I leave it so long? Fright, I suppose, and that awful — that awful *embarrassment*, that *shame*. Children blame themselves in these cases, you know, and feel they must keep silent. But April, my poor April — I couldn't let it go on. So I plucked up my courage and went to Uncle Bill" — he turned to Phoebe — "that's William Latimer, the Minister. I went to him and told him what was going on. At first he wouldn't believe it, of course — who would, after all? — but in the end he had to. Then I went to Pa and told him what I had done, and said that Uncle Bill was going to go to the Guards, though I have to say I'm not sure he would have, thinking what a scandal there would be — Little Willie, as Pa used to call him, was already well on his way up the greasy pole and had no intention of sliding down again. It didn't matter. The fact that I had told someone — anyone — set me free in an odd way. Can you understand that? So I confronted him, confronted Pa. We were in the garden, by the summerhouse. I was crying, I couldn't stop, it was so strange, the tears just kept flowing down my face, though I didn't feel in any way sad, but angry, more like, and — and *outraged*. Pa said nothing, not a word. He just stood there, looking away. I remember a vein in his temple, beating — no, fluttering, as if there were something under the skin there, a butterfly, or a wriggly worm. It was in the summerhouse that Ma found him, late that evening. The weather was so beautiful, I remember, high summer, and a golden haze, and the midges in it like champagne bubbles going up and down." He picked up the revolver and looked at it. "I wonder why we didn't hear the shot," he said. "You'd think we'd have heard it, a gun this size, going off."

They were on the long curve towards Sutton. Now and then a single snowflake would come flickering haphazardly through the air and melt at once to water on the windscreen. Phoebe had drawn herself into the corner of the seat with her arms crossed tightly, clinging on to herself.

"This is terrible, Latimer," Quirke said, "a terrible thing to hear."

"Yes, it is," Latimer agreed, in a throwaway tone. "Terrible is the word. We were bereft, of course, April and I. Despite everything, we loved our father — does that seem strange? Ma didn't count, of course, we took no notice of her, she might as well not have been there." He heaved a whistling sigh. "But it was wonderful, then, what April and I developed between us. Pa had trained us for it, you see, and we were grateful to him for that. True, the world would have frowned on our — our union, if it had known about it, but somehow that made it all the more precious for us, all the more — sweet." He broke off. "Have you ever loved, Quirke? I mean, really loved? I know what you feel about your" — he cupped a hand beside his mouth and lowered his voice to a stage whisper, as if to keep Phoebe from hearing — "about your darling daughter here." He coughed, resuming a normal tone. "What I'm talking about is *love*, a love that is everything, a love that pushes everything else aside, a love that consumes — a love, in short, that *obsesses*. This is nothing like the stuff you read about in novels, or nice poems. And poor April, I really think she was not up to it. It was too much for her. She tried to escape, but of course she couldn't. It wasn't just that I wouldn't let her go — I paid the rent in her flat, did you know that? Oh, yes, I paid for all sorts of things — but that she couldn't free herself. Some bonds are just too strong" — he glanced back at Phoebe — "don't you think so, my dear?"

At Sutton Cross he directed Quirke to turn right, and they began the long ascent of the hill. There were cows in frosty fields, and people trudging along at the side of the road in hats and heavy coats, like refugees fleeing a winter war. The flakes of snow were multiplying now, flying horizontally, some of them, while others seemed to be falling upwards.

"So the child was yours," Quirke said.

Behind them Phoebe made a small, sharp sound and put a hand to her mouth.

Latimer turned to her again. "Are you shocked, Miss Griffin?" he asked. "Well, I suppose it is shocking. But there you are. God allows certain things to happen, seems even to want them to happen, and who are we, mere mortals, to deny a divine wish?"

"Did you know she was pregnant?" Quirke asked. He was leaning forward, peering hard past the clicking windscreen wipers into the snow.

"No," Latimer said, "I didn't know, but I can hardly say I was surprised, given my training. I could have done something to prevent it, I suppose, but somehow one doesn't think clearly in the throes of such passion. Do I feel guilty, you'll ask me? Guilt is not the word. There is no word for it. That was the thing, with April and me, there were no words adequate enough. — Ah, here we are!" They had gained the summit, and pulled into the parking place. The dusty ground was whitened here and there with frost, and before them and on two sides the sea stretched away, pockmarked and pistol-grey. "You can stop here," Latimer said. "This will do — no, leave the car facing that way, the view is so nice."

Quirke brought the car to a stop, and did not switch off the engine. Phoebe suddenly needed very badly to pee. She said nothing, only cowered back farther into the corner of the seat, her hands clasped in her lap and her elbows pressed to her sides. She shut her eyes; she thought she might scream but knew that she must not.

Quirke turned to Latimer. "What now?"

Latimer seemed not to have heard; he was gazing down the hillside, nodding to himself. "This is where I brought her, that night," he said. "I stopped the car just here, and lifted her out of the back seat, wrapped in a blanket. She felt so light, so light, as if all the blood

316

she'd lost was half her weight. You'll laugh at me, I know, Quirke, but the moment had a strong sense of the religious, of the sacramental, though in a pagan sort of way — I suppose I was thinking of Queen Maeve and the thunder on the stones and all that. Silly, I suppose, but then I can hardly have been in my right mind, can I, given all that had happened in the previous few hours — all that had happened, indeed, in all those years when April and I had only each other, and when it was enough?"

When he stopped speaking they could hear the wind outside, a faint, vague moaning.

Quirke said: "You went back and mopped up the blood, made the bed."

"Yes. That too was a religious ceremony. I felt April's presence very close — she was with me — she's with me still."

"It was you who was watching my window, wasn't it?" Phoebe said.

Latimer glanced at her, frowning. "Your window, my dear? Now, why would I do that? Anyway, enough questions, enough talk." He lifted the pistol and pointed it at Quirke and then at Phoebe, waggling the barrel playfully. "Get out now, please," he said, "both of you."

"Latimer," Quirke began, "you can't —"

"Oh, shut up, Quirke," Latimer said wearily. "You have nothing to say to me — nothing."

They got out of the car, all three. Latimer held the gun down at his side to conceal it, though the place was deserted, except for, way off down the hill, a man in a duffel coat and cap, plodding along with a white dog at his heels. Quirke took Phoebe by an elbow and drew her in behind him, so that she was shielded by his bulk.

"Are you going to tell us what you did with the body?" he said. "Tell us that, at least."

Latimer waggled the gun again limp-wristedly. "Stand over there, by those bushes," he said. "— Go on, go on."

Quirke did not move. He said: "You didn't bring her out here at all, did you? This is not where you left her. I know you're lying."

Latimer, still pointing the gun in their general direction, had opened the door on the driver's side and was climbing in behind the wheel. He paused, and smiled, making a rabbit face and twitching that ridiculous moustache. "Obviously I can't fool you, Quirke," he said, shaking his head in rueful mock-admiration. "No, you're right, I didn't bring her here. In fact, I'm not going to tell you where she is. Let her be gone into the air, like dust, like — incense."

"*No!*" Phoebe cried, stepping out from behind Quirke's sheltering back and freeing her elbow from his grip. "You can't do that," she said. "It's the last insult to her. Let her have a grave, or a place, at least, some place where we can come and — and remember her."

For the first time Latimer's look hardened, and his mouth compressed itself into a narrow, bloodless line. "How dare you?" he said softly. He was behind the wheel now, with the door still open and one foot on the ground. "You think I'll let her be anywhere for you and the rest of her so-called friends to come and pretend to

318

mourn her? She was mine and she'll stay mine. You were the ones who tried to take her from me, you and that Hottentot, and the guttersnipe reporter, and that other slut. But you couldn't take her, and you can't. She's mine for ever, now."

He drew in his foot and slammed the door, then rolled down the window. He was smiling again. "Really, this is such a nice car, Quirke," he said. "I hope you aren't too attached to it." He winked then, and turned to face the windscreen, and the engine roared as he trod on the accelerator and the great car leaped forward, over the frozen dust and through the gap in the low wall there. They walked forward, father and daughter, to the wall, and stopped there and watched the Alvis bump and roll its way down the steep, slanting track. Then they heard the flat crack of a gunshot, and the car wallowed drunkenly to the right and the wheels on the driver's side sank into the heather and the machine reared up sideways and seemed to hang for a long moment before pitching over on its roof and then turning in clumsy, lateral somersaults down the long, uneven slope, until they could see it no more. There were cliffs down there, and they waited, as if they might hear, from all that distance, the terrible splash of the car going into the sea, but there was nothing, only the gulls crying and the man's white dog way off there in the bracken, barking.

It was hard going on the hillside, and Quirke and Inspector Hackett had scrambled only half-way down when they had to give up. The heather was slippery under the slushy snow, and there were hidden rocks that they knocked their ankles on and loose stones on which they slipped and slid. "Ah, let them young fellows at it," Hackett said, stopping, lifting his hat to scratch his head. A long way down in front of them three young Guards in climbing gear and stout boots were negotiating the last steep stretch before the cliffs fell sheer away into the sea. The turn-ups of Quirke's trousers were soaked and his shoes were wet through. Hackett sat down suddenly in the heather, his hat on the back of his head, and planted his elbows on his knees. There were flakes of snow in his eyebrows. "By God, Dr Quirke," he said, "this is a queer thing altogether."

There were two Garda cars and a jeep parked above them, behind the low wall. Quirke had taken Phoebe down the hill road on the other side, to a café there. It was shut at this still early hour, but he had banged his fist on the door until a woman came and let them in. Quirke told her there had been an accident, that a car had gone over the cliffs, and he would have to telephone the Guards. His daughter was in shock, he said, and needed something hot to drink. The woman stared at them, then bade Phoebe to follow her out to the kitchen, where she would make tea for her and give her something to eat, she said. Phoebe, dull-eyed, did as she was told. At the door to the kitchen she stopped and turned to look back at Quirke, and he made himself smile, and nodded, and told her it would be all right, that everything would be all right. Then he went back up the hill to wait for Hackett and his men.

He had sat there on the wall, smoking, his overcoat buttoned to the throat and the brim of his hat pulled low against the randomly billowing snow. He did not know how much he should tell Hackett of what Latimer had told him. He thought of Celia Latimer sitting by the fire in her husband's study with her hands folded in her lap, weeping for her lost child. Then he had heard the sirens in the distance.

Now Hackett from where he sat in the heather was squinting up at him with that lazy, shrewd eye of his. "You don't make an easy time for yourself, do you, Dr Quirke?" he said. He found a clump of tough grass amongst the heather and plucked a blade of it and put it in his mouth. Melted snow shone slick on the shoulder-tabs of his American coat.

"None of this was my doing," Quirke said.

Hackett grinned. "Sort of an innocent bystander, is that it?" He heaved himself to his feet, grunting. The snow, indecisive and sparse, was making the morning air soggy and coldly damp. Going up, they found a stony pathway through the heather. At the top, where the Garda cars were parked, the detective halted and stood with his hands on his hips, surveying the view of hill and sea and distant islands. "Isn't it a grand spot," he said, "snow or no snow?"

They turned in the direction of the squad cars. A Guard got out of one of them. He wore a cape and a cap with a shiny peak. It was the bony-faced sergeant from Pearse Street. He gave Quirke a hard look. "I hope you got the insurance fixed up," he said, "on that car of yours."

The inspector looked at Quirke and grinned, and together they turned and gazed off through the snow down the hillside, towards the steadily greying sea.

CHAPTER
THIRTEEN

There were only the three of them now, Phoebe, Isabel, Jimmy Minor. They met in the Dolphin Hotel at half past seven as usual, though everything else was different, and would never be the same again. Patrick Ojukwu had been deported. Inspector Hackett, under instructions from the Department of External Affairs, and accompanied by a second plainclothes man and a civil servant, had escorted him to the airport that morning and put him on a flight for London, from where he would travel on direct to Lagos. None of them had been allowed to see him before he went. He had gone back from Isabel's house to his flat in Castle Street, where he was picked up by the Guards and brought to the Bridewell station and held in a cell there overnight. There had been no question of an appeal. Patrick was gone, and would not return.

Phoebe felt strange. She was calm, despite everything that had happened, calm to the point of numbness. It was like the feeling she would have if she had not slept for many nights. Everything around her seemed unreally clear and defined, as if bathed in a sharp, strong light. She had sat in the kitchen of the café in Howth for an hour, drinking cup after cup of horribly strong sweet tea, and then Quirke had driven her home. He had wanted her to come with him to the flat in Mount Street and rest there, but she had preferred to be in her own place, amongst her own things. She had walked through the day in a sort of dream. She could not remember now how she had filled the hours. She had not gone to work, but had phoned Mrs Cuffe-Wilkes and told her she was sick. Then she had sat by the window for a long time, she remembered that, looking down into the street. She had not realised before how interesting it could be just to watch the world as the day slowly passed by. People came and went, housewives going to the shops and returning again, schoolchildren trudging along with their satchels, mysterious, shabby old men about their feckless doings. A Guinness dray had come and delivered barrels of stout to the pub across the way, the big brown-and-white horse standing in harness and now and then stamping one hoof, and lifting it again and setting it down on its tip as delicately as a ballet dancer. Though it was an overcast day the light underwent many subtle, almost surreptitious changes, through all the shades of grey from pearl to lead.

For a long time she did not think about April at all, or about April's brother. It was as if her mind had set up a barrier, a *cordon sanitaire*, to protect her. The worst thing of all, now, was not knowing for certain if April was dead or alive. Was Oscar Latimer to be believed? He was a madman, and could have been making it all up. It was true that Patrick had seen poor April after she had done that terrible thing to herself

324

and had described what a perilous state she was in, but that did not necessarily mean that she was going to die. Maybe Oscar had been able to stop the bleeding — he was an expert doctor, after all — and then had taken her somewhere and hidden her until she recovered and was well enough to go away, to England, maybe, or — or America, or — or anywhere. She could be there now, on the other side of the world, embarking on a new life. April would be capable of that, Phoebe was sure of it. April could cut herself off from everyone and everything she had known and not look back once.

Phoebe thought of the watcher below her window. Oscar Latimer had denied it was he who had stood there on the edge of the lamplight, night after night. If it was not Latimer, who was it, then?

Now, in the Dolphin, she did not tell the other two that she had been in the car with Quirke and April's brother. She might have confided in Isabel, but not Jimmy; she did not trust Jimmy any more. For his part, Jimmy said he was sure she knew what had happened on Howth Head, and was furious that she would not tell him. How was it Oscar Latimer had been in Quirke's car? Did Oscar know where April was or what had happened to her, had he said? Phoebe stayed silent; she owed it to April to keep her secrets. She could feel Isabel watching her, though; Isabel was not fooled.

Jimmy Minor complained violently of Patrick for keeping silent all that time and not telling them what he knew of April and the trouble she had got herself into. He believed that Patrick was the father of April's child, and Phoebe said nothing to enlighten him. She watched him as he sat there, his little legs dangling, going over and over and over it all, or all of it that he knew, and it came to her that what he felt for Patrick was not, in fact, hatred, but something else entirely. She received this illumination calmly, almost with indifference; nothing, she felt, would surprise her ever again.

She finished her drink and said she would have to go, that she was to have dinner with her father and Rose Crawford. She could see they believed she was lying. Isabel said she too would have to leave shortly, that she was on in the second act and would be in trouble already and would get shouted at for not being there for the first. She was pale, paler even than usual, and looked tired and disconsolate. She had sat for the past half-hour nursing her gin and tonic and saying nothing of April, or Patrick, or of any of it. Phoebe knew there had been something between Isabel and her father, and she supposed it was over now, and that Isabel was sad.

They knew, all three of them, that this was the last time they would meet here like this, that the little band was not only diminished in number, but was no more.

When she came out of the hotel it was snowing still, not heavily, though the street already had a thin, frail coating of white. She decided to walk to the Shelbourne. Her hat, the black velvet one with the scarlet feather, would be ruined, but she did not care. The lights from the shop windows shone on the snow, making her think of Christmas. There would be real Christmases again, now, Rose Crawford would make sure of that. Phoebe pictured the three of them, her and

Rose and her father, sitting round a table with a turkey on it, the crystal sparkling and a big bowl of holly in the middle, its polished leaves reflecting the fairy lights on the tree. When she tried to imagine her father's face, though, the expression on it, she felt a prick of doubt in her heart.

The doorman at the Shelbourne scolded her with mock-seriousness for venturing out into the snow with those thin shoes and that poor little hat, the feather of which was thoroughly bedraggled by now. She went up in the lift to the top floor, and through the door with the green baize on it that led to Rose Crawford's suite. A waiter in a tailcoat let her in, and escorted her to the sitting room. Rose was there, and Quirke, and Malachy Griffin, too. Rose came to meet her, and kissed her on the cheek. "My Lord" — she pronounced it *Lawd* — "but you're cold, darling! And look at your shoes! Take them off at once, while I find you some slippers."

Quirke wore a black suit and a red silk tie, and his shirt was starched and very white. When he got dressed up like this he seemed to her very young, a big schoolboy, scrubbed and awkward, out for a treat with the grown-ups. She noticed he was drinking water with ice and a slice of lime — at least, she hoped it was water, and not gin. He would need to be on his best behaviour tonight, for she was sure it was tonight that Rose would make her announcement, that this was the reason they were here, the four of them. Rose went off to one of the bedrooms to search for a pair of slippers, and the waiter came and asked Phoebe, in the confidential way that waiters did, what she would like to drink. Nervously she asked for a sherry, and when he brought it to her she spilled some of it because her hands were unsteady. She was so excited she felt that she was herself a glass filled to the brim that she had been given to carry and which she was terrified she would let spill, or drop. Malachy asked her if she was all right, and she said yes, and he said that Quirke had told them what had happened on Howth Head. She turned quickly to her father — how much of it had he told? — but he would not meet her eye.

"Yes," Rose Crawford said, coming back into the room, "that poor man, killing himself like that. What was the matter with him? — was he so upset about his sister disappearing?"

"You're lucky he didn't take you with him," Malachy said.

"And your lovely car!" Rose cried.

Quirke looked into his glass.

For dinner they were served roast pheasant, which Phoebe did not like but which she made herself eat, determined to do nothing that might impede in the slightest way the steady progress of the evening towards the moment that she knew would come, when Rose would put down her glass and look about the table, and smile, and begin to speak —

"More potatoes, Miss?" the tailcoated waiter murmured, leaning down at her shoulder. He smelt of hair oil.

Time dragged. Rose talked of her visit to America. "Boston looks so bare in wintertime, the grass on the Common turned to straw by the cold and the pond iced over. I always feel sorry for the ducks — they look so puzzled, slipping and sliding on the ice, not able to understand what's happened to the water." She turned to Phoebe. "My dear, everyone, but everyone, asked after you and told me to be sure to give you their love, especially" — she put her head on one side and arched a mischievous eyebrow — "that nice young Mr Spalding from the Chase Manhattan, you remember him?" She glanced at the two men. "*Very* handsome, *very* rich, and a great admirer of Miss Phoebe Griffin."

Phoebe was blushing.

"What's this?" Malachy said. "—You had an admirer and you didn't tell us?"

"He wasn't an admirer," Phoebe said, concentrating on her plate. "And anyway he had a fiancée."

"Oh, she's long gone," Rose said. "Mr Spalding is quite free and unattached." Malachy coughed, and Rose glanced at him and lifted that eyebrow again. "Yes," she said, with a mild little sigh, "I guess it's time." She put down her glass. Phoebe felt something swell up suddenly inside her, and she went hot, and accidentally knocked her fork against her plate, producing a ringing chime. "We have a little announcement to make," Rose said, looking at her and then at Quirke. "I confess" — she picked up her napkin and put it down again — "I confess I'm feeling somewhat nervous, which as you all know is not like me." Quirke was watching her, and frowning. The waiter came to clear the plates but Rose told him to leave them until later, and he went away again. Rose by now was looking decidedly flustered. "I had my speech all prepared," she said, "but I'm afraid I've clean forgotten it. So I'm just going to say it right out —"

She reached forward and took —

Phoebe stared, baffled.

It was Malachy's hand that Rose took — Malachy's, not Quirke's.

"— that Mr Malachy Griffin has kindly asked me to be his wife, and I, well, I have kindly accepted."

She laughed helplessly. Quirke had turned to Malachy, and Malachy smiled, shyly, sheepishly, queasily.

The rest of the evening passed for Phoebe in a hot fog of stupefaction, anger and pain. There would be no cosy Christmases after all, no sea voyages to the isles of Greece, no games of happy families. How could she have thought that Quirke would marry Rose, that Rose would marry him — how could she have allowed herself such a foolish dream? She looked across the table at Malachy, sitting there in what seemed a befuddled amazement, and she almost hated him. What was Rose thinking of? She would make the poor man's life a misery. Quirke she tried not to see. She could have hated him, too. She knew it was Sarah he had wanted, all those years ago, and instead of marrying her had let her go with Malachy. Now he had done it again. Would he be maundering in regret over the loss of Rose, too, twenty years from now? She hoped so. He would be old, then, and Rose would probably be dead, and the past would repeat itself. She saw the two of them, Quirke and Malachy, shuffling along the pathways in Stephen's Green, picking over together the lost years, Quirke sourly unmarried and Malachy a widower again. They would deserve each other.

When finally the evening was over, and Phoebe was putting on her shoes and her poor, ruined hat, Rose took her arm and led her aside, and looked at her searchingly and said: "What is it, dear, what's the matter?" Phoebe said nothing was the matter, and tried to break free, but Rose held her all the more tightly. Quirke and Malachy were still at the table, sitting in silence, Quirke smoking and drinking whiskey and Malachy doing nothing, as Malachy usually did.

Phoebe turned her face aside; she was afraid she might begin to cry. "You said it was my father you were going to marry," she said.

Rose stared. "I did? When?"

"That day outside the American Express place, you said it then."

"Oh, my," Rose said, and put a hand to her cheek. "I probably did. I'm sorry. I always think of Malachy as your father — he *was* your father, for so long." Dismayed, she let go of Phoebe's arm at last. "My poor, dear girl," she said. "I'm so sorry."

Quirke had finished his drink, and the waiter brought his overcoat and his hat. There were goodnights. The waiter held the door open. Quirke followed Phoebe out, and through the green baize door. She felt the tears welling in her eyes now but forced herself to hold them back. She did not take the lift but hurried to the top of the stairs. Quirke was at the lift, calling to her to wait, and saying something about a taxi. She went on, down the staircase. The doorman smiled at her. Across the road, in the Green, behind the black railings, the branches of the trees were laden with snow, she saw them through a shimmer of unshed tears. She turned and walked away along the pavement, hearing only her own muffled footfalls and the dinning tumult in her heart.

Quirke came out of the lift and went through the revolving door out on to the steps. That morning he had got a call from Ferriter, the Minister's man. The Minister, Ferriter had said, in his soft, smooth voice, was sure he could count on Dr Quirke's discretion in the matter of his nephew's tragic death. Quirke had hung up on him, and walked into the dissecting room, where Sinclair was sawing through the breast-bone of an old man's corpse and whistling to himself. Quirke had thought of April Latimer, whom he had never known.

Now he looked up and down the street, but his daughter was nowhere to be seen. A taxi drew up, and he climbed in. The driver was a sharp-faced fellow in a cap, with the stub of a cigarette stuck in one corner of his mouth. Quirke sank back luxuriantly against the greasy upholstery, chuckling to himself. Rose Crawford and old Malachy — ha!

The driver turned to him. "Where to, squire?"

"Portobello," Quirke said.